uk6

M40

ulI

3.

THE LADY OF CAWNPORE

Elisabeth McNeill titles available from Severn House Large Print

Hot News
A Bombay Affair
The Golden Days
The Last Cocktail Party
The Send-Off
Unforgettable

THE LADY OF CAWNPORE

Elisabeth McNeill

Severn House Large Print
London & New York

This first large print edition published in Great Britain 2005 by
SEVERN HOUSE LARGE PRINT BOOKS LTD of
9-15 High Street, Sutton, Surrey, SM1 1DF.
First world regular print edition published 2004 by
Severn House Publishers, London and New York.
This first large print edition published in the USA 2005 by
SEVERN HOUSE PUBLISHERS INC., of
595 Madison Avenue, New York, NY 10022.

British Library Cataloguing in Publication Data

McNeill, Elisabeth
   The lady of Cawnpore. - Large print ed. - (The India series)
   1.   India - History - 19th century - Fiction
   2.   India - History - Sepoy Rebellion, 1857 – 1858 - Fiction
   3.   Large type books
   I.   Title
   823.9'14 [F]

ISBN-10: 0-7278-7471-3

Printed and bound in Great Britain by
MPG Books Ltd, Bodmin, Cornwall.

The Bibighar, Cawnpore,

July 14th, 1857

Through the open arch of a colonnaded terrace where she lay on a pile of rags, Emily stared up at swathes of stars strung out like glittering diamonds against a background of deep purple velvet.

Sleepily she thought that she loved the stars of India. Her mother did too. Where was she tonight? Up there in the heavens? Religious people believed in heaven and perhaps it did exist, but Emily was beginning to doubt it. She believed in hell though, because she was in it now. There was not a shadow of doubt about that.

When she and Lucy were small, their mother would often sit with them in the garden at night, and point out the constellations. Lucy, with her quick mind, swiftly learned which was which, but Emily, who was three years younger, could never transform them into the lions, winged horses, and great bears that her mother said they were. All she saw was an infinite spread of sky

5

spangled with pinpricks of light. They represented eternity and that was magic enough. Even tonight, in this terrible place, the grandeur and immensity of the heavens softened her terrors and made it possible to sleep.

A fretful movement beside her stopped the merciful drift into unconsciousness, and Lucy sat up, eyes wide and staring in frightful distraction. 'Where are we? Where is little Bobby?' she asked in a loud voice.

All around them, in the filthy, stinking building, other women were moaning, sobbing, or grinding their teeth. Children, who could not be soothed, called fretfully and when Lucy's voice rang out, a woman answered sharply. It was Colonel Hancock's domineering wife Alice, who, even in this hellish place, clung to her superior position and took precedence by right over the other women.

'Do be quiet, and let us sleep,' she cried, but most of the other hundred and thirty-two survivors of the Satichaura Ghat massacre were already awake and listening.

In an effort to calm Lucy, Emily gently took her sister's hand and whispered, 'Sssh my dear, Bobby's safe with his ayah. Go back to sleep.'

'I can't. It's too hot. That punkah wallah's stopped working again. Tell someone to beat him in the morning,' said Lucy, still in a loud voice, completely unaware of the moaning people around her.

Lucy was in some other world because there was no punkah and not a breath of air in the stifling building. In fact they hadn't enjoyed the luxury of fans or fan pullers for a long time but, mercifully, distraction of mind made her unaware of all the terrible things that had happened.

She tried to stand, pulling Emily's arm up with her. They were both tall girls, but Emily was the stronger and managed to hold her sister down because she knew making too much fuss would alert the guards who might come in and lash at the captives with long canes.

Lucy protested at being restrained. 'Let me up, Emily. I must change my clothes because Matthew will be here soon and I can't let him see me looking like this. You look dreadful too. Call for the dhobi,' she said, plucking at her ragged clothing with distaste. All she was wearing was a filthy chemise and the tattered remains of an underskirt with pink ribbons threaded through the frilly hem. It was badly stained because they had no way of washing clothes, and no dhobis to do the washing for them.

Though she was her sister's junior and, till now, always in awe of her, Emily felt like an older woman with Lucy in her care. 'Lie down and stop worrying, my dear. There's

7

no dhobi and you've nothing else to wear. You can't go around naked,' she coaxed.

She was equally ragged and dirty, wearing a flimsy cotton dress with long, flounced sleeves and a scooped-out neckline, but she knew there was no point complaining or trying to do anything about changing it. Some other women in their prison took clothes off women who died, but Emily drew back from doing that.

Lucy raised her eyebrows. 'Don't be silly, Em. Of course there's a dhobi and I've lots of other clothes. Please go into my box and fetch me a skirt.'

A moan interrupted her orders, and she turned to look at Mrs Murray, an old friend of their mother, who was lying alongside them on the paved floor inside the colonnade. Her teeth were chattering with fever and she was raving in a delirium which, every now and again, made her give a piercing shriek and call out her husband's name in an anguished plea: 'James! James! Get up, my dear. Waken the children. They're coming, they're coming...'

'What's wrong with Mrs Murray?' asked Lucy sharply, suddenly seeming aware of what was going on around her.

'Mrs Murray is dying of fever,' whispered Emily. Over the last month she had seen many people die in horrible ways, but recently it had been fever or malnutrition that claimed one-third of the women and children who were shut up in the Bibighar, the house of a long-dead Englishman's native mistress near the Nana Sahib's palace. The girls' own mother, Mary Crawford, was among the dead. She'd succumbed from dysentery only four days ago, after two hellish weeks of stoically endured imprisonment.

Lucy stared at her sister with round, astonished eyes. 'Is Mrs Murray really dying? Of fever? Is there fever here?'

'Yes, she has fever,' Emily slowly said, afraid that her sister was returning to sanity, for it would be better if she could stay distracted and unaware.

'If there's fever in this place, we must leave at once,' said Lucy jumping up again. 'Where's mother? Tell her to dress and call for the horses. Fetch Bobby. Tell his ayah to make him ready...BOBBY! MOTHER!' Her frantic calls rang out across the crowded courtyard again and made more women protest.

Mrs French, who had been Cawnpore's most fashionable dressmaker and in those days very obsequious to the Crawford family, called angrily to Emily, 'Mrs Maynard, try harder to keep your sister quiet. She's upsetting everyone. At least let poor Mrs Murray die in peace.'

Emily groped in her pocket for her little

nacre pill box, which the guards had not considered worth stealing, and with careful fingers, fished out a tiny black ball of opium she'd been saving for emergencies. She slipped it into her sister's mouth, and said, 'Lie down, dearest. Bobby's quite safe. Swallow that and I'll brush your hair.'

Hair brushing usually soothed Lucy but tonight she was fractious, struggling and still calling for Bobby, and had to be held tight against Emily's knees as the brush was gently pulled through the tangled strands that had been so beautiful and shone like corn silk when it was coiled up into a thick plait. Now it was dull, greasy, and infested with lice, like the hair of everyone else in the Bibighar.

Squalor was horrifying to the sisters, who had always been very fastidious. Two days ago, distressed by Lucy's constant scratching, Emily cut off six inches of her long yellow hair with nail scissors but the lice were still there. She cut her own hair too but that was a lesser sacrifice because it was only pale brown and not as glorious as her sister's.

Little by little, the scrap of opium, allied with the rhythmic brush strokes, soothed Lucy, who stopped calling out for Bobby and closed her eyes as Emily hummed a nursery rhyme they used to sing together in the nursery. 'Hickory, dickory dock, the mouse ran up the clock...' At last she fell

10

asleep, and Emily hoped that, when she woke, she would have reverted to insanity, for life in the Bibighar would be insupportable if she recovered her mind.

Emily envied Lucy's ability to blank out the memories. How fortunate to forget that a pack of red-eyed mutineers stabbed her husband Matthew to death as he lay beside her in bed in the Meerut cantonment. She'd also forgotten running out of the house with two-year-old Bobby and his ayah to hide in the stable dung heap while sepoys sacked her house before rampaging off to kill other *feringhees*.

Lucy escaped from Meerut and took her son to join her parents, Colonel and Mrs Crawford, in Cawnpore, which was thought to be a safe place, for the scale of the sepoy mutiny was not yet realized. Emily, also a refugee from a similar but less bloody rising in Barrackpore, had reached Cawnpore earlier and the family had a few days respite together before that city was also besieged and, unbelievably, eventually capitulated to the army of the local ruler, the Nana Sahib. He promised the garrison safety if they capitulated, but he broke his word and a terrible slaughter on the river bank at Satichaura Ghat followed.

Colonel Crawford died that day. His wife survived to be shut up in the Bibighar with her two daughters and little grandson, but

11

now she too was dead. Emily, Lucy and Bobby clung to life as they mourned her – but no one knew for how long.

The most merciful thing was that Lucy's madness saved her from realising that precious little Bobby and his ayah were no longer with them. Over and over again during the last two days she had asked where he was and, so far, accepted the various excuses for his absence.

Emily calmed her anxious sister by saying, 'Don't worry. The ayah is playing with him in the garden,' or 'He's sleeping, so we must not disturb him.' But even in the distraction of her mind, Lucy would not go on accepting these excuses much longer. What would she do if she realized the child was no longer in the Bibighar? After her mother died, Emily gave him to the ayah and told her to carry Bobby out in the darkness as if he were her own. The last sighting she had of him was sitting limpet-like on the ayah's hip with a dirty old cloth over his head to hide his golden hair.

Surely, Emily thought, this hellish confinement must end soon in one way or another. Either the rebels and the Nana Sahib's fiendish mother, who visited the captives every day to rant and jeer, would murder them all, or a rescue party would arrive to save them. She clung to the hope of rescue, especially because persistent rumours were circulating among the rankers' wives, who seemed to have more reliable information than their social superiors, that a relieving force under Henry Havelock was advancing on Cawnpore.

Believe it, I must believe it! I must believe that the Company army is invincible, she told herself. She must believe that the mutineers were only a breakaway rabble of disloyal natives out for plunder. As Mrs Hancock persisted in saying, when they amassed enough loot, and their blood lust was satiated, without British officers to give them orders, they'd disperse. Surely, oh, surely she was right!

Clinging to that hope, she drifted into disturbed sleep but was wakened again when Lucy stirred and whispered into her ear, 'Happy birthday, Emily.'

'What?'

'Happy birthday, my dear. It must be midnight by now.'

How had Lucy managed to remember my birthday? Emily wondered, for she had forgotten it herself. She frowned, and did a quick mental calculation, counting the days off in her mind. If midnight had passed, it was the fifteenth of July.

'You're right. My birthday's on the fifteenth,' she whispered to her sister.

'I know, but I haven't a gift for you,' said Lucy in a voice of disappointment.

13

Emily forced a laugh. 'Oh my dear, that doesn't matter.'

'But it does. I must give you something. You're eighteen today. It's such a good age to be. I married Matthew on my eighteenth birthday.'

A feeling of almost unbearable sadness swept over Emily as she remembered that wedding day, only three years ago, when they were all happy and carefree. She closed her eyes and saw the laughing faces of her dead parents at the banqueting table, their glasses raised in a toast to the bride and groom, while beaming servants bustled around. Most of the people who celebrated with them that day were now dead, including the groom.

A suppressed sob made her swallow deeply, making it impossible to speak, but Lucy was sitting up in renewed animation, pulling a golden necklet, the last piece of jewellery she had managed to save, out of the top of her chemise.

'Happy birthday, dear sister,' she said, putting the chain into Emily's hand.

'No, I can't take this. It's the necklace Matthew gave you on your wedding day,' gasped Emily, her voice choked by tears.

'I want you to have it. I know you will keep it safe,' said Lucy.

Emily sat up too and stared at her sister. Lucy's eyes were shining as if she'd seen a vision. Was it possible that she was more aware of what was going on than she pretended? The necklace hung from Emily's fingers. 'I can't take this from you,' she said again.

Lucy firmly closed her sister's hand around the fragile links and said, 'You *must*. Perhaps one day, when you have no more need of it, you'll give it to Bobby.' Then she lay down, turned on her side and closed her eyes.

Holding the necklace between her fingers, Emily silently wept. Before she lay down too, she folded her hands in prayer, looked back at the stars and thought, 'Dear Lord, if we are going to die, please be merciful and make it as quick and as painless as possible. And take care of my sister's little boy. Keep him safe, even if none of us ever see him again.'

Cawnpore Bazaar,

April 1919

The room was sparsely furnished, shadowy and airless. Brilliant sunshine dappled the baked earth of a dried-up garden outside and the leaves on a few spindly trees rustled like scraps of brittle paper in a hot, unsettling breeze.

Brushing back tendrils of damp hair, and panting from her bicycle ride under a blazing sun, Jenny leaned over an old woman lying on a string bed near the door. A limp left hand hung down beside the bed and Jenny grasped it, gently chafing the fingers. They felt cold.

She fell on to her knees and put her other hand on the sick woman's neck, searching for a pulse. It was there, but feeble. One of the female watchers in the room gave a convulsive sob and said something in a language that Jenny did not understand, but she looked up and nodded in reassurance.

'Don't worry. She's not dead,' she said.

It was as if her voice brought the patient

out of a spell. Pouched eyelids fluttered and slowly opened. Obviously confused, the old woman looked vaguely from one face to another, at first recognising no one, then her right hand went to her throat and the thin lacquer bracelets on her wrist tinkled faintly as she groped to grasp at a gold chain around her neck.

Touching it seemed to revive her. She sighed, blinked, tried to focus her eyes and looked up into Jenny's face. 'Oh, dearest Lucy, thank God you've come back. I've still got your chain,' she whispered, holding out the gleaming links and struggling to sit up.

Relieved that her patient was coming round, Jenny said softly, 'No. Lie still. Don't worry. I'm not Lucy. I'm Jenny.'

A tall, middle-aged woman in a silk sari stepped forward and asked in halting English, 'She can drink? Char? Pani?'

'Only a little sugar cane water or grape juice,' said Jenny firmly because she had already decided that a possible cause of the old woman's unconsciousness was a diabetic coma. Her order was passed back to the door and a scared looking servant girl, who only a few minutes ago had led Jenny into the maze of the bazaar from the Mission hospital, ran off to fetch the drink. It appeared in an elegant tumbler with a silver filigree holder and a curved handle, which Jenny abstractedly admired as she held it to her

17

patient's lips.

'Only a sip at a time and please don't move. You'll feel better soon,' she said in a soothing voice.

The patient nodded but her eyes sharpened, appearing to gather light, which showed that she was coming back to consciousness. The juice moistened her pale lips, and she sighed as if in disappointment and said, 'I thought you were Lucy, but, of course, you're not. What are you doing here?'

'You were taken ill, and your maid fetched me from the hospital. I'm a doctor,' Jenny explained.

'A doctor! Nonsense! You're only a girl.' The sick woman seemed to be gaining strength by the minute and the others in the room muttered in relief. They were obviously in awe of her.

Jenny was used to reactions of disbelief when people in Cawnpore heard what she did for a living. 'It's not nonsense. I really am a doctor. Now let me take your pulse again,' she said in her professional voice.

For a moment it seemed as if the old woman was going to refuse to hold out her hand, but after a momentary hesitation, she yielded it to Jenny who looked down into the wrinkled face on the pillow, smiling in reassurance. With surprise she noticed that the patient's eyes, though faded with age, were very blue. Her black hair was obviously dyed, which was not unusual among older Indian women, but apart from brown hands and forearms, any areas of exposed skin on her body were very pale – alabaster white in fact.

But there was something else. Jenny mentally kicked herself for overlooking the most surprising fact of all about this old woman. She'd been so engrossed in reviving her patient that she hardly registered they were communicating in English. What was more, the woman on the bed spoke in the commanding and imperious tone of voice of all well-to-do British ladies in Cawnpore. Hers was the voice of privilege that rang out loudly all over the Raj.

She's not a native at all. This woman is English! What is she doing in a place like this? Jenny thought in amazement.

She had been the only doctor on duty in the outpatient room of the Edinburgh Medical Mission Hospital when a distraught girl came rushing in, grabbed at the sleeve of her white coat and abruptly tried to pull her towards the door.

Sadie, one of the two Anglo-Indian nurses helping Jenny, stepped in and cuffed the girl, shouting at the same time, 'Get out! You can't mishandle a doctor like that.'

But there was something so urgent, and so sincerely anxious, about the importunate girl that Jenny restrained the angry nurse. 'Ask her what she wants,' she said.

'Huh, she's only a beggar from the bazaar. She wants you to go with her to treat some old woman who is dying,' was the reply.

'I'll take my bike and go,' said Jenny immediately.

'Don't be silly!' snapped the nurse. 'It's not safe for a white woman to go into the bazaar on her own. How do you know this girl won't take you to bad people who'll rob you – or worse?'

'But this is a Mission hospital and it's my job to look after poor people. I haven't anything worth stealing anyway except my medical bag and I'll make sure there's not much in it,' said Jenny.

'What's not much to you is a lot to a beggar. The *badmashes* in the bazaar will kill you or sell you into white slavery,' said Sadie in a warning voice.

Jenny thought this ridiculous. 'Nonsense, Sadie. Don't worry, I'm a big girl. I'll fight back,' she joked.

The nurse glared and rolled her eyes. 'I'm not talking nonsense, Doctor. You've only been out here a few weeks and don't know what those bazaar people are like. You'll learn soon enough not to trust them.'

But the frantic messenger was still pulling at Jenny's sleeve and there were tears in her eyes as she went on pleading. 'I'm going,' said Jenny firmly and pulled off her white coat.

With the messenger running by the side of the bike to show her the way, she eventually arrived at a hidden compound in the middle of the bazaar where, to her surprise, she found an old Englishwoman in a diabetic coma.

The patient's room was spartan. Its floor was made of hard packed mud without rugs or carpets and there were no curtains on the window, only a rolled up chick blind. In the farthest dark corner loomed a high four-poster bed looped round with white mosquito curtains. Its pillows and bedding were also white. At its foot stood a battered looking tin trunk, dark green coloured but painted with panels of flowers. An enormous brass padlock secured its hasp.

The only other furniture was the string charpoy where the patient lay, surrounded by a pile of multi-coloured cushions. They were the sole concessions to comfort or luxury for there were no pictures, no ornaments, no fripperies of any kind.

The house did not appear to have electricity for there was no ceiling fan but from the main roof beam hung a primitive punkah – a strip of cream-coloured linen suspended longitudinally from a long horizontal pole – which was being pulled to and fro by a little boy who sat in the open doorway with the string from the fan tied to his ankle. Though

21

he seemed to be dozing, his foot kept moving to and fro making air waft over the woman on the bed.

Outside the open door were a conjoined series of low, whitewashed buildings grouped around a well and the square of sun-baked garden. A high, white-painted wall completely surrounded this property and closed it off from the teeming bazaar outside.

Everything and everyone was very quiet, waiting for Jenny's diagnosis. In the doorways of other rooms that opened into the compound she could see shadowy figures of men, women, children and dogs, silently and unsmilingly watching every move she made. She hoped they would not become aggressive if her patient died.

Fortunately that was not about to happen because the old woman appeared to be recovering. Relieved, Jenny straightened up from the bed and smiled at a helper who rushed forward, twittering like an excited bird as she offered Jenny a glass of sherbet. Hot and thirsty, she gratefully drank it down and was looking around for someone to talk to about the patient when a tall, dignified man in an immaculate white shirt and narrow-legged trousers appeared in the doorway.

The woman pulled Jenny towards him, gesturing for her to sit down on a bench

22

against the outside wall. When he bowed and sat beside her, she saw he was a very handsome Indian in late middle age with large, slanting eyes; a high-bridged, hooked nose; a neatly trimmed grizzled beard and thick black hair, streaked with broad bands of white. His appearance was very striking and reminded her of the Mughal paintings of elegant men astride prancing horses or sporting with beautiful ladies in flower-filled gardens.

In strongly accented English he said, 'I am Vikram Pande. Thank you for helping my mother. We were afraid that she was dying, but you have brought her back to life.'

Jenny nodded in a reassuring way and said, 'Don't worry. Your mother's getting better. Can you tell me how she's been feeling and behaving lately?'

He gestured with his left hand towards the waiting women to bring them closer and spoke to them in their own language before passing their replies on to Jenny.

'They say my mother has been very weary and short-tempered but they put that down to the season. She is always listless and irritable when the temperature starts rising,' he said.

'Has she been drinking more water than usual?' Jenny asked and was told that had been noticed. Apparently the old lady also complained of pains in her legs, but, after all, said Vikram Pande, she was about eighty years old, though no one seemed to be exactly sure of her age, which she kept a secret. Her eyesight was failing too, so much so that she had given up embroidery, previously her favourite hobby.

'Has she been losing weight?' Jenny asked and was told that for the past year, though the patient was previously 'well built', her size had been visibly dwindling.

'Tell me exactly what happened today,' she asked next, and the son said that his mother, to whom he referred, in a tone of great respect, as 'the Begum', complained of a headache at midday, ate nothing of the food brought to her, and went into a coma about three o'clock.

When his wife and the other women of the household were unable to rouse her, they realised she needed a doctor and the maid-servant offered to fetch one from the Mission hospital at the edge of the British cantonment. That was how Jenny came to be summoned.

He looked anxious as he asked, 'What is wrong with the Begum, Doctor?'

'I'm pretty sure she is suffering from diabetes, but it seems to be manageable at the moment. It's a fairly common disease among old people.'

He frowned and asked, 'Are you absolutely sure it's diabetes? My wife thought she was

24

having an apoplectic fit.'

She shook her head. 'I'm almost certain it wasn't that, but I'll do a urine test to re-assure myself. When I felt her skin, it was cold, and she wasn't running a temperature. If she'd had a stroke, it would be up and she'd be very hot. And her breath smells sweet, like fermenting apples – that's a sure sign of diabctes. When she started to come round she could speak and move her hands, so I gave her sugar cane juice to sip and it brought her round properly. If she starts to feel ill again, sugar cane or grape juice will help her. She must eat a light diet and keep warm – even in this climatc she'll feel the cold.'

'I'll tell my wife what you say. You are very clever,' said the man with great solemnity and Jenny flushed.

'I'm only doing my job. I'm sure your mother will feel better soon but she is an old lady, and though she sccms to have recover-ed, she has an illness which has to be moni-tored. If you like, I could call back tomorrow and check up on her again,' she told him.

He smiled. 'The Begum is loved and hon-oured by us all. The whole household jumps to her orders so we cannot spare her. It will be much appreciated if you come back. Thank you very much, Doctor. Can I pay for what you have done today?'

This flustered Jenny because she hated

dealing with money. That sort of thing was always taken care of by Dr Mason, the hospital superintendent, so she explained, 'I work for the Edinburgh Medical Missionary Society and it's mainly financed by people at home, but patients give whatever they can afford. The best thing would be for you to speak to Dr Mason about the fee the next time you are passing our hospital.'

'That's what I will do,' he said with a smile that showed his magnificent teeth. She smiled back, impressed by his physical presence.

Before leaving however there was one other question she wanted to ask. 'What's your mother's name and where does she come from?' she said, but instantly realised that she had made a mistake, for the friendly expression on his face changed to one of reserve and he replied in a guarded tone, 'Everyone calls her the Begum but that's only a nickname. She's not royal. She is known here in Cawnpore as the widow of Dowlah Ram and she has lived in seclusion in this house for more than fifty years. Why do you ask?'

'Because she speaks English like an Englishwoman...' Jenny felt herself floundering.

'She speaks it only rarely,' he said so abruptly that she decided to stick to professional matters. As she prepared to leave, he added in a more mellow tone, 'We are all very grateful to you. It's growing dark and you mustn't ride alone through the bazaar in the dark. There are bad people about. I'll call a tonga to take you and your bicycle back to the hospital. Please come again tomorrow.'

Edinburgh Medical Missionary Society Hospital, Cawnpore,

April 1919

When Jenny did not turn up for dinner at seven o'clock, Molly Mason, wife of the medical superintendent, began fretting about her house guest.

'Where can she be? There's terrible rumours going around about trouble in Amritsar – some blacks attacked a white woman there the other day and people say they raped her! I hope Jenny's not been attacked,' she said to her husband Harry who sat opposite her at the dining table, his face obscured by the *Times of India*.

'I heard the rumours too. The woman wasn't raped. She was knocked off her bike by some rough boys and her arm was broken. Anyway, there's no rioting here, so don't let's start imagining things and spreading alarm. Perhaps Jenny decided to miss dinner,' he suggested.

'But she must be hungry. She works very hard and she's terribly thin. The climate is wearing her down. She's only been here for three months after all, but we're acclimatised after twenty-five years in this place, though sometimes even I find it takes some enduring. It would be nice to take her to the hills. Darjeeling is lovely... I don't mind for myself, but a place like that would buck her up and she'd meet more people of her own age. She looks terribly sad and lonely sometimes.'

Molly's voice ran on and on in a high trill, interspersed now and again with little sighs. Long ago, in childhood, she had cast herself as a martyr who would preserve an uncomplaining exterior through all vicissitudes, and help everyone, whether they wanted to be helped or not. Having married a medical missionary, she was determined that *A wonderful wife and helpmate to a saintly man* would be her epitaph.

The doctor rustled the pages of the newspaper as he said, 'By people, I suppose you mean men. I don't think she's ready for that yet. Anyway, you know perfectly well that we can't go to the hills. Apart from the girl, I'm the only doctor in the hospital till Allen gets back from the war. We're lucky to have her.'

Molly sighed again. 'I can't imagine what Allen was thinking about running off like that to fight in France, especially after Marshall died of the plague, leaving us to cope here. We're always left to carry the burden.'

'How inconsiderate of Marshall!' said the doctor sarcastically. 'But you don't have to cope. You only write letters and play mah-jong or bridge with your friends. The girl and I do all the work round here and she's turning out to be an excellent doctor – better than Marshall, or Allen as a matter of fact.'

Molly said, 'That's good, but seriously, I worry about her. If she's attacked, or gets ill and dies, what will we tell her mother?'

Mason grunted. 'We'll tell her what we told Marshall's parents.'

Molly shuddered, remembering Marshall's swift and untimely death. 'I mourned for him, really mourned.'

'You once told me you didn't like him,' reminded her husband, turning over a page of the paper.

'How can you say that? I thought he was a bit uncouth but I never said I didn't like him. Anyway, that doesn't change what I feel about Jenny. She's a sweet girl and I worry about her because she's so sad sometimes.'

'She's probably homesick. It takes people a while to get used to this place, and anyway she's got something to be sad about, hasn't she? You can't expect her to pick up and start dancing about after what's happened to her. You'd say she was unfeeling if she did,' said her husband.

'I don't expect her to start dancing about,'

30

Molly primly replied, 'but it's up to us to do something to cheer her up. We could throw a little party perhaps and invite some eligible men to meet her.'

Her husband groaned. He hated his wife's little parties but knew he was not going to be able to avoid this one because Molly was on a cheer-up-Jenny crusade.

Just then they heard the sound of bicycle wheels on the gravel outside the dining-room window. Molly jumped up and leaned out of the open window, calling, 'Oh Jenny, thank goodness it's you. We were so worried. Come in and have some dinner. It's roast mutton – goat really, but we have caper sauce with it and that makes it taste like mutton!'

They heard Jenny laugh, and a few moments later she came into the room to sit down beside them.

'Where have you been, my dear?' asked the doctor in a kindly voice.

'I was called out to see a sick woman in the bazaar,' said Jenny.

'I hope you took someone with you. It's not safe for a white woman to go into the bazaar now. Haven't you heard about that poor soul in Amritsar? Some of the blacks seem to dislike us so much. It's like the Mutiny. They're just waiting for an excuse to kill us all, I think,' exclaimed Molly.

Molly's like Sadie, thought Jenny, who

took this line of talk with a pinch of salt. 'I rode my bike but I went slowly and the girl who came to fetch me ran alongside. The bike and I came back in a tonga so I was perfectly safe,' she said.

Molly moaned. 'How foolhardy of you! No white woman should ever go into the bazaar on her own. What am I going to tell your mother if you get killed? You really mustn't take risks with those natives. They're not to be trusted, two-faced cheats and rogues, every one of them, especially since that man Gandhi has been going around stirring up trouble and putting ideas into their heads.'

While his wife was speaking, the doctor behaved as if her conversation was a background noise that could be ignored, like a ringing in his ears, but eventually he interrupted and said firmly, 'Hold on, Molly. I've already told you this isn't Amritsar and nobody here has shown any sign of wanting to attack us.'

Turning to Jenny he asked, 'What was wrong with the woman you went to see?'

'She's better now, but she was in a diabetic coma when I got there. I wouldn't have gone if you'd been available but her servant girl was very insistent. She thought her mistress was dying,' she told him.

He nodded. 'Diabetes is very common. Lots of them get it in old age, especially the women, because they eat all those sweetmeats they love so much – what age was she?'

'Late seventies, perhaps over eighty. Her son was a bit vague.'

'Hmmm. Not many make it to that age. Was she otherwise well?'

'Not too bad. She'd lost weight recently apparently and her heartbeat was a bit irregular at first but it was all right by the time I left. I said I'd look in on her again but if you'd rather go, I've got the address of her house. It's in the middle of the bazaar.'

He shook his head. 'I'll leave her to you, my dear. She probably prefers a woman anyway. Was she in poor circumstances?'

'No, though the house was very bare, but I'm learning that local people don't seem to live like Europeans. She had lots of people looking after her and seemed to be very comfortable. They called her The Begum, as if she was a princess. Oh, and something else about her surprised me – she spoke perfect English.'

The doctor only raised his eyebrows but his wife said with conviction, 'The ones who speak English are the worst. They're very pretentious. Did she speak it with a chi-chi accent?'

'Not at all. Her voice sounded very well bred. In fact I think she might actually *be* English,' Jenny replied.

Molly laughed. 'That's not very likely.

33

What would a well-bred Englishwoman be doing living in the bazaar?'

Dr Mason, however, was obviously intrigued and said, 'How interesting, but some high-born Indian women are very well educated. If your estimate of her age is right, she'd be born around 1840, before the Mutiny. She'll have seen lots of changes if she's been around since then.'

Next morning, after they finished breakfast, Jenny accompanied him to the hospital that stood next door to the medical superintendent's bungalow. Their stiffly starched white coats crackled as they walked, and, as usual, a noisy crowd of patients clamoured for their attention in the wooden dispensary that reminded her of the cricket pavilion beside Inverleith Park back home in Edinburgh where she used to go to watch games with her father before he died.

The two Anglo-Indian nurses, Sadie and Flora, were attempting to control the crowd by raucous shouting, but as soon as they saw the doctors, some of the more determined female patients struggled forward to ask for help for the sick babies they carried in their arms. Some of these little scraps of humanity had thick lines of kohl painted round their huge eyes, and they made Jenny's heart ache because almost all of them suffered from malnutrition, evidenced by swollen bellies and spindly legs. Her own frustrated longing for a child, which she feared would never be satisfied, made her want to reach out and hold them to her breast.

Their mothers were as demanding of pity as the babies for many were little more than children themselves. Most were low-caste sweepers or labourers from the gangs who worked on building sites or mended the roads, and few could expect to live to be more than twenty-five – thirty at the most if they were exceptionally lucky.

Dr Mason made his way through the throng like a cutter in heavy seas, gesturing at Jenny to follow him to his private office. 'It seems that you're getting a reputation,' he said when the door was closed behind them.

She looked puzzled and asked, 'Am I? What sort of reputation?'

'As a soft touch, and magic healer. That's a tremendous crowd out there and they all want you. It's not good for my self-respect!' But he was only joking because it was said with a laugh.

Jenny flushed and said, 'I do what I can, but it's all very different to working at home.'

'You're coping well, my dear. I'm very pleased with you, but my wife thinks you're working too hard. She doesn't want you to overdo it and make yourself ill. The trouble about this place is that it seduces some people, it gets into their hearts. They want to give everything they have but, believe me, it's a cruel country. It sucks us in, uses us up and spits us out again, yet the flood of people needing help never slows down. You're a young woman. Take some time to live your own life as well.' His tone was solemn.

She stared at him. She had seen this man in action, cuffing trouble-makers, throwing out sycophants, malingerers or thieves, but in spite of his surface gruffness, and frequent complaints about the natives, he was tender-hearted. He had to be or he would not have stayed in this small Mission hospital for so many years, coping with every disease known to man. He was a legend among the missionary doctors of India and she felt privileged to be working with him.

All morning after their chat she bandaged sores, wiped mucus from sticky eyes, peered into ears and down inflamed throats, put splints on broken bones, tried to prescribe for a woman debilitated by excessive bleeding because of unsupervised childbirth, and delivered an apparently lifeless baby.

The doctor's right, it's a cruel country, she thought, as she held the bloody and inert child in her hands. The hopeless future facing most of her patients made her heart ache. Though she had treated poor people in the slums of Edinburgh while she was a student, until she arrived in Cawnpore she'd had no idea such truly brutal deprivation could exist.

Most of the people who sought her help every morning in the Mission hospital had no homes – not even a slum room – for they lived out on the streets where they'd been born and where they would die. Dr Mason's analogy was a good one because trying to make their situation better was as ineffectual as attempting to hold back the tide.

At noon, he came upon her despondently washing her hands at a deep porcelain sink after the baby finally died. He patted her on the back and said, 'Don't let it get you down. Even the little we do helps, you know. Go back to the bungalow for something to eat and a bit of a rest before the rush begins again.'

She shook her head. 'I've already had a banana and a cup of tea. That's enough lunch for me. I'm planning to go back to see that diabetic woman in the bazaar who I was called out to yesterday, then I'll come back for a nap because I don't have to be on duty again till half-past five.'

Dr Mason looked out through the open doorway at the brilliant world outside. 'It's too hot out there to take your bicycle. Put on a solar topi and hire a tonga. The Mission will pay for it. The son of your patient in the bazaar came in to see me this morning and gave me a thirty rupee donation. He seemed very grateful for what you did for his mother.'

A payment of thirty rupees was unusually generous because the normal fee paid for a consultation or treatment was five. The man from the bazaar must be well off in spite of the starkness of his home.

The tonga Jenny hailed in the roadway outside the hospital was drawn by a high-stepping chestnut pony with skin that gleamed like satin. Its harness was decorated with strips of multi-coloured ribbon and tiny tinkling bells, which showed it was the pride and joy of its owner, and its life was probably far more comfortable than the lives of most of her patients.

It trotted briskly through the bazaar until it reached the narrow street where she had been the previous evening. When she descended into the roadway, she was disappointed to see that the alley leading to the house was closed off by a high wooden gate, firmly closed and padlocked. There was no bell and she looked around in confusion, wondering how to get in.

Next door was a large, open-fronted shop selling beautiful materials. Over the doorway was a big board bearing the name Celestial Silks and the interior was full of rolls and swathes of glistening fabrics, many of them shot through with gold or silver thread. Loops of material – purple and crimson, brilliant green and peacock blue – hung in festoons from canes above the heads of the customers.

When Jenny climbed up two steps from the roadway into the shop, a young man immediately descended on her, rubbing his hands in anticipation of a sale. 'You want to buy some silk, memsahib? We have the very best materials here, princesses buy their silks from us,' he said.

She shook her head. 'No, not today thank you. I'm trying to get into the house next door but the gate is locked. If they have a doorman, do you know how to get him to open it for me?'

'That house belongs to the owner of this shop. I will call him now,' said the shop assistant officiously.

She was gazing in wondering admiration around the Aladdin's Cave of silks when the handsome man she'd met the previous evening emerged from the back of the shop. Again he was dressed in spotless white and his beard looked as glossy as his beautiful materials. He smiled when he saw her and said, 'My mother is much better, thank you, Doctor.'

'I'm glad, and I want to thank you for your very generous donation to the Mission. I said I'd look in and check up on your mother again but I can't find my way into your house,' she told him.

He laughed. 'We live like people in a citadel, I'm afraid. Mother likes it that way.

39

Come, I'll take you through the door we use when this shop is open. She'll be happy to see you.'

In fact the Begum, who was still lying on her string bed, did not look overjoyed when her son showed Jenny into her presence. Her head was propped up on the silken cushions, and from the rafters above her the punkah sent a soothing breeze through the room.

'She is feeling much better today. She says there is no need for a doctor,' the man told Jenny in an embarrassed tone after his mother poured out a stream of words in a native language when she caught sight of the visitor.

His wife, standing in the background, came forward frowning and also said something, so he told Jenny, 'But my wife says that is not true. In spite of what she says, the Begum spent a disturbed night and we are glad you've come back.'

Hearing this, the old woman shot a sharp look at her daughter-in-law and told her off in no uncertain terms. Jenny guessed that she was deliberately speaking Hindi to indicate that she did not want to be bothered with the doctor.

'Tell your mother not to worry. I'll not trouble her if she doesn't want to see me. I only came to make sure she's better. And why is she not speaking English today? She spoke it very well yesterday,' she said.

The old woman's eyes flashed even more dangerously when she heard this and she snapped – in English, 'Has my son not paid you? Is that why you have come back?'

Jenny flushed but defended herself stoutly. 'He paid me very generously – far too much in fact. I came to see you because I don't like leaving things half done.'

Her refusal to be intimidated softened the old woman slightly, but she was still a formidable opponent. 'You can't have been a doctor very long. Are you practising on me?' she asked in a challenging voice.

Even her son was taken aback by this. 'The doctor is only here for your good, Mother,' he protested.

She glowered at him from under lowered eyebrows and asked Jenny, 'How do we know you're a real doctor? Where are you from?'

'Edinburgh,' said Jenny.

'How old are you?' was the Begum's next question.

'I'm twenty-six.'

'So old! Have you come to Cawnpore looking for a husband? Most of the girls who come out fishing for a man are younger than you. Or are you one of those religious fanatics who pray over poor people and try to save their souls? That's a waste of time. Converts only pretend to agree with you so they can get medicine or free rice. Why should they become Christians when they have perfectly good religions of their own?' The Begum obviously enjoyed sparring with words and did not worry about her listeners' feelings.

Jenny protested, 'I'm certainly not husband-hunting and I have no intention of praying over anybody. Our Mission's not like that. It's a real hospital. I came out to work in it because it is a place where I can do good medical work. I'm not here to make converts. Do you want me to take a look at you or not? If you don't, I'll leave.'

She was rattled, but her ability to fight back was appreciated by the patient. When her son spoke sharply to his mother, she meekly rendered up a hand to Jenny for pulse taking. When that was done, with a nod of her head, she indicated the pillows, and said, 'All right. I'm sorry. Sit down. Don't go. You're really very kind. Sit down and tell me how to cope with old age and illness.' Amazingly, she was smiling when she spoke.

Jenny was still bristling inside, however. 'All I can advise you to do is be careful. Don't eat the wrong things. You seem to have been keen on sweets and that's not good. Don't overtire yourself, and listen to your body,' she said.

'And slip quietly into death,' added the Begum mockingly.

Jenny looked her in the eye. 'If you are lucky,' she said.

That made the old woman flinch as if at a bad memory but she said in a more chastened tone, 'I suppose I asked for that. After all I'm very old and none of us are immortal.'

'Your son told me you're about eighty but how old are you exactly?' Jenny boldly asked.

The faded blue eyes stared hard at her. 'I'm eighty if you count by the English way and eighty-one if you do it the Indian way.'

Jenny already knew that Indians reckoned their age from the date of conception instead of the date of birth, so she nodded and said, 'That means you were born in 1839.' It seemed a very long time ago.

The Begum nodded in assent and Jenny took another chance when she added, 'And you're English, aren't you?'

'Am I? What makes you think that?' They were sparring again.

'Your eyes, the colour of your skin, and especially your voice.'

'I was born in India, but I went home for schooling for a few years and then came back when I was sixteen,' said the old woman.

'But you *are* an Englishwoman,' persisted Jenny.

The Begum sighed. 'All right, I am, if what you mean is both my parents were English.'

Jenny gently laid the hand she had been holding after taking the Begum's pulse back on the silken lap and said, 'Tell me. What is an Englishwoman doing in the middle of Cawnpore bazaar?'

The old woman laughed lightly. 'If I told you, would it make any difference to the way you treat my illness?'

Jenny shook her head. 'No, I don't suppose it would, but I'd like to hear it none the less.'

'Perhaps one day I'll tell you my story if you tell me yours, but not now because I'm beginning to feel very tired,' said the Begum.

'I've no story,' said Jenny stonily, her face changing.

'Most people have a story and I can tell that you have one, too,' the Begum told her. Then she closed her eyes and that was Jenny's dismissal.

Back in the hospital, the waiting room was crowded and the nurses irritable because of the wailings and groanings of the patients. Jenny waded into battle, rolling up her sleeves as she went, and it was two hours before they were able to sit down, rest their aching feet and talk to each other.

After they'd discussed the day's cases, Flora asked Jenny, 'Did you go back to see your patient in the bazaar today?'

'Yes, I did. And she is an Englishwoman. She told me so herself,' said Jenny.

The nurses were surprised. 'She must be

Eurasian, probably a soldier's widow. Some of them marry local men if their first husbands die,' said Flora.

Jenny shook her head. 'If she was, her first husband must have been an officer because she's really rather grand and well bred,' she said.

Sadie turned and walked away towards the medicine trolley. 'Not all the ordinary soldiers are peasants from the bogs,' she snapped.

Jenny flushed. The two nurses were her friends, and she did not think of them as Anglo-Indians, or 'chi-chis' as she had heard people calling women of mixed blood.

'I didn't mean that,' she said, and Flora jumped in to move the conversation along.

'What does she look like?' she asked.

'Dark hair, though I'm pretty sure it's dyed because the roots are white. But blue eyes, and very white skin, except for her hands and forearms which are brown they look dyed too in fact!' Jenny laughed.

'It's a terrible thing to be born brown, but we can't all be Caucasian,' snapped Sadie, who had still not thawed.

Jenny looked at Flora for help, but the other nurse turned away, obviously reluctant to continue with the subject. Sadie was not though. 'And why do you think she's *grand*?' she asked.

'Because of her voice.' Jenny wished she

45

had never started this.

'What does it sound like?' persisted Sadie.

'A bit like a duchess's voice. She has a very upper-class accent, slurs her vowels and pronounces some words strangely.' Jenny could not really think of what else to say.

'You mean she doesn't speak chi-chi, like we do?' said Sadie.

Flora whirled round from where she was standing and said, 'Come on, Sadie. Jenny doesn't mean anything bad.'

Sadie retorted, 'She doesn't know what it's like to be neither one thing nor another, does she?'

Then she slammed down the medicine trolley lid and flounced out of the room. Distraught, Jenny looked at Flora and said, 'I didn't mean to hurt her feelings. Why is she so touchy?'

'It's because of her grandmother,' said Flora with a shrug.

'Her grandmother? Was she English?' asked Jenny.

'Not exactly. She was part Indian and part Irish apparently, but she was famous in her day. Her name was Miss Dolly.'

'That's a nice name,' said Jenny, bemused.

'Not exactly a nice person though. She died in the Mutiny.'

'Why does that upset Sadie?'

'Because the British killed her.'

This was all too confusing. 'By mistake do

46

you mean?'

'No. They meant to kill her all right. They hanged her because she was a traitor who took the mutineers' side. Sadie's very defensive about her, though most people have forgotten the scandal by this time, but she still doesn't like to talk about what happened. Perhaps I shouldn't have told you,' Flora replied.

'It must be hard for her, having a traitor for a grandmother,' Jenny said.

'Yes, among white people and some Eurasians it is, but not among Indians. Some of them think of Dolly Mullins as a heroine – like the Rani of Jhansi who led her army out against the British,' said Flora.

Jenny asked, 'Do you mean that there's still such bad feeling against us?' and was taken aback by Flora's closed expression as she stood up and began making herself busy with the medicine trolley, before saying, in a tone of finality, 'Neither black nor white people make it easy for themselves in this country. What the mutineers did was awful, especially here, but afterwards the revenge was terrible, too. There's a lot of hatred on both sides. It's best to forget these things.'

Amritsar, April 13th, 1919

Reginald Dyer was nervous. Sweating heavily in his khaki uniform and polished gaiters, with his solar topi set firmly on his head, he stuck a leather covered swagger stick under his left armpit and marched up and down his office floor in front of the English officers, who stood crowded at the door watching him.

'Get the men ready. Tell them that they have to obey orders, no matter what. Any man who doesn't will be shot. I'll do it myself if necessary!'

Major Paterson, a pleasant looking younger man, said in an anxious tone, 'Surely it won't come to that, General Dyer. The people are gathering in the Jalianwala Bagh park to celebrate a big Sikh festival that starts tomorrow. There'll be women and children in the crowd so they won't start any trouble.'

Dyer, an unintelligent man with little experience of India because he had only recently arrived in the country, whirled round and glared, eyes popping, at Paterson.

'That's a bloody mob gathering out there, isn't it? I know a mob when I see one.'

Paterson nodded in apparent agreement. 'Yes, there are a lot of people and there's more joining them all the time, but I've spoken to the organisers myself and they've promised me that there'll be no trouble.'

Dyer sneered, 'You're one of those pro-Indian fellows. They spot the softies and take you for a ride every time. The moment the agitators get out there, they'll whip that crowd up and they'll be rioting and killing for days.'

'I don't think so,' said Paterson quietly. 'None of them are armed.'

'What do you mean by armed?' asked Dyer.

'They haven't any rifles or guns,' said Paterson.

Dyer, beside himself, shouted a series of questions. 'But they have knives, don't they? This is Amritsar, the city of the Sikhs, and every bloody Sikh in India carries a knife, doesn't he? It's part of his religion, isn't it?'

He gestured at his office window, through which could be seen a clutter of roofs. In the distance the glittering dome and pinnacles of a huge temple rose above them. This was the Golden Temple, the Sikh holy of holies, and Dyer, the commander-in-chief of the British army in Amritsar, who would never set foot in or near the temple, was striding up and

49

down in its shadow.

One of the other officers intervened to help Paterson and suggested, 'Perhaps we should approach this business quietly, General. The protesters *are* going to use the festival to express their grievances about the Rowlatt Acts – and perhaps they have a point – but if we stand back and let them get it off their chests, the heat will go out of the meeting.'

'It's attitudes like yours that made the Mutiny possible. I've been sent here to keep order and I'm not going to stand by and let it happen again,' shouted Dyer.

Old India hands among the officers looked at each other in despair when they realised that Dyer was so ignorant that he did not know the Sikhs had not rebelled against the British during the Mutiny of 1857.

They also knew that he had no idea how high ill feeling was currently running among all Indians about the recent Rowlatt Acts, which continued wartime regulations of press censorship, the arresting of suspects without a warrant, and detention of political agitators without trial. The Sikh community was particularly outraged because hundreds of their men fought gallantly on the British side against the Germans in France where they suffered many casualties. In recognition of their support for Britain, they had expected a measure of self-determination after the war finished, but this new denial of civil

50

rights was seen as a poor reward for loyalty.

Dyer was beyond reasoning with, however. All he knew was that he'd been sent to Amritsar because of rioting and civil disaffection. Before he arrived, two European men had been killed and an Englishwoman missionary beaten up. Now, as he saw it, a mob of agitators was flooding into a public park in the middle of the city and yelling for blood. He was mortally afraid of what might happen next.

Frenzied, he yelled at his staff officers, 'Don't all stand here arguing with me. Get out and get moving. Mobilise the men. Arm them with machine guns. We have to show these niggers that we are the rulers here.'

When they disappeared, he went to his desk and fished a bottle of brandy out of the bottom drawer. Without bothering to find a glass, he pulled out the cork and held the neck of the bottle to his mouth, glugging it down. When he'd wiped his mouth, he felt better, ready to take on anything. What he did not know was that his name would never be forgotten in India, and because of him, the date was to become one of the most significant in the history of the country.

An official car, with his General's pennant flying from the bonnet, and driven by an impassive faced British sergeant, was waiting outside in the roadway for him. Dyer and his adjutant climbed into the back seat and he said, 'All right, sergeant. Take us to this Jalianwala place.'

It worried him that the force under his command was not large – less than fifty white men including officers and NCOs. They were lined up in a narrow street leading to a walled park which was already jam-packed full with a seething mass of local people. Over the heads of this crowd floated banners and placards – some of them in Hindi script, others in English. Those that Dyer could read proclaimed things like, 'End the Rowlatt Acts' and 'India for Indians'.

In the front of the crowd, facing the khaki-clad military contingent of both white and native soldiers, were grim-faced men wearing the plain-coloured homespun clothes that Mohandas Gandhi advocated as suitable wear for his followers.

The crowd went quiet when Dyer's open car drove into the narrow lane that led to the park, and stopped with its nose pointing towards the crowd. He stood up and stared at the men in the front rank of the crowd. Some of them began chanting – 'English out! English out!' The others took it up and a huge noise of roaring voices rose to the blue heavens.

'Bloody rabble,' hissed Dyer. He knew he had to show courage so he stood still and very straight, staring menacingly at the mass of yelling people facing him. Fierce-looking

52

turbaned Sikhs were prominent in the crowd, and, as Paterson had said, there were also women, dressed in plain saris and shouting as loudly as the men.

Dyer's eyes swept over the sea of faces in the park before he looked down at his adjutant to ask, 'How many do you think are in there?'

'About six or seven thousand, I'd say, sir.'

'More than that, and they're still coming,' said Dyer, pointing across to the far side of the open space to another entrance, through which more people were crowding like ants into an ant hill. In a few minutes the mob increased to a terrifying ten thousand, a crowd of hostile faces and open shouting mouths that made Dyer's bowels melt with fear.

Very conscious of his vulnerability because his force numbered only a fraction of their opponents, he thought, If this lot go rabid, even without arms they'll tear us all apart. Sweat stood out on his forehead and his heart fluttered. He wished he'd brought the brandy with him. Because he'd been posted behind the front lines in France, he'd survived the fighting there, but now it looked as if he was about to meet his maker in an Indian public park. Not if he could help it!

Bending down, he lifted a trumpet shaped megaphone that was lying on the front seat beside the driver. Heart palpitating and legs trembling, he put the megaphone to his mouth. 'In the name of the king emperor, I order you to go home. Disperse immediately,'he shouted in English because he knew no Hindi. The words echoed and re-echoed off the twenty-foot-high stone walls that encircled the park.

People were still coming through the only entrance on the far side, and the response to Dyer's order was derisive. One turbaned Sikh in front of the crowd imitated the general's English accent and shouted back, 'You *go home,* General. This is India and it is our country. We fought for you in the war and now you are disdaining us. Is that how you treat your supporters?'

Dyer's natural high colour deepened to purple and he felt a strange popping noise in his ears, which made him afraid he was on the verge of a stroke. 'I'm warning you, if you do not disperse immediately, you will suffer retribution,' he yelled back into the megaphone.

The only response was more chanting, more flag waving, and more derision.

He tried again. 'Go home. I'm warning you, if you don't, I'll order my men to shoot.'

Uncaring because they were disbelieving, the mob yelled back. He looked down at his adjutant for support and saw that the man's face was set in a strange, immobile expression. He was on his own, like a frightened child. He put his hand on the loaded revolver he carried in a holster on his belt but it was little comfort to him.

The faces looking up at him from the crowd were resolute. These were proud people with a grievance, who would not draw back from bloodshed if sufficiently provoked. One tall man in the front had a peculiarly piercing stare that seemed to penetrate Dyer's innermost soul. That man knows I'm frightened, he thought, and lost his head completely. He was no longer thinking rationally.

'Reverse the car,' he told the driver.

With a grinding of gears, the car inched backwards and Dyer was thrown down into his seat. The crowd laughed, thinking they had won and he was withdrawing, but they made no move to follow him. Paterson, mounted on a bay horse, was waiting in the alley when the car stopped beside him.

The general, face contorted like a gargoyle and incandescent with fury, leaned out yelling at him, 'So this is your peaceful demonstration, is it? What are you going to do about it, Paterson?'

'I still think we should stand by and let them have their say in the park, sir. When they've got it off their chests, they'll go home,' was the reply. Paterson had fought in France with soldiers from the Punjab and respected them greatly. Privately he thought they'd been given a raw deal, but resignedly accepted that it was useless to plead the Indian side with Dyer, a dyed-in-the-wool British supremacist who knew nothing about the country or the psychology of its people.

'Rubbish! We've got to make an example of them or we'll never be respected here again,' the general shouted hysterically.

Paterson looked at the adjutant who he knew shared his point of view. The man deliberately looked away.

Dyer was standing up in his seat again, staring over to where a detachment of British soldiers was standing beside machine guns pointing towards the leading demonstrators at the opening to the park.

'Get the men ready to fire,' he ordered.

'Surely not!' was the major's involuntary reaction.

Dyer screamed, 'Do as I tell you. Tell them to get ready to fire.'

Even the most hardened sergeant in charge of the machine gunners stared at the general in disbelief, and Paterson tried again to remonstrate with him. 'Are you sure, sir? These people are all unarmed, and look at the women...' he pleaded.

'Do what I tell you or you'll be bloody well court-martialled,' yelled the general.

Stony faced, Paterson raised his arm and shouted, 'Prepare to fire!' He hoped the men in the front of the crowd heard him and did not dismiss the order as an empty threat.

The guns were levelled, eyes narrowed, fingers tensed on triggers, and more men stood beside the gunners waiting to reload.

Dyer shouted again at the crowd, 'For the last time, disperse!'

The crowd was so thickly packed by now that it was difficult for most of the people to move, far less run away. They all went quiet and stared back at him in disbelief.

'We have no guns,' one tall man yelled back, spreading out his arms.

Dyer lost his head completely. 'Fire!' he yelled, brandishing his arm at the machine gunners.

Paterson closed his eyes. Dyer must have gone mad, he thought, but short of pulling out his revolver and shooting the general, he could do nothing.

The crowd, pressing close to the mouth of the lane, seemed to be frozen in shock, unable to believe that these soldiers really intended to shoot them down.

'Fire, fire! Kill them!' Dyer was screaming, and the British sergeant, a man called McKay, raised his arm in a desperate gesture.

'Get ready, load, FIRE!' he yelled. A terrible volley rang out from men too well trained to disobey orders.

Paterson turned his head away, ashamed to look at what he knew would be carnage.

The front row of marchers, including the man who'd mocked Dyer, fell at the first volley. Terrible spreads of scarlet marked their white clothes and turned them into martyrs. Brave men in the second row attempted to rush the line of gunners but a second order rang out, and, amid the rattle of machine gun fire, they fell too.

Seeing what was happening, terrified people farther back in the crowd turned and tried to run away, but the crowd was so dense that it was impossible to escape through the single narrow alley that led out from the far side. People milled around, screaming and stepping over dead bodies, but they were trapped like rats in a barrel – and all the time Dyer kept yelling at his men to go on firing.

The rain of death kept falling as men and women vainly tried to escape by climbing up the high surrounding walls or hiding behind trees and bushes. There was a well in the middle of the park and some desperate people jumped into it, only to drown there because others jumped in on top of them.

The gunners did not stop firing until they ran out of ammunition. In a space of less than ten minutes they fired 1,300 rounds into an unarmed and defenceless crowd who did not fire one shot back.

When McKay shouted that there was no ammunition left, a stony-faced Paterson gave the order to retire. Dyer's car reversed rapidly out of the lane with the general sitting exhausted in the back seat. No one went into the park to help the wounded or the dying who lay heaped in front of them.

A Sikh called Lal Singh, who had been in the front of the crowd, crawled out from under the body of his dead brother, and knelt in anguish as he watched Dyer's car driving away. 'I curse you, I curse you all, I will have my revenge,' he called out, raising his eyes to the sky.

That night, while the officers were at dinner, reports arrived at headquarters that 380 protesters had been killed and over a thousand wounded. There was no tally taken of the drowned in the well. Grimly, Paterson reported these figures to Dyer and his fellow officers at the mess table. 'There were no casualties among our men,' he added in a cold voice.

'Well done, well done. That'll teach them,' cried a jubilant and very drunk Dyer.

Next day he received a telegram from Sir Michael O'Dwyer, Lieutenant Governor of the Punjab, complimenting him on his action and hinting at promotion to Brigadier General because of it.

'I've shown them who's master in this place,' said Dyer, who was still very drunk when the telegram arrived.

Meanwhile in the army lines of the cantonment, both officers and sepoys were stunned with shock, horrified at what had been done. A grey-haired subadar called Abdul, a long-time soldier, rose from his seat by a guttering bonfire and went to the latrines where he hung himself from the rafters.

Another proud and upright sergeant called Sher Singh, recently returned from France where he had distinguished himself by conspicuous bravery, slipped off to the temple and prostrated himself in prayer for a long time.

Later he joined Lal Singh and a group of shaken survivors of the massacre to tell them of his terrible remorse about what had happened. 'I was confined to barracks or I would have turned my gun on Dyer when he gave his order. None of us believed he would shoot into the crowd but I will atone for my cowardice by taking revenge somehow,' he said.

'On Dyer and on O'Dwyer, the governor. They both deserve to die,' said an army office clerk who had deciphered the governor's telegram to Dyer.

The little group in the temple shook hands on the vow and the word of it passed round native India like the flickerings of a hardly discernible but potentially disastrous fire.

Cawnpore, April 20th, 1919

Harry Mason always opened his personal mail at the breakfast table, and the women did the same.

Most of the Masons' letters came from their two children, both of whom were 'at home' – a nineteen-year-old daughter Susan living with an aunt in Hove and their son, also Harry, now seventeen, who was finishing his schooling in his father's old school, George Watson's College, in Edinburgh, and planned to study medicine in the city's medical school.

Neither of them had been able to visit their parents during the war years and they were becoming strangers to each other. When Molly read their letters, she was amazed at how adult her children seemed, for she still thought of them as the young people she left at home in 1911. Her next visit back had been scheduled for the spring of 1915 but, of course, it never happened.

The separation was very painful for her, and, she suspected, for Harry too, but neither of them talked about their sadness.

61

She confided in God, however, and prayed every day that soon they would be able to go home, perhaps for good, though she knew that Harry would find it difficult to settle away from India and his precious hospital.

Jenny's mail consisted of the occasional letter from friends and a weekly missive from her mother, to which she always replied by return, writing enthusiastic descriptions of the beauties and customs of the strange country where she was now living. In her last letter she had told about the mysterious Begum, describing her secluded home and the close family life that went on in it. Her letters gave her mother colourful material with which she regaled her friends at the weekly whist drives she attended in the Edinburgh suburb of Blackhall.

On a sweltering morning Harry opened the last letter in his pile and raised his eyebrows in surprise. It was written on a single scrappy sheet, in what looked like an indecipherable scrawl, which he pored over for some time before looking up and saying to Molly, 'Well, my dear, your prayers have been answered. Allen's coming back.'

So he knows about my prayers! thought Molly, as she looked up with her face suddenly enlivened. 'When?' she asked.

'Soon, he says. In fact he's probably on a ship now. He's been in hospital but he's recovered and wants to get back to work as soon as possible. He sends his regards to you, my dear.'

Molly's eyes were shining. 'Does that mean we can have our leave at last?' she whispered.

'That's exactly what it means. We'll be catching the old P&O steamer by the beginning of July at the latest. It'll be stinking hot in Calcutta then but you won't mind that if you're on your way home, will you?'

She clasped her hands. 'Oh no! I'm so pleased. I must write and tell the children. I can hardly wait to see them.' For once her voice did not carry its 'martyred' tone, but was filled with unalloyed delight.

Both the Masons looked at Jenny, and Harry said, 'You'll be working with Allen while I'm away, Jenny. He's a good fellow when you get used to his manner.'

'What sort of manner has he?' she asked, wondering about the changes that lay ahead for her.

'He's rather abrupt, doesn't waste words or suffer fools gladly. The Gymkhana Club set don't like him much, I'm afraid,' said Harry, who had little time for the gymkhana set himself, and Molly chimed in, 'He *is* rather a rough diamond. Daphne Villiers once said to me that she thinks he's an Irishman from the bogs, but the patients respect him because he doesn't kowtow or expect to be kowtowed to. The nurses will be pleased to hear he's coming back, though. They all like him, especially Sadie.'

Harry said nothing. He knew that Sadie had more than a marked fondness for Allen, but he'd never talked about that to his wife.

Jenny frowned. 'When you return from your leave, will I still be needed in the hospital if Dr Allen's back?' she asked.

Her contract stipulated that she was to work for at least a year before she qualified for a paid passage home. After her first year, however, if both she and the hospital superintendent were satisfied, she would be offered an extension.

'Of course you will! You're doing a good job here. And you'll be needed while I'm on leave because Allen will be rusty about the sort of things that crop up with us. He couldn't run the place on his own,' said Harry.

'How long will you be away?' Jenny asked, still doubtful.

'Six months,' said Molly quickly, before Harry could start cutting their time down.

Six months from July will take us up to December and, in January, it will be a year since I first arrived. When Harry comes back, as he certainly will, the hospital will be over-staffed, Jenny thought.

The man at the end of the table read her mind. 'Don't worry. There'll certainly be a job for you if you want it. I won't let them send you back if you don't want to go. The work load has increased a lot since you arrived because the local women have heard good things about you, and we can afford another doctor. In fact I was thinking of asking the board at home for funds to give you a maternity and gynaecological clinic all to yourself.'

Jenny tried to look pleased but privately she was disappointed in Harry, and dismayed because she did not want to be relegated to the areas that her old professors considered the only suitable areas of medicine for a woman. One of the things she enjoyed most in Cawnpore was being treated like a man as far as work was concerned.

Harry let her do surgery, and she also enjoyed coping with the rush and bustle of the accident and emergency department. Most of all she relished the intellectual stimulus of helping him diagnose and treat difficult diseases in both men and women. Every day, thanks to him, she was gaining experience and expertise.

'I don't know how I'll feel about continuing when my year is up,' she said cautiously.

The Masons looked at her in consternation. 'Aren't you happy here, my dear?' asked Molly anxiously.

'Very happy, I enjoy the work and I enjoy living with you, but after a year I might be ready to go home. I love India and I know already that I'd miss it if I left because it's a fascinating country, but in a way I could be cutting myself off from professional advancement if I stay away too long.' The Masons listened with solemn faces while she stumbled on.

When she'd said her say, Molly leaned forward with hands clasped. 'We want you to stay because we enjoy having you here. You're like a daughter to us. Perhaps you won't want to leave if you meet someone nice to marry,' she suggested.

'Molly!' snapped her husband in a warning tone, but she paid no attention. Smiling at Jenny she said, 'I've organised a bridge party for tomorrow night and I want you to play because there's a special bachelor coming who you might get to know.'

Harry groaned.

In party mood, the bridge enthusiasts draped themselves over the wicker sofas and chairs in Molly's drawing room with full glasses in their hands. Though they saw each other almost every day of their lives, they shrieked, boomed and gossiped as if they'd been parted for months. They were all excited and intrigued by the stimulus of introduction of strangers to their close circle – and not just one stranger, but two. There was the recently arrived girl doctor, plus Daphne Villiers' nephew, a high-ranking policeman.

66

Daphne was the wife of Philip Villiers, Cawnpore's senior man in the Indian Civil Service, and, as his consort, she was top woman in the highest echelon of local society. She only deigned to attend this party because Dr Mason's wife played a demon hand of bridge, and, when she and Molly played together, they always won.

It was Jenny's first party because she was disinclined to venture into society. Though she had been introduced to one or two of Molly's friends after Sunday morning church services, she turned down their invitations to morning coffee or ladies' lunches, pleading pressure of work.

Attendance at this party was unavoidable, however, and she stood in a corner with a fixed smile on her face, trying to make conversation and stay out of the way of the wandering hands of a lecherous Scotsman who managed the Elgin Mills in the city. To the other women guests, she was the least interesting of the strangers because she was only another female, and a do-gooder at that.

They weighed her up in a glance, deciding that, though impressively tall and pretty enough, she was not a startling beauty, and, thankfully, no femme fatale so no threat as a husband stealer. They scrutinised her clothes without envy because she was very plainly dressed in a cream dress of tissore silk. Jenny

Garland, they decided, was boringly serious and not sufficiently upper class, just a 'nice' girl.

Daphne's nephew, Chief Inspector Robert Ross, was a more intriguing subject altogether and for weeks they had listened to his aunt boasting about how capable and handsome he was. 'He's a rising star in the police service, and his speciality is undercover work. He's terribly brave, and he often dresses up as a native and goes into the bazaar. He recently exposed a group of political plotters in Calcutta, so if they're sending him to Cawnpore, they must suspect that something is going on here too,' Daphne said portentously.

Excitement was running high because Daphne always took care to be the last to arrive at a party. When her car drew up on the gravelled drive, the other guests, convulsed with curiosity, all craned forward in their chairs to watch her entrance. Though she was wearing a beautiful dress of draped fawn chiffon and a long rope of real pearls that gleamed with a succulent lustre, it was her companion that attracted most interest.

Waving a ringed hand in his direction, she said to Molly, '*So* kind of you to invite us. This is Robert, my *older* sister's son. As I told you, he's with the police.'

The word 'older' was stressed because the nephew was at least thirty, and Daphne's age was a topic of considerable speculation. Childless and stick thin, she never appeared without heavy make-up, even in the early morning or when going swimming in the Cawnpore Club pool. Harry Mason was of the opinion that if he met Daphne without her maquillage, he would be unable to recognise her.

The man who followed her into the room was not a disappointment, and an almost visible frisson of sexual excitement swept through the female guests at the sight of him – tall, and dark haired, with a strongly boned face and dominating nose that made him look like a proud Roman emperor, he was wearing an immaculately pressed cream linen suit, and his broad shoulders seemed to block the whole width of the drawing room door. With solemn and unsmiling eyes he surveyed the gathering and, under their gaze, the other men seemed to shrink into insignificance, intimidated by his masculine glory.

Jenny looked across at Dr Mason and saw an amused look in his eyes as the handsome policeman stepped into the gathering. In spite of herself she smiled too, and an un-expected surge of gaiety, and a desire to flirt, suddenly rose in her. It was a surprise because she thought she'd left feelings like that behind in her student days. Tonight might be amusing after all.

There were twelve people at the party. Pairs were swiftly arranged and the players seated. Daphne and her nephew were playing together and, at another table, Jenny and Dr Mason, neither of whom were enthusiastic bridge players, were partnered with each other. The doctor was very erratic and did not care if Jenny made mistakes too, but, in spite of their failings, they succeeded in winning two rubbers before dinner was announced.

After they ate, Molly announced that everyone must draw for new partners and, to her disquiet, Jenny found herself paired with the intimidating Ross. Unlike the doctor, he took the game very seriously, furrowing his brow as he stared at his hand and pronouncing his bids in a tone that sounded solemn enough for an official warning.

There was to be no flirting with this man. Flustered by his solemnity, Jenny either overbid or underbid and their opposition – Molly and Daphne – had no trouble in wiping the floor with them.

It was a relief when Molly announced that the evening's finale was to be played out between the four people with the highest scores. Jenny was not one of them and, because of her, neither was Ross. While the last game was going on, she accepted a glass of gin and soda from the bearer and strolled on to the verandah where a faint breeze was blowing the scent of night jasmine in from the garden.

Putting the glass on the step, she sat down with her elbows on her knees and her chin on her hands, staring at the mysterious purple shadows beneath the trees. Were wild animals lurking out there, staring back in amazement at the people in the party, she wondered?

It took a few moments before she became aware of two highly polished brown shoes beside her and a voice asking, 'May I sit beside you?' It was the handsome policeman.

Looking up, she smiled at him and moved along a little to give him space. 'Of course,' she said.

A faint whiff of coal tar soap that reminded her of the hospital came from him as he settled on the step by her side.

'I understand that you're a doctor,' he said.

Not another one who thinks it isn't a suitable job for a woman! she thought, but nodded in agreement, and said, 'Yes, I am.'

'We don't get many lady doctors coming out to India,' he told her.

'You'll probably get more now. A lot of male doctors were killed in the war,' she said.

He nodded solemnly and agreed. 'That's true. Where did you study?'

'Edinburgh.'

'A famous medical school I believe. Were there many women studying with you?'

'Twenty in a class of a hundred and forty when we started, but only eight of us graduated,' she told him.

'Why was that?' He seemed genuinely interested.

'Several reasons. The professors in the medical school aren't keen on women students and are much harder on them than on the men. Some of the girls gave up because they were not exactly encouraged to stay,' she said.

'What do you mean?' he asked.

She frowned. 'Women are regarded as inferior in the medical world, I'm afraid. Because of male prudery, we weren't allowed to attend many of the lectures with the men, but we had to pass the same exams. It was considered immodest for both sexes to look at naked bodies together, so we couldn't share anatomy lessons either. There's even a separate dissecting lab for women students, very grudgingly provided I may say. I thought it was so stupid. Some of the men students were as bad as the teachers and used to barrack us during lectures and they were never told to stop.'

He shook his head and said, 'It all seems very ungentlemanly.'

Encouraged by his sympathy, she laughed and said, 'It toughened up the survivors, but as far as most of the medical profession is concerned women are on sufferance in a man's world. Even some of my friends who got their degrees gave up and settled for marriage.'

'But you didn't,' he said.

She turned her head to look full at him as she asked, 'Gave up, you mean? If I had I wouldn't be here now, would I?' Her eyes were so wide and frank, he couldn't decide if she was being sacrcastic. She was a handsome young woman, he noted as he said, 'No, I meant you didn't get married.'

She shrugged slightly as she replied, 'Actually I did.'

There was silence for a few moments while he reached into his pocket and brought out a silver cigarette case. 'Do you smoke?' he asked.

She shook her head, glad that she didn't have to speak because her eyes were stinging as they always did when she talked about her marriage.

'Do you mind if I do?' he asked.

She shook her head again and the light from his Vesta flared up in front of his face, highlighting the strong cheekbones and prominent nose. When his cigarette was burning satisfactorily, he asked a question to which he already knew the answer from his gossipy aunt, who had been told Jenny's story by Molly.

'Where is your husband now? Is he in Cawnpore too?'

'He's in France, in a military graveyard.' Her voice was flat.

'I'm sorry for being so intrusive,' he said quietly.

'Don't worry. I'm practising being able to talk about it. The Masons know the story, but they're very kind and tactful about avoiding the subject because they're afraid of upsetting me. I'm Mrs James Hope. He was a doctor too – a couple of years ahead of me in medical school. A week after the wedding, he was sent to France.'

He drew deeply on his cigarette, and asked, 'When was that?'

'Three years ago. In 1916. He was on the Somme. We were luckier than some people, I suppose, because he lived long enough to have seven days' leave before he was killed. I got a telegram....' Her voice trailed off, but soon she was able to add, 'When I graduated, I applied to go to France and work as a surgeon at the Front, too, but they wouldn't take women ... so I worked in the casualty department of Edinburgh Royal Infirmary instead. It was almost as dangerous.' She laughed slightly bitterly and he shook his head, but whether in agreement with the authorities about women doctors at the Front or not, she could not tell.

'It's been a terrible war. Many of my

friends died in it, too. I missed going to France because I'd joined the Indian police before war broke out and they needed me here. The authorities are afraid of civil insurrection, you see, and that saved my life, I suppose,' he told her.

She stared at him, thinking that if he dressed up as an Indian to go undercover, as his aunt said, he'd get away with it. 'You were lucky,' she told him.

'Was I? I feel guilty when I think of the friends who were killed.'

'You shouldn't. You're doing a worthwhile job here, aren't you? You had to obey orders, just as they did. Now you must do the things they would have wanted to do if they'd lived.'

Her voice sounded tired and he asked, 'Is that why you've come out to India – to do something your husband wanted to do?'

'Perhaps. James was a great idealist. He wanted to help sick people anywhere in the entire world. But I came to India because I needed to get as far as possible away from the places I knew – and to be useful as well, I suppose.' She felt her voice quaver slightly as she spoke but he did not seem to notice, and when he replied, his tone was hard.

'You'll find plenty to do here,' he said.

In an effort to change the subject and lighten the atmosphere, she said, 'Molly said you're newly arrived in Cawnpore. Where were you before?'

'In Calcutta. I've been promoted, and Cawnpore seems a pleasant enough place. Better than Calcutta anyway. That's grim but interesting. I want to travel around a bit when I'm here because I've a family connection with Lucknow. My grandfather and grandmother were in the siege at the Residency and I was brought up hearing about their adventures,' he told her.

'So many of the English people I've met out here seem to come from families with long connections in the country. It makes me think that there can hardly be a family in Britain that hasn't a link with India,' she said.

'That's true, especially among Army families, but my lot were box wallahs. Grandfather had an indigo farm up river from here and my grandmother's father was also in trade. They told me so much about India that I wanted to join the I.C.S. like Daphne's husband, but, unfortunately, I failed the exam. The police took me though,' he solemnly told her.

She nodded and said, 'Even I have an Indian connection, though it's a small one. My father was born in this country but he was only a baby when he left and he never talked about it much because he couldn't remember it at all. He died when I was seven, so we never really talked to each other much anyway. I'm sorry about that now.'

'Has he no relatives who could tell you about his background?' asked Ross.

She shook her head. 'No, unfortunately not. His parents died when he was small and he was an only child.'

'We shouldn't forget that British sacrifice built this country,' said Ross in an intense tone of voice. 'All this talk of power sharing is stupid. The blacks are incapable of ruling themselves, and they'd cut our throats if we showed any weakness. The Mutiny could happen all over again if the authorities are not careful. Even that Gandhi chap needs watching though he preaches non-violence. But the police are watching. We won't be taken by surprise this time.'

His eagerness to convince her made him lean over and say earnestly, 'Don't let any do-gooders persuade you that the Indians are different today compared to 1857. They're not. Some of them *in this very city* are plotting insurrection at this very moment. I know that for a fact and it's up to me to stop them.'

There was such an intense tone in his voice that she shivered, cold in spite of the warmth of the night, and had to steel herself not to move along the step away from him, but she sat still and said, 'It must be galling to have your country ruled by a foreign race. Scotland's had a taste of that and we don't like it. I've noticed that some British people out here behave very badly towards the locals, and bad things happened on both sides in the Mutiny, didn't they?'

'We took a hard revenge, but who can blame us after such atrocities? At least we didn't harm women,' he said.

Jenny shook her head and told him, 'But we did sometimes. I know a woman whose grandmother was hung as a traitor by the British because she sympathised with the mutineers.'

He was immediately interested. 'Really? What was her name?'

'Miss Dolly Mullins, I think,' said Jenny.

'That's some name, more like a music hall singer! Where did you meet her grand-daughter?' He sounded interested.

'She's a nurse in the hospital where I work. She's called Sadie. I'm not sure of her second name but it's probably Mullins.'

Before he could reply, they heard the sound of the party breaking up and Daphne's voice calling for him. As he rose, he said, 'When I have the opportunity, I'll look up the Mutiny records and send you any information I can find about your Miss Dolly Mullins.'

Robert Ross had a compulsive nature. If he got an idea into his head, he would pursue it to the bitter end. When he saw the young doctor sitting forlornly on the verandah steps with her chin on her fists, he decided there and then that he was going to marry her.

It wasn't that he'd fallen in love or anything. That was not part of his plan. His was a pragmatic decision that would probably suit them both, because his aunt had already told him that Dr Mason's new assistant in the hospital was a war widow. When the survivors came back from the war, she might be out of a job. Most patients, the men certainly, were chary of being treated by a girl. He wouldn't stand for it himself.

Ross was thirty-four years old and fiercely ambitious. Because he was daring and ruthless, he quickly made his mark in the Indian Police service and his early career path was smoothed by the deaths of contemporaries, three of whom were assassinated in their up-country postings by agents of the political opposition. The war or old age removed other men who blocked his path to advancement and he was given promotion to Chief Inspector in a relatively short time. Now he required a suitable wife to ease his path in society. Single men over a certain age were suspect, as his aunt had not hesitated in pointing out when she told him about Jenny.

Because life for single women in their expatriate community was as anomalous as it was for single men, Daphne reckoned that Jenny was also looking for marriage. From

Molly she'd learned that the new doctor was twenty-six, but did not look her age because she was tall, slim, and girlish. At her age, however, it would be more difficult for her to find a husband than for one of the young 'fishing fleet' girls who came out straight from school to India. Clever women were a bit of a bore as far as Daphne was concerned, and this new girl must be intelligent or she'd never have passed her professional examinations, but that could be overlooked.

'She's just what you need. She's still at the weepy stage about her husband but she'll get over that in time. It's up to you to lay claim to her before someone else moves in,' she told her nephew as they drove home together after the bridge party.

One of the first things Ross did when he reached his office next morning was to look up the files of police and military reports from Mutiny times and search through them for mentions of Dolly Mullins. The only reference he found was to Dorothy Mullins who was arrested in Cawnpore bazaar in December 1858, and taken under guard to Lucknow. That had to be the one.

A few days later, having heard that the biggest archive of Mutiny material was in Lucknow, he took a day off and covered the forty miles to that city by car, driving himself and tearing along tree-lined, rutted and dusty roads, irritably blasting his horn and scattering bullock carts, pony-drawn tongas, pedestrians and wandering animals on all sides.

The results of his labours among the Lucknow files were posted off to Dr Jenny in Cawnpore, and she received four pages of neatly written notes in a big brown buff envelope a day later.

The first page read:

Dorothy or Dolores Mullins, also known as Miss Dolly, a Eurasian woman, aged 36, was executed by hanging at Lucknow on Eighteenth December 1858. On the previous day, she had been found guilty by a military tribunal of treason and incitement to murder.

She worked as a prostitute in the Meerut bazaar from around 1850 till 1857 and her clients were native sepoys from the various regiments of foot stationed there. She refused to sleep with Europeans.

It was well known that she was actively engaged in incitement to mutiny even before the unrest began, haranguing her clients to sweep out the British rule and refusing to accommodate any men who drew back from murder. Not only that, but she organised other prostitutes to follow her lead. This had a strong impact in forcing undecided men towards rebellion. She was said to have advocated the killing of British women and children as well as Company soldiers.

Ross added a note that, as far as he could find out, Mullins was the daughter of an unruly Irish sergeant who served with the East India Company army from 1830 till 1848 when he died, leaving a half-caste widow and two handsome Eurasian daughters, both of whom married British soldiers.

Dorothy's choice was an Irishman like her father, but he too turned out to be a drunken brawler who was frequently disciplined by his superiors. When her husband died of unspecified causes, poison was suspected, but no investigation was ever launched, and she did not take the usual army ranker's widow's option of marrying one of his comrades. Instead she left the cantonment and took up prostitution in the Meerut bazaar.

According to the evidence, she seemed to have early links with plotters and was aware of the planned insurrection before it erupted. Dolly helped to incite religious fears of contamination among both Hindu and Moslem sepoys before the actual outbreak of rebellion in Meerut on May 10th 1857.

When the maddened mutineers did their work and moved on through the country to

Delhi, she and a band of other women like herself turned up in Lucknow and then Cawnpore, still preaching the doctrine of hatred against the whites. In the aftermath of the rebellion, she went to ground, but was betrayed by an unknown woman. Dolly was found hiding in Cawnpore bazaar, arrested, taken to Lucknow for sentencing, and hung the next day.

Signing off, Ross scrawled:

I found this information in the records and thought it might interest you. She sounds like a wicked woman. There was no reference to any children, but she must have had at least one if you know her granddaughter. Perhaps we can talk about it when we next meet.

Best wishes R. Ross

Jenny read the notes and wondered what turned a half-Irish girl into a rabid hater of her father's people. Why was Dolly so bitter? Something terrible must have happened to her.

Later that morning, working in the hospital alongside Sadie, she surreptitiously watched the nurse as she bustled about, efficient and economical in her movements, with capable hands that never seemed to fumble. If Jenny needed a special instrument, Sadie seemed to read her mind and was holding it out even before she was asked.

When she died, her grandmother Dolly would only have been a few years older than Sadie was now. Was she as quick-witted and capable as her granddaughter? Was the apparently sensible and collected Sadie hiding a character prone to terrible violence? Could she turn into a virago urging men to murder? In telling Jenny about Miss Dolly, was Ross showing her the hidden underside of India? Was he telling her not to be naïve?

Cawnpore, April 26th, 1919

In defiance of the Jalianwala Bagh protest, the Rowlatt Acts were rigorously applied and an official blackout imposed on news from Amritsar. No newspapers were allowed to print the story of Dyer's massacre in the park, so it was days before news of what had happened spread through the rest of India. But spread it did, in much the same surreptitious way as incitement to Mutiny in 1857 was signalled by the passing of chapattis from hand to hand across the vast country.

From bazaar to bazaar, along the ancient roads and tracks that carried news even before the arrival of *feringhees*, the story spread by word of mouth. Also the native press was not as easily gagged as the English-language outlets. Churned out on rickety presses, operated by inky printers in the back streets of little towns, flimsy news sheets carried the terrible story on their front pages.

Eventually an official government version had to be released to counteract the more outrageous rumours. According to this propaganda, Dyer was a hero, and Amritsar a cauldron of incipient rebellion that was made tranquil because of his timely actions. People were assured there would be no repetition of the riots or murders that had occurred in the city in previous months.

Reading their newspapers in bungalows scattered throughout the sub-continent European men and women felt quavers of fear because memories of the Mutiny were only dormant and they were uncomfortably aware that they were a tiny minority, dominating a country of millions. If the Indians were to rise, they could sweep the foreigners into the sea. After all, they'd almost succeeded in doing that only two generations ago. Beleaguered whites scanned the faces of their servants and workers and wondered if their loyalty was as staunch as it seemed.

At breakfast, Harry Mason suddenly laid his newspaper beside his plate with a look of the deepest distaste. 'Bloody hell!' he said to the coffee pot.

Since he was a man who rarely swore, his words made the two women eating alongside him sit up in surprise.

'Harry!' exclaimed Molly in a tone of deep disapproval.

He slapped both hands palm down on the white tablecloth and said again, even louder,

'Bloody hell.'

'What on earth is the matter?' asked his horrified wife.

'Look at that,' he said, throwing the folded paper across to her.

She lifted it and read aloud, 'Rioters dispersed and peace restored at Amritsar because of General Dyer's timely action...'

Lifting her head, she said, 'I don't know why you're surprised. There's been a lot of trouble there recently. General Dyer seems to have put a stop to their nonsense so things will calm down now I expect.'

'Will they? That's exactly what you're meant to think. But Dyer and his men were armed – the Indians weren't. That madman could start another mutiny with this.'

Molly's face flushed. 'It's always the same with you, Harry. The Indians are always right. I think if one of them came rushing in here and tried to kill me, you'd find some excuse for him.'

Dr Mason stood up. 'I hope for your sake that isn't about to happen, but I'm not so sure it won't after this,' he snapped and stormed out of the room.

Jenny sat silent, listening to their exchange, and when a tearful Molly flounced off in the direction of her bedroom, she reached over and picked up the discarded newspaper from the floor. The report of the shooting at Amritsar was obviously one-sided, but it could not hide the fact that General Dyer's troops had fired on a mass demonstration of men and women, killing or wounding many of them. Nobody fired back.

The report said that Sir Michael O'Dwyer, Lieutenant Governor of the Punjab, was hailing Dyer as a hero who, greatly out-numbered, faced a mob with bravery and resolution. Messages relayed back from the government in London echoed O'Dwyer's opinion and Dyer was to be promoted to Brigadier General.

At the same time as Jenny was reading the newspaper, Robert Ross sat in his office in police headquarters with a telegram on the desk in front of him.

It was signed by his equivalent in the Amritsar police and said, 'Reliable informa-tion Sikh insurgents on way to Cawnpore to contact sympathisers. Expect trouble. Please follow up.'

Exactly how? he thought. There were a million-and-a-half people living in and around Cawnpore city – no one was sure of the exact number and among them had to be thousands of malcontents. How many were dangerous plotters?

He liked difficult tasks, however. They put him on his mettle. He laid down the tele-gram and lifted one of his English-language newspapers. A report on the British government's approval of Dyer's action in Amritsar filled the front page, but towards the end of the piece there was a paragraph saying that some people at home felt the action was 'unfortunate' and 'ill judged'.

Ross snorted. 'Bloody woolly thinkers,' he said aloud. Lying beside the pro-Dyer *Times of India* was a local news-sheet, written in Punjabi. He had a good working knowledge of the language, enough to make out that the local opinion was very different to the English one.

According to the Punjabi paper, Dyer was a cold-blooded killer and the British authorities guilty of disdain for making him a hero because he shot unarmed Indian people. The paper called for all patriots to unite in opposition to an overbearing government that would not give Indians the opportunity to play a part in ruling their own country.

'Rabble rousers,' said Ross to an engraving of Britannia on the back wall of his office.

He leaned back in his chair and let the breeze from the electric punkah blow round his bare knees beneath his stiffly starched khaki shorts. The time had come to do a little snooping round, and he knew where to go to start his enquiries, but before that he wanted to check on the security of his own staff, all of whom were new to him. He'd lay a little trap by pretending to ignore the message of the telegram and going to the Mission hospital to pay court to the woman doctor. As he left his office, he locked its door.

Jenny was helping Flora and Sadie to sterilise the surgical instruments. She preferred the nurses to do that task because the male laboratory assistants boiled up the instruments well enough, but went on to pick them up with their bare hands, indifferent to the fact that they were only contaminating them again.

Flora looked up when a large open car drove into the compound and parked beneath the sterilising room window. 'Who's this?' she asked, for few, if any, of their patients arrived by car unless the driver had inadvertently run them over.

Jenny went to the window and looked out as well. 'It's that policeman, Mrs Villiers' nephew. I met him playing bridge the other night,' she said.

'I bet he's come to see you, Jenny,' teased Flora but Jenny shook her head. 'I do hope not,' she said.

Of course Ross *had* come to see her. After an exchange of pleasantries with Dr Mason, the pair of them appeared in the sterilising room door and Harry said cheerfully, 'This gentleman wants to invite you out to lunch, Jenny.'

She looked around for an excuse. 'I wasn't planning on eating lunch. It's rather hot and my appetite seems to have disappeared,' she said.

Ross smiled. 'Then you need a glass of something long and cool and my club does very good snacks, especially Scotch woodcock or anchovy toast if you like that. Anyway it would be a pleasure to talk to you.'

'Yes, go. Things are quiet today,' encouraged kindly Harry Mason and his smiling face told Jenny that he wanted her to take this opportunity of breaking her routine. So, rather grudgingly, she pulled off her white coat and walked out of the room with Ross.

As he solicitously showed her into his car, he said, 'This will be a good chance for us to talk about Dolly Mullins. Did you get my notes?'

While Ross was escorting Jenny into the police club, one of his clerks used a skeleton key to slip into his office while the others were outside eating their tiffin. He had to work quickly and the telegram on the desk top was read first, then he went quietly and efficiently through a pile of papers in a wire tray beside it. Ross's notes on Dolly Mullins especially intrigued him.

He read them through and took care to replace them exactly as they had been. What he did not realise was that, before he went out, the wily Ross had lain two hairs across the top of the exposed papers on his desk, one on the telegram and the other on top of the Dolly Mullins notes. On his return he wanted to know if anyone had been snooping.

In the club, Jenny looked across the table at her escort and was struck by how good looking he was. She would have expected him to be married at his age, but perhaps the police service was like some commercial companies that did not allow recruits to marry until they proved themselves worthwhile employees – and that usually took eight to ten years.

It was pleasant to be sitting under shady trees, waited on by assiduous bearers and plied with tasty snacks and ice-cold drinks. The spartan life of the hospital seemed very far away, though it was only on the other side of the city.

'It's much greener here than where I live,' she said, looking around the carefully tended lawns.

'Yes, this is the best side of Cawnpore. The race course is over there,' he said pointing at a distant group of trees.

'I've never been to the races,' she said.

'Haven't you? It's tremendous fun. There's a meeting next week. My aunt always takes a party and the champagne flows like water.'

She laughed. 'I've never gambled or tasted champagne either. In my student days beer was the strongest drink I ever had.'

'Good heavens, you have led a sheltered life. We'll have to corrupt you a bit – or are you very straight-laced, being a missionary and all that?'

'I'm sailing under false colours there a bit, I'm afraid. I'm a doctor first of all and not out to make converts, though people often assume that I am,' she told him in a defensive tone.

'That's good,' he said, and then asked, 'What did you think of my notes on Dolly Mullins?'

'She sounded a bit mad to me. Or else terribly angry and resentful.'

'Well, she was half-Irish, and they're fiery people. She got the mutiny up and running in Meerut, and she was in Cawnpore at the time of the killings here too,' he said.

Jenny rested her chin in her hands and said reflectively, 'If she was pro-Irish, perhaps she associated herself with the Indians as another downtrodden race or something. After all, the 1850s was not long after the time when her father's people had died of hunger because of the potato famine. They had every reason to hate the English. I don't expect that excuses her though.'

He snorted. 'There's always people like her around, blaming other people for their own

93

bad luck, or for the way they mess up their lives. I haven't any time for them. I'm surprised the authorities didn't realise what trouble she was causing among the sepoys. They should have put a stop to it before things went too far. We wouldn't let it happen now,' he said firmly.

Big cubes of ice – tremendous luxuries in this weather – chinked in her glass of lime soda as she raised it to her lips and asked, 'How could you stop it?'

'Our information system is much more efficient. We have reliable informers and can put a brake on troublemakers before they get out of hand. That Gandhi fellow can't make a move without us knowing about it. I've been posted here to monitor incipient troublemakers because I'm a surveillance specialist...'

She stared at him. 'Do you seriously think there'll be trouble here?'

He frowned, 'After Amritsar there could be trouble anywhere, but cities like Cawnpore and Lucknow are very possible because they are famous names in Indian history as well as British. The niggers don't talk about the Mutiny, you know. They call it the War of Indian Independence! An insurrection in Cawnpore would be a rallying cry for trouble-makers all over the country, and believe me there's plenty of them.'

Jenny looked around the idyllic setting,

disbelieving that it could erupt into chaos. Smiling waiters were hovering around tables spread with gleaming silver and sparkling glasses. There had been nowhere as sybaritic in wartime Britain.

'But it's so peaceful here. The people are pleasant and they seem very contented!' she exclaimed, wondering if Ross, in his way, was as mad as Miss Dolly.

He shook his head. 'Don't you believe it. What you see is only the surface. As a policeman, I'm always worried when things go too quiet. It means we're being lulled into false confidence. Like people were before the Mutiny.'

He seemed to have the Mutiny on the brain, she thought as she said, 'I do hope you're wrong.'

He shook his head. 'Unfortunately I'm not wrong. We're battling against ignorance and prejudice and greed and cruelty here. We try our best, but the blacks want us out and they'll never appreciate us, no matter what we do. I hope you don't expect to be thanked for your work among them.'

During her short time in Cawnpore, Jenny always recoiled when she heard white people referring to natives as 'niggers' or 'blacks', and she mentally withdrew from the man opposite her when he used the offensive words.

'I don't find them ungrateful. In fact I'm

95

often embarrassed by the touching way some patients thank me for doing my job,' she told him.

'Oh they're very good at flattering us. *Muska* polish, they call it. *Muska* means butter – buttering up,' he told her. Jenny was taken aback by his sudden vehemence, as well as by the disparaging way he talked about the Indians.

'Perhaps I'm very naïve but I like most Indian people I've met since I arrived here,' she told him. The courtesy of local people always impressed her, especially when compared to the over-bearing and snobbish behaviour of some of the whites.

'Like them by all means, but don't take any chances with them. Believe me, under their smiles they resent you,' Ross told her. He seemed galvanised with dislike for the people among whom he had cast his lot.

'Perhaps they have good reason to resent us,' she retorted, though she knew it would be better to say nothing and let him rant on.

He stared at her as if he doubted her sanity.

'How can you say that when you're living in Cawnpore? Surely you know what happened here? You've heard of the Bibighar where over two hundred women and children were slaughtered – chopped to pieces and shoved down the well. The mutineers even made the women *eat* bits of their murdered children! Can you imagine that? It was an act of infernal cruelty that we should never forget or forgive.'

He was galvanised, urgent in his need to convince her. She shivered with horror and put her empty glass down on the table. It was time to return to work.

After Ross dropped her back at the hospital, he returned to his office and immediately noticed that his papers had been disturbed. The hair on the telegram was still in place, so it did not matter because it would have been read and talked about by the clerks already. What else would interest a snooper?

The Dolly Mullins information obviously. That hair was gone.

He pulled out the sheets and read them again. Were they important? He trusted no one. The clerks in the Lucknow archive would certainly have noticed and commented on his search through the archives, and his detective instinct told him that if someone was bothering to find out what he'd noted down, he may be on to something.

The fact that a snooper had taken the chance to go through his papers when he was out was the really significant thing though. Casually he strolled into the outer office where four clerks sat on high stools behind wooden desks piled high with buff cardboard files tied up with red ribbons. The saying about 'cutting through red tape' had come from India where subordinate officials were notoriously tardy and reluctant to give up their routines and their secrets.

He perched himself on an empty stool and surveyed his clerical force. 'Did you all go out to eat your tiffin?' he asked.

A grey-haired old fellow said he did. The others said they ate at their desks.

'You work too hard. Have all you fellows been here for a long time?' Ross asked in a cordial tone.

Narayan, the grey-haired man, a southern Brahmin by the look of him, nodded and said, 'Thirty years, sahib.'

His neighbour, Jadhav, a dark-skinned man from Maharashtra, chipped in, 'And I've been here for ten.'

The two youngest were a Moslem with a pale skin and a proud face, who said, 'I am Akbar, sahib, and I came five years ago,' and a fat fellow chipped in, 'And I'm Balraj. I joined last month.'

'You're Bengali, Balraj, aren't you?' said Ross.

'Yes, I'm from Calcutta, sir,' was the reply. He said 'sir', not 'sahib'. What did that mean?

Ross strolled back into his office, deliberately leaving the door half open and watched the men in the outer office through the gap. Balraj was new and the others well established. Perhaps he was a decoy. If household servants wanted to do a bit of stealing, they always took the chance when someone new joined the staff. It was the same with police clerks – if one of them was spying, he'd take care to divert the suspicion on to someone else. But it wasn't worthwhile taking chances with any of them. He'd have them all followed.

After the clerks went off for the night, he walked past the police lines in the hope of spotting a sergeant he'd asked to be transferred from Calcutta with him. This man, Ali Bey, a beetle-browed native of Lucknow, was an old associate. Together they had gone into the stews of Calcutta after various criminals and Ali Bey equalled Ross in courage and cunning, though they always treated each other with cautious reserve because Ross made sure that Ali Bey knew which of them was the more senior and important.

In Calcutta they always held their clandestine meetings about sundown and Ross knew that Ali could be looking out for him at that time – and he was. They knew better than to have any discussions within sight or earshot of other policemen, so exchanged greetings like old associates coming across each other by accident, had a little innocuous conversation and parted – but Ross let slip a code word that indicated he had information to impart. Later that night, when darkness fell, Ali slipped like a wraith across Ross's lawn and appeared at the verandah rail of his bungalow.

He was given his orders and slipped away unseen. The surveillance of the clerks was under way.

Cawnpore, April 30th, 1919

The hospital was very quiet when Jenny walked into the empty outpatients' department. Outside the sun blazed down. Somewhere in the distance she heard voices and the insistent thudding of a far-off drum and smelt the tang of a wood fire because it was time for the servants' midday meal that would be followed by a two-hour siesta for everyone except the nurses, unless some emergency interrupted it.

The heat rising from the earth pressed down on her like a blanket and her cotton dress clung damply to her back. She felt a painful kinship with the women who must have heard the same sounds and sweated in the same uncomfortable heat while they huddled together in the Bibighar. The story told to her by Robert Ross had preyed on her mind ever since.

At school she had thrilled with horror over the terrible stories of the Black Hole of Calcutta, the siege of the Lucknow Residency, and the massacre at Cawnpore, but in the schoolroom, these tales never seemed quite real. Now, in the place where such things happened, they did. Ross's fierce insistence that women like her were forced to eat the flesh of their own children made her shrink with horror. Could that possibly be true?

Could the servants who saluted her as they passed, white teeth flashing as they smiled, turn against their employers and coldly cut their throats? Was Ross right? Were all Indians dissemblers? She found that hard to believe but feared she was being ingenuous in taking Dr Mason's line and uncritically siding with the native people.

One of the things she had meant to do ever since she arrived in the city was visit the Garden of Remembrance which had been created as a memorial to the British people killed in the rising. She'd not yet gone to see it though Molly Mason kept urging her to do so.

'It's a lovely place, created by Lady Canning so that we would never forget what happened to these poor murdered souls. It's only open to white people. They don't let Indians in. I sometimes go there for a walk and the tranquillity makes me feel consoled. They say the ghost of a little blond-haired boy can sometimes be seen laughing and running around in the garden as if he hadn't a care in the world. I think that shows the dead are at peace, don't you?' Molly said in her anxious way.

The afternoon was wearing on as Jenny pulled a solar topi off a peg in the office, stuck it on her head and hurried to the shed to wheel out her bicycle. The sun blazed down near the horizon like a globe of molten metal and dust devils danced on the pathways as she rode along a line of hard, dry earth between the serried ranks of Molly's beloved rose bushes that were sadly wilting in the heat though they were watered morning and evening.

The Remembrance Garden was not far away – only about fifteen or twenty minutes desultory pedalling. She dismounted from her bicycle at a tall, wrought iron gate, and was saluted by a uniformed guard who sat by it in a wooden sentry box with a rusty old rifle propped up beside him.

On the other side of the gate a little bit of England had been created. As Jenny stared in she thought it looked like the park of a stately house back home, with groups of shady trees and carefully tended flower beds running along a broad, carefully raked path that led to a tall, white marble statue of an angel with huge, swan-like wings. The angel's hands, holding palm fronds, were crossed over her breast, her head was slightly bent and her eyes downcast in sorrow. Lady Canning, wife of Viceroy 'Clemency' Canning, who some of his more vengeful fellow countrymen considered to be too merciful towards the mutineers, had chosen her sculptor well when she commissioned the statue.

This was the site of the infamous Bibighar, where English and Eurasian children and adults were imprisoned and brutally murdered. The house itself no longer existed because, after the Mutiny, it was knocked down for it held too many terrible memories to be allowed to remain. The well into which the bodies of the dead were thrown was blocked up too.

When she walked towards the angel, Jenny was overcome by an immense feeling of awe. It seemed to draw her to it and she wondered if vengeful spirits of the dead still lurked beneath the trees, or, as Molly hoped, were all old wounds healed, and hatreds forgiven?

Her own ever-present sadness about James was increased by the realisation that terrible deeds had been done and sacrifices made here, too. As she thought about her dead husband, she flinched and a familiar stab to the heart made her catch her breath, so she stood looking up at the marble angel with tears running down her cheeks and hoping that for her too there could, in time, be forgiveness and healing.

A marble bench stood at the angel's feet and when she sat down on it, the stone felt cool beneath her legs and her sadness was slightly soothed by the sounds of the river Ganges flowing peacefully at her back.

She doubted if she would ever completely forget her hatred of the Germans and forgive the pointless slaughter of the trenches. Oh, my darling James, she thought, is there any tranquillity and feeling of forgiveness where you are lying? Will anyone put a statue of an angel above your grave? But James' body had not been found for, as far as she was able to find out, he'd been blown up in a massive German bombardment of his field hospital.

She missed him so badly it was a physical pain, deep in her gut like an incipient cancer. Their marriage had been so short that sometimes she found it hard to remember what he looked like, but she could still vividly remember the thrill of their bodies against each other, and the feel of his mouth on hers.

Thank God they'd been passionate lovers, seizing their pleasure like greedy children during the short time they had together. Immediately after the wedding, they spent two nights in London before he left for France, and then had a few days in Edinburgh when he came back on leave.

Her final exams began the day after she waved him off from Waverley Station. Looking back now, she realised that, somehow, she knew in her heart that she'd never see him again, but had refused to accept the knowledge. Even three years later she still found it difficult and every morning woke up with the happy expectation of turning towards him, but within seconds she always had to suffer the agony of realisation that he was dead. Would that daily pain never end?

The immediate shock of his death meant that she had no period for several months and clung to the hope that she might be pregnant, but it was not to be. On the day she graduated she was bleeding heavily and feeling that her life had ended at a time when she ought to be jubilant.

She remembered the stricken faces of her mother and uncle as they walked away together from the degree ceremony. Her uncle tried to be positive, addressing her as 'Doctor', and telling her how proud he was that she had triumphed over the chauvinism of the established medical authorities. He was the manager of a bank near the Royal Infirmary, where many medical college professors had accounts, and he knew how little they relished admitting women into their profession.

'What are your plans now, my dear?' he asked.

'James used to talk about going to work in India. I've seen an advertisement asking for a doctor in a missionary hospital in Delhi and I'm going to apply. Perhaps they won't be as prejudiced against women as some other places seem to be,' she said.

Her first application for missionary work in Delhi was not successful either, and she was still smarting about the rebuff when she volunteered to serve at the Front. Secretly she'd hoped to go there and be killed, just as James was, but they didn't accept women doctors either. However, because her uncle knew a board member of the Edinburgh Medical Missionary Society, she tried again, and was accepted. In January 1919 she found herself shipping out to Calcutta, en route for a position as assistant to Harry Mason at Cawnpore.

It was troubling that her mind was going over these past events in the Garden of Remembrance, but she hoped the peaceful place would bring her some solace because she knew she must try to rid herself of gloomy thoughts. It would be too easy to be plunged back into the crippling misery that claimed her after James was killed.

She straightened up and looked at her watch. It was a quarter to six. A merciful breeze was blowing in from the river, and, gratefully, she turned her face towards it. A group of elegant long-legged wading birds were stalking along the water's edge and she remembered that Cawnpore was famous for its bird life. The garden was such a tranquil, silent place that it was hard to appreciate that, less than a mile away, enormous mills were churning and thundering day and night. In post-Mutiny times, the city had become an industrial spinning and weaving centre, making money for both Indians and Europeans.

A quarter to six was too early to go back to the hospital or to her room in the bungalow, for the Masons usually went out to their club at half-past seven and Molly would be sure to press her to accompany them if she was in the house. She didn't want to go because being a single woman in a gathering of couples and predatory bachelors depressed her and made her lonelier than she ever felt sitting at home with a book on the verandah.

As she looked around, she realised that the atmosphere of the garden was changing. Its very English look, the silence, solitude and beauty that she'd appreciated when she first entered, began to feel sinister, and she feared that the place really was haunted. If a yellow-haired child came out to run around the marble angel, would he be looking for his murdered mother?

The sound of crunching footfalls on the path made her heart jump with fear, but out of the gloom beneath the trees came the guard from the gate wheeling her bicycle. 'Gardens closing now, memsahib,' he told her.

She stood up, smiled and took the handle-bars from him. 'Thank you,' she said, mounted the bike and rode back through the wrought iron gates, out of that very silent and now sinister garden into the bustling, noisy throng of India.

During her time by the statue, a line of little market stalls along the main road had opened up for business. Hissing Tilley lamps hung from their roofs and the counters were heaped with artistically piled displays of fruit – enormous water melons, with artful slices cut to show luscious red flesh; heaps of glistening grapes; pyramids of oranges; hands of different coloured bananas – yellow, green and rosy pink – interspersed with triangles of green limes.

People were out shopping, dressed in freshly washed clothes, the women with sweet-smelling garlands of tuberoses tied in the knots of their gleaming hair. Though she rang her bicycle bell continuously, they were oblivious to Jenny trying to make her way through them, and eventually she was forced to dismount and walk, pushing the bike beside her.

The crowd enveloped her, making her one of them, and she enjoyed the experience. Moths buzzed round the lamps in the booths, touts hustled for business, and music – Indian and European – was blasting out from wind-up gramophones inside some of the stalls. As she passed one, she was surprised to hear Harry Lauder singing the

109

soldiers' plaintive song, 'There's a long, long trail a-winding into the land of my dreams'.

She didn't mind being slowed down by the crowd, for the spicy smells and colour of the little market helped lift her melancholy mood. At the end of the line of stalls she came upon one displaying lengths of multi-coloured, poor-quality sari cloth, which was nothing like as luxurious as the materials sold by the Begum's son in the bazaar. The sight of the loops of cloth over her head brought her mysterious patient back into her mind however. How was she? Was she sticking to her diet? On impulse, Jenny remounted her bicycle and pedalled rapidly off to the big bazaar, determined to find the cloth sellers' street again.

It was even more crowded than the little market for every Indian family in Cawnpore seemed to be out taking the air. At Celestial Silks, the Begum's son saw Jenny looking up at his glorious display from the roadway and smiled as he rose from his seat on a mound of plump white pillows to greet her.

'Ah, Doctor Jenny, it's good to see you again. Have you come to buy?' he said.

She smiled back. 'No. I was passing and thought I'd look in on your mother. How is she?'

He frowned, 'It's good you came. She is not well. She has been very tired. She weeps and talks much of dying. Perhaps she needs

110

some fortifying medicine.'

Jenny was concerned. 'I'm sorry to hear that. There's not a lot I can prescribe for her illness, I'm afraid, especially at her age. Just keeping to the diet and resting as much as possible is all that can be done really.'

'She bullies the servants into giving her sweet things. They are too afraid of her to refuse,' he said sadly.

'Has she fainted again?' asked Jenny and he nodded. 'Yes, once, but we did as you advised with the grape juice and she revived.'

'Do you want me to have another look at her?' was Jenny's next question.

'If it isn't too much trouble. Tell her not to drink so much sherbet. I'm afraid that if she goes on, she will die.'

'It sounds as if she likes sherbet,' Jenny said.

'Too much, and she will take no advice,' was his reply.

'I'll scold her for you,' she said with a little laugh.

The Begum was looking more sprightly than expected when Jenny was shown into the room in the hidden compound. The old woman was resplendent in a wrapper made of green silk with gold embroidery down the front and round its neck and her eyes were heavily made up with kohl. Her dyed hair was oiled, parted in the middle and drawn tightly back from her thinning face. As usual, the women of her family were fluttering around her like acolytes at a shrine.

'You're looking very grand. Are you expecting visitors?' Jenny asked in English, when a stool was drawn up for her.

The old woman obviously decided to be mischievously obstructive. 'No speak English. Talk Hindi or Punjabi,' she said.

Jenny laughed, amused by the Begum's effrontery. 'Don't start that again. Of course you speak English and you know I can't speak a local language. How are you feeling today?'

The Begum laughed too, as if pleased at being caught out. 'I'm better, but this weather has never suited me. It doesn't suit anyone, in fact. European women used to die like flies in the summer, and the heat drove men mad. The Mutiny broke out in May, you know. Even Indians are at breaking point then.'

'You could go to the hills,' said Jenny.

'Pschaw! I don't travel any more. I did all my travelling long ago and I've no desire to take to the roads again.'

'Where did you go when you travelled?' Jenny asked, lifting the old woman's hand to check her pulse.

The eyes that looked up at her were guarded. 'All over – Delhi, Barrackpore, Lucknow, Jhansi.'

Jenny was impressed. 'That's a long way.

Did you enjoy travelling?'

'I suppose I did, but I wouldn't want to start again.'

'Why not?'

'Because I was afraid most of the time.'

'What were you afraid of?'

'Of being killed, I suppose, but now that I'm near death, I wonder why I was so frightened.'

Her pulse was normal and as Jenny laid her patient's hand down, she said, 'Nobody knows when they're going to die, do they?'

'The gods know. They write the date of everyone's death inside their heads when they're born – like a hat label!'

The Begum gave a splutter of laughter that surprised Jenny, who said, 'I don't think your label's worn out yet, providing you don't drink too much sherbet.'

'You've been talking behind my back to my son. He scolds me but I don't listen. I think I might as well die enjoying myself, and I enjoy sherbet.'

Jenny shrugged. 'That's your decision. I won't argue with you. But at least take it in moderation if you want to go on living a little longer. You're lucky you have the choice.'

The Begum's eyes were fixed on her face. 'Ah, what's wrong with you, Doctor? Is the weather getting you down, too?'

Jenny shook her head. 'I don't think so. I don't mind the heat.'

'What do you do with yourself? Have you any friends? Do you play cards, swim, play tennis or ride horses?' asked the Begum curiously.

'No. I work mostly, and I don't know many people yet.'

'You're a nice-looking girl. Before long, bachelors will be besieging you with invitations. You'll be married before the year is out.'

Jenny shook her head. 'No, I won't.'

'Why not?' The question was sharp.

'Because I'm married already.'

The Begum's eyes flashed with curiosity. 'Where is your husband?'

'Dead.' One word only and as she said it, Jenny had a sudden flash of memory and saw James' smiling face looking boyish and cheeky. His wide mouth curled up humorously and his eyes crinkled, making him seem impish.

'In the war?' asked the Begum, more softly.

'Yes.' Jenny was incapable of saying more.

'Life can be cruel,' said the old woman.

'I know. I went to visit the Garden of Remembrance this afternoon and it made me think that when terrible things happen it's necessary to forgive...' The words slipped out without thinking.

The Begum drew back against her pillows as if she was afraid. 'I've never been there. It's a terrible place, terrible.'

'I thought it was very peaceful considering what happened, and the statue of the angel's beautiful,' said Jenny.

'It's a sentimental gesture,' said the Begum fiercely.

'I thought the angel represented consolation,' said Jenny.

'But they don't let Indians in so the consolation is only for white people. The grief and loss wasn't all one sided, you know. People were cruelly treated *on both sides*. When the British took back Cawnpore they hanged innocent men all round the Bibighar and made passers-by go down on their knees and lick the bloodstains off the floor. Even I thought that was wrong, and I had reason to hate. It's like the war your husband died in – there are weeping widows on the German side, too. Don't forget that.'

The Begum's voice was so intense that Jenny asked, 'You were here during the Mutiny?'

'I was.'

'In this city?'

'For some of the time.'

'And you survived? How?'

'You're making me weary. I must sleep. Please go away,' said the Begum, closing her eyes. She was doing her usual trick of shutting out questions, refusing to cooperate.

Jenny knew she was beaten and stood up. It was obvious that their interview was over, though many unasked questions thronged in her brain. She decided that, before she left, she'd risk some more.

'What is your real name?' she asked.

'What do you mean?' The Begum opened her eyes sharply when she spoke.

'I mean what should I call you? To say Begum all the time is very formal.'

'Being formal suits me very well.' The tone was frosty.

Jenny, though rebuffed, decided to try one more question.

'Did you know Dolly Mullins?' she asked.

The old woman's eyes opened wide in surprise. 'Why do you ask me that?' she snapped.

'Because I know her granddaughter,' said Jenny.

'Her granddaughter? I didn't know she had one. Does she know you come to see me?' asked the Begum.

'I don't think so. Her granddaughter is a nurse in the hospital and a very good one. I only heard about Miss Dolly the other day and it intrigued me. I'd like to know more about her.'

'If you knew Dolly Mullins, you wouldn't get much profit from the acquaintance. She was a wicked woman. Go away now please,' said the Begum sharply, waving her hand towards the door.

When Jenny left, the Begum's daughter-in-law was disturbed to hear the old lady sobbing. She rushed in, full of concern, and asked what was wrong.

'It's that girl, the doctor. She asks too many questions. She disturbs my mind,' said the Begum.

To calm her, a small dose of opium was administered and she drifted off into sleep – but it was not a peaceful sleep because she tossed and turned in frightening dreams till morning came.

The Bibighar, July 15th, 1857

Just before dawn began to break, Emily woke but lay still, going over in her mind the events of the last terrible weeks.

How did this horror start? she asked herself for the hundredth time. Though it seemed like a century, it was only two and a half months since the Sunday morning when she and her husband, Dickie Maynard, to whom she had been married for just under a year, rode to church in Barrackpore where he was posted with his regiment, the 34th Native Infantry.

On their return, she was surprised to see what she thought was a line of hats stuck along their bungalow railings. Dickie rode ahead, and then came racing back to tell her, 'Turn your mare around and go to Cawnpore. Your father's there and he'll look after you.'

She stared at him in astonishment. 'But I have to pack first!'

'No!' he said and grabbed her arm roughly. 'Do as you're told. Turn the horse round and *go*! I'll send two trustworthy men after you.

I'm off to Delhi to tell them what's happened.'

It was then she realised that the line of hats were actually the decapitated heads of their household servants. Mutiny had broken out.

She and Dickie did not embrace on parting because their short marriage had gone sour for both of them. In other circumstances, they would have welcomed the opportunity to be apart.

She was a resilient and adventurous seventeen-year-old, buoyed up by enough of the confidence of the young to believe that she was immortal, and, once clear of Barrackpore, she enjoyed the five-day journey to Cawnpore, riding her big, strong bay and sleeping under the stars. She was perfectly safe because she had the protection of two loyal sepoys, who rode back to join her husband's regiment when they delivered her to her parents.

Her beloved older sister Lucy, with her baby son and his ayah, arrived a few days later in a group of refugees from Meerut, where, on the tenth of May, a more dangerous and bloodthirsty mutiny than the skirmish at Barrackpore broke out. Though Lucy was grieving for her murdered husband, the sisters were comforted to be together.

The period of peace did not last long, however. First of all, news came that the sepoys at Lucknow had mutinied – and Lucknow was only forty miles away. Soon they heard the residency there was under siege. A week later the Cawnpore garrison, swelled by hundreds of fugitives from the city and surrounding countryside, was also besieged. The commander, Sir Hugh Wheeler, who thought of the attacker, the Nana Sahib, as his friend, was confused and unsure of what to do.

The girls' father, Colonel Crawford, was one of Wheeler's senior officers, but his warnings against the Nana Sahib were not taken seriously, nor was his advice about how to defend the cantonment against the ferocious Marathas who made up the Nana's besieging army. Wheeler completely lost his nerve and when the Nana Sahib sent an envoy to promise the beleaguered Europeans a safe conduct down the river Ganges to Calcutta if they vacated their entrenchment without any more fighting, he accepted the offer, though Crawford doubted it was genuine.

Emily shuddered as she remembered how hundreds of men, women and children from the fort were transported on elephants or bullock carts to the river bank where the promised boats were lined up waiting to take them to safety – or so they thought.

Her father, still doubtful, kept his family back till the last, but eventually his wife, with

120

Emily, Lucy, two-year-old Bobby and the ayah, were loaded into one of the last bullock carts. They were alighting from it when the killing started. The Nana Sahib's men, lined along the river bank behind a little temple used by local fishermen, suddenly shouldered their rifles and started firing on the people in the boats. Every man, including Emily's father, was shot down. She sheltered behind their cart with the other members of her family, and watched the slaughter.

People in the boats were jumping up, hands raised and shouting, but there was to be no mercy. More shots rang out, volley after volley. Blood mingled with the water of the holy river as the dead toppled out of the boats. A few who survived the first fusillade tried to crawl back up the muddy bank, but sharpshooters coolly targeted them and they too died, with their hands feebly grasping at tufts of coarse river grass.

When the Ganges was running red and corpses bobbed like horrific buoys around the shallow boats which had never been untied from their moorings, the shooting stopped and the traumatised survivors were rounded up to be taken back into the town. They were herded into the house known as the Bibighar, facing the end of a bridge that took the road to Lucknow across the Ganges, and there they had stayed in conditions that grew worse every day.

That was when Lucy completely lost her reason. She did not scream or rave but slowly retreated into another world, away from horrible reality.

Most of the men of the garrison were dead, but a few civilians with about two hundred women and children survived, though some were wounded and would soon die too. The strongest of them set about organising things, finding the best places to establish themselves and attempting to browbeat their jailers. Conditioned by years of being rulers, they could not believe what was happening to them.

Eventually, however, even the most courageous was intimidated when the Nana Sahib's terrible mother, the Rani, appeared and started screaming insults and threats at them. This woman, who looked like a witch with long, flowing black hair and a hawk's beak of a nose, took out on them her resentments after years of being disdained by the white people. More dangerous even than her treacherous son, she gave off vibrations of evil.

'You're all going to die and I'll enjoy watching it happening,' she screamed and some of her listeners wept, while others, like Lucy, were traumatised into shocked silence. For hours after her first visit, all of the prisoners moved about like people in a trance.

After that she came back every day to gloat over the dead and the living. Her captives lived in fear, and like a dog, she seemed able to smell their terror. Though she constantly threatened them, amazingly they were not immediately killed, and the deaths that did happen were caused by previously inflicted wounds or sickness. The only explanation Emily could think of for this clemency was that live hostages were valuable because they could be used as a bargaining token by the Nana Sahib, if and when Brigadier General Henry Havelock, who was rumoured to be advancing on Cawnpore, retook the city.

Little by little, as the days passed, the more resilient of the captives began to believe that they might escape and created a little world inside the Bibighar, dividing up and quarrelling over the few possessions left behind by the dead and forming their social groups that clung together and kept others out.

Lucy was impervious to all this. The only time she showed any animation was when Bobby perched on her knee, and she prattled to him in the baby talk that only he understood.

Heartbroken and lonely, some captives kept journals or wrote farewell letters to their families and hid them behind loosened bricks in the inner walls of the harem. Emily did not bother to do this because, apart from Bobby, Lucy, and her sick mother, there was no one for her to care about – she had no children; her father was dead, and she did not care a fig if she ever saw her husband again. Being separated from him was the only good thing about her present situation.

She did, however, keep a record of the people who died, scraping their initials and little crosses on a paving stone with nail scissors. When her mother died, she decided to save Bobby. On day fifteen, she gave him into the care of the ayah, and also passed over the small sum of money she still had with her.

'Take him to Delhi. My husband Captain Maynard is there. Tell him to look after Bobby,' she said.

Tearfully, the ayah nodded her head and in the middle of the night, she and the baby slipped away, as soundlessly as ghosts. In case her captors were aware of her death list on the paving stone and wondered where Bobby had gone, Emily scraped his initials there as a decoy.

When seventeen days passed and she and Lucy were still alive, she began to allow herself a little hope that they might come out of the ordeal.

Today is the eighteenth we have been here. Surely Havelock will arrive soon, she told herself on the morning of July 15th, as the light grew stronger in the square of sky above her head. In the distance, beyond the walls, the usual early morning noises of India could be heard – chirping birds, a bell clanging in the distance, shouting, running feet, hawking and spitting.

Alongside her, other captive women and children began the return to painful awareness, some of them weeping or cursing their fate; others, like Lucy and poor Mrs Murray, too ill or confused to fully comprehend what was happening to them.

Emily rolled over, stretched and clutched her ragged clothing around her before she went to the latrine. It smelt horrific because no effort had been made to clean it out for days and she gagged while she squatted in a corner, looking out through the open arch at her fellow prisoners.

Colonel Hancock's wife was sitting up with her head in her hands; the padre's wife was kneeling in prayer; Lucy too was awake and combing her fingers through her hair like an obedient, tidy child. Emily stood up, determined to get back to her sister before she wandered off to another part of their prison but as she was pulling her skirt back in place, she heard a voice saying softly, 'Missee, Missee Crawford!'

She turned and looked to her left. It was still not completely light and there were deep shadows behind the pillars that held up the roofs of the terraces where the women slept.

'Missee,' said the voice again, and she

strained her eyes to see. A tall Indian in a stained scarlet-and-white uniform was standing behind the nearest pillar.

'What do you want?' she whispered in Hindi, and repeated the question in Punjabi for she was fluent in several local languages.

'Keep quiet, Missee Crawford,' said the man.

He'd used her maiden name. She stood very still and strained her eyes to make out his face. When he stepped forward a little way, she recognised him as one of her father's soldiers who used to guard their bungalow in the Cawnpore cantonment when she lived there with her parents before she was married. It seemed like centuries ago.

She'd always noticed him because of his physical beauty, the brilliance of his eyes and teeth, and because he was invariably courteous towards her. But here he was now, in a stolen officer's uniform, one of the treacherous mutineers, holding her captive in this filthy place!

During talks with the other captives over the past two weeks, she'd been horrified by tales of the lasciviousness of the native guards towards white women and now cold fear gripped her. What did he want? There was no point shouting for help. There was no one to help her.

'You're one of my father's soldiers! You

should be ashamed of yourself! What are you doing here?' she asked, angrily going on to the offensive. To show anger and make a noise was obviously a mistake however because, like a wraith, he disappeared, almost melting away from behind the pillar.

At the same moment, a loud shouting and clattering announced the arrival of the palace servants bringing in huge pans of lentil stew to feed the captives. The foul-smelling stuff was ladled out into bowls and shoved into eager hands. Some of the senior wives still stood by protocol and sent their inferiors to fetch food for them. They were always served first.

A Eurasian girl, who ran eagerly forward to fetch some food for her sick mother, was cuffed and pushed aside by a major's wife. 'Take your place at the back of the queue. Officers' wives first,' she was told.

Emily was not hungry but she wanted to feed Lucy so she stood in line behind a large woman called Mrs Maguire, the wife of a sergeant from her father's company, who turned towards her and asked, 'Are you keeping your pecker up, m'dear?'

'It's not easy,' Emily admitted.

'Don't you worry, lovey. General Havelock's nearly here. He was at Fatehpur yesterday and should be here tomorrow,' said Mrs Maguire, who could be relied on to have all the latest news, which apparently

127

came to her through the palace servants. She was always chattering to them.

'Are you sure?' asked Emily doubtfully. She'd heard those cheerful rumours before.

'It's as true as I'm alive. The Nana Sahib's taken his army and marched out to meet Havelock. It's like sending Mr Punch to fight a giant, isn't it? The Nana Sahib's a milksop. Our men will wipe the floor with him.'

'But Havelock's meant to have been coming for days. I'm surprised it's taken him so long,' said Emily, but Mrs Maguire shook her head. 'Well he's coming this time. Take your sister to lie down beside the back wall in case there's a bombardment. He'll probably shell the palace and he might not know we're in here.'

Emily grabbed a bowl of food and ran over to tell her sister. 'I've brought you breakfast, and some good news. Mrs Maguire says we'll be out tomorrow,' she whispered.

Lucy looked up with a more lucid expression than she'd shown for a long time, but shook her head and said, 'Out of here? That would be lovely if it was true. Hold my hand. I had an awful dream last night and I'm afraid something bad is going to happen. Don't go away again. We must stay together.'

Emily, still exhilarated by Mrs Maguire's news, tried to cheer her sister. '*Nothing* bad is going to happen. I think we're in for a very good day. Havelock's army is nearly at

Cawnpore. The Nana Sahib and his men have ridden out to challenge him. They won't stand a chance. We'll be saved tomorrow!'

All Lucy said was, 'But what if Havelock doesn't beat the Nana Sahib?'

'Of course he will. The Nana Sahib's no general. He'll take to his heels and run at the sight of Havelock's army. I'm sure he's running now.'

They had often seen the Nana Sahib at social functions at the palace. When he was trying to ingratiate himself with the English he seemed simpering and silly. Most of the people who accepted his hospitality rarely bothered to thank him, and some of them made open fun of him to his face, imitating his unfortunately prominent buck teeth; effete, lisping way of talking and eye rolling mannerisms.

The person who could imitate him to the most hilarious degree was Colonel Hancock's spirited wife, and, though she was sharing the captivity of the other women now, that had done nothing to soften her behaviour towards their captor even after he revealed himself in another guise as a killer of the men of the garrison, including her own husband.

About a week ago he'd come into the Bibighar to speak to his captives, and reassure them that he would not harm them.

Mrs Hancock, who adopted the position of leader because she was the only surviving wife of a senior officer, haughtily spoke back to him, lisping in an exaggerated way, and his face had darkened.

On that occasion he was accompanied by two women – his mistress, the fifteen-year-old Eurasian daughter of a dressmaker in Cawnpore city, and his mother, the Rani, who noticed and resented the jibes aimed at her son. Even bold Mrs Hancock was wary of the Rani and did not lampoon the Nana Sahib too harshly when his mother was around.

Lucy clung to Emily's hand and said pitifully, 'I hope you're right about Havelock but I had such a bad dream last night.'

'Don't worry. Dreams are always opposite to what's actually going to happen,' said Emily, who did not want to have her own good spirits brought low by hearing about Lucy's dream.

They were starting to eat when a huge gong clashed somewhere outside and the main door was thrown open to admit the Rani, glittering with diamonds though it was still early in the morning. Brilliant pendant stones flashed like icicles from her ears, and glittered in a collar round her scrawny neck.

With her were a cluster of soldiers, some women of her court and another woman who looked English. She was older than the

Nana Sahib's nubile mistress and dressed European style in a bold, low-cut gown with a ruched skirt. Round her neck was a necklace of big rubies. There was a broad smile on her face and she looked as if she was drunk or drugged, perhaps both.

The Rani marched into the middle of the floor and pointed at Mrs Hancock. 'You daughter of a dog! You are going to die. You and your kind have laughed at us long enough but now we will laugh at you. Kneel down!'

Instead of kneeling Mrs Hancock stood up taller. 'Your Highness,' she said but not meekly, 'I kneel to no one except my own Queen.'

'Victoria!' The Rani could not pronounce 'V' and said 'Wictoria' which made Mrs Hancock smile derisively. The smile was not missed by the woman with the rubies who ran up and slapped the Colonel's wife across the face.

'English bitch!' she screamed.

Mrs Hancock did not flinch. 'What are you doing here, Dolly? Get back to the bazaar brothel where you belong.'

The woman addressed as Dolly went berserk. Shrieking like a banshee she began running around aiming blows at the watching prisoners, kicking children and stamping on women who were too sick to rise from their bedding. When some tried to fend her off, the Rani's guards stepped in to stop them and she went on raving, as unrestrained as a maniac.

Lucy and Emily huddled together behind a nearby pillar and Emily whispered to her sister, 'I remember that woman and you should too. It's Dorothy Mullins. Her husband was in father's regiment at one time, but he died a few years ago.'

She pulled Lucy back out of sight, wishing that they could melt into the back wall unnoticed. But that was not to be. Still rampaging, Dolly came running towards them, pointing at Lucy.

'Ha ha ha! It's Colonel Crawford's pretty daughter and her sister! Two for the price of one. You were very fine young ladies, weren't you, but look at you now. Not so grand any more. I used to watch you being high and mighty, and I hated you, *hated you.*'

Lucy said nothing but lifted her head and stared at the woman with a look so cold that it chilled Emily. Dolly stared back, large, dark eyes burning in her head. It was obvious that she was so drunk she was beyond reason or control.

The Rani, who was enjoying the rampaging, suddenly clapped her hands and shouted something back over her shoulder at a detachment of soldiers drawn up on the open ground outside the door.

At her call, one of the men stepped forward

and said something but she hissed in rage and hit him across the face with a clenched fist. Dolly went running back and screamed at him too, but he turned his back on both of them and marched away, followed by the other men.

Shouting, the angry women ran after them and Emily heard their insults – 'Cowards, fools, you'll be shot for disobedience...' But they did not turn round, only kept on walking while the terrified prisoners inside the building watched them go.

Mrs Hancock said very loudly, 'She told them to shoot us and they wouldn't do it.'

No one else said anything. Some stared in silent horror, some clutched each other, some bent their heads or fell to their knees in prayer, others clutched their crying children and tried to cover them with the remnants of their ragged skirts. Emily and Lucy held on to each other and Lucy began babbling in madness again, 'Where's little Bobby? Where's my poor, dear husband?'

Emily abandoned lying. Now was the time to tell the truth. 'Don't you remember? Matthew's dead. He was killed at Meerut, and I sent Bobby away with the ayah. She's smuggled him out to take him to Delhi. I gave her a note for Dickie if she can find him. It was better than keeping him here.'

Lucy stopped weeping, sense came back and her face brightened. 'Thank you, thank you. I'm so glad! He has a chance, hasn't he? The ayah loves him.'

Weeping, Emily nodded. 'She does. She'll guard him with her life. I'm sure he'll be safe.'

The sisters clutched each other again and were huddling together when the Rani came storming back with Dolly. Behind them was a party of low-caste butchers from the bazaar and the palace kitchen, some of them little more than boys. All were clutching knives or hammers.

While the Rani screamed orders at them, and Dolly Mullins screeched like a mad woman, waving her arms, they rushed among the captives, slashing around indiscriminately. The Rani incited the butchers to 'Kill, kill, kill...kill the English!'

Brave Mrs Hancock, standing straight as a tree, was the first to be hacked down. Sick Mrs Murray was decapitated with a single blow of a butcher's knife. Others, after a few moments of disbelief, began shrieking and screaming, running around in an effort to avoid the killers. The noise they made was blood-chilling and Emily pressed both hands over her ears in an unsuccessful effort to shut it out.

Then she saw that a squat man with glittering eyes was advancing on her with a knife pointed at her heart. Suddenly filled with immense strength, she whirled around, hauling Lucy to her feet and ran towards the latrine. There was a trapdoor on the back wall there through which the chamber pots were emptied in the early days when basic luxuries were supplied for the prisoners. It was big enough to let a woman through.

Lying on the latrine floor was a long stave, and she lifted it up, swinging it wildly at her pursuer. Lucy clung to her skirt like a dead weight. She did not seem able to run properly, or even to appreciate what was happening.

'Come on, come on,' screamed Emily, trying to push her sister through the trapdoor but it was like pushing at a dead animal. Lucy would do nothing to help herself. The killer was closing in on them, when Dolly Mullins appeared behind him, still laughing wildly.

Emily knew it may be useless trying to escape the slaughter but she was not going to let them kill her without putting up a fight. She struck the man full across the face with her stick, and was going for Dolly too when a grinning boy also appeared, brandishing a blood-stained knife, and caught hold of Lucy.

She saw a way out. If she could get under the boy's arm, she could bolt for the open main door. She yanked at her sister but, to her horror, Lucy threw herself on the ground, eyes rolling. Dolly Mullins stood over her as she fell and gestured to the blood-maddened boy to kill her. He bent down and stuck his knife in Lucy's heart.

Howling in rage and grief, Emily let go of Lucy's hand and ran towards the door.

Then everything went black.

In the house in Cawnpore bazaar, as dawn was breaking sixty-two years later, the old woman called the Begum woke up screaming.

Cawnpore, June 6th, 1919

The Begum's son and his wife worried about their mother, because the fierce spirit that used to fire her seemed to be disappearing fast. As the heat rose and the leaves of the trees in their enclosed courtyard lost their green and turned to greyish red because they were coated with dust, she grew more listless, but though she was always tired, her nights were disturbed by bad dreams and she seemed to be afraid to go to sleep.

She used to enjoy her food but now her appetite dwindled until she was living on lassi, coconut milk and the occasional banana. The most disturbing thing however was that she stopped interfering in the goings on of the household, every detail of which she had dominated for sixty years. If an argument broke out, she did not shout a command to be quiet as she used to, or demand to know the reason for the dispute. It was all very upsetting.

From time to time during the day, members of the household tip-toed into her room to try to talk to her and cheer her up,

137

but she rarely responded though she was always awake. If anyone said, 'Try to sleep,' she summoned up a rare burst of anger and retorted, 'I don't want to sleep. I'll be sleeping for ever soon.'

Throughout the long nights she fought to stay awake and during the day, even in the enervating heat of the afternoon when most people took their naps, if one of the family checked up on her unexpectedly she was awake, cheeks stained with tears and eyes wide open. No one ever actually heard her sobbing but she was obviously sunk in misery.

The worried women consulted with Vikram Pande who wanted to send for Dr Jenny again, but they vetoed the idea. 'The Begum doesn't want to see that girl. She thinks she is too curious,' said his wife.

'We should fetch an ayurvedic doctor from the bazaar,' suggested her sister, and this was done. Within the hour, a venerable man with a long grey beard and ash marks on his forehead was ushered into the Begum's presence.

He felt the pulses in her arms and neck, peered into her eyes and prescribed cupping, as well as a concoction of bitter-tasting herbs to be administered to the patient before sunrise and after sunset.

The cupping was painful and she complained feebly as she lay with heated glass globes pressed into her back. 'What is this meant to do for me?' she asked the healer.

'It draws the poison out,' he told her.

'I doubt if you'd get it all out of me even if I was cupped for months,' was her acid reply.

The old man laughed. 'You cannot be so bad, my lady.'

'Oh yes I can,' she snapped.

During the night after the cupping she vomited copiously, and in the morning her worried household summoned yet another doctor whose consulting room in the bazaar sported a huge, garishly painted sign that gave his qualifications as a graduate of Benares University. He was a confident young fellow of twenty-five who shook his head when he saw his patient and wasted no time examining her.

'There's little I or anyone else can do now for your mother. She is very old and will die soon. Make her comfortable as she slips away,' he said to the Begum's son.

'But she cannot be made comfortable. She only catnaps and will not go properly to sleep because she is very uneasy in her mind,' was his anxious reply.

The doctor scribbled a prescription for a strong opiate. 'This will calm her. She'll definitely sleep if she takes it,' he said as he handed it over.

Unfortunately this transaction was tactlessly done in the patient's room and within her hearing. When the doctor departed, she summoned some of her old energy and said sharply, 'Don't bother buying any of his medicine. In spite of what that young puppy says, I'm not taking opium, if that's what he's given me. It'll make me sleep and I don't want to do that because I've been having very bad dreams and I'm afraid that if I die in the middle of one of them, I'll be in it for ever. I'll be trapped in hell for eternity. I want to die with my mind at peace.'

'Please let me fetch a holy man or a priest to talk to you,' suggested her son.

'No.' The reply was as sharp as a shot from a gun.

'But they could soothe the state of your mind if something is bothering you. Can you tell me what it is? Are you in pain?'

'No, my pains are the same ones I've had for ten years. I know what ails me. Memories I've tried to quell for a very long time are crowding in on me and they are affecting my body.'

'Can you talk to me about them?' he asked but she shook her head and said, 'I don't think I can talk to anyone. They go too deep down in me.'

Vikram Pande was desperate. 'Let me bring back that English doctor from the Mission. She was the only one who has had any real idea of what is making you ill.

140

Perhaps the dreams have something to do with your sickness. She helped you once. She can do it again.'

At last, after days of pestering, the Begum, who was visibly weakening, reluctantly agreed. That morning, the servant who first took Jenny to the house in the middle of the bazaar, stood in the hospital's outpatient waiting room wringing her hands while Sadie shouted and pushed in a vain attempt to get rid of her.

'Go away. Dr Jenny is busy. She cannot see you now. Come back tomorrow,' she said but the girl mutely shook her head and would not leave.

'Tell Doctor Jenny to come to see my lady,' she kept saying.

Eventually an exasperated Sadie, who liked to keep to her prearranged routine and had taken against the girl's persistence anyway, went into the treatment room and said to Jenny, 'There's a beggar out there who won't go away until she's seen you. It's the girl who took you to the bazaar to see the old lady.'

Jenny was stitching a deep cut in a small boy's leg and she looked up in surprise to say, 'I'll go but this is going to take another fifteen minutes or so. Tell her to wait.'

When she eventually went into the waiting room, the girl ran over to pull at her sleeve, gabbling out words.

'What is she saying?' Jenny asked Sadie.

'She says you must go with her to see the Begum again because she is being plagued by evil spirits. I didn't know you'd been treating royalty.'

Jenny laughed. 'I'm not. It's that mystery Englishwoman in the bazaar. Her son has the big cloth shop there and he calls his mother the Begum. It's a sort of joke I think.'

Sadie's eyes sharpened. 'Do you mean Celestial Silks, Vikram Pande's shop?'

'Yes, that's his name, Vikram Pande,' said Jenny.

'I know of him, and I know the shop but I didn't know his mother was English,' said Sadie.

'Well, she is. She told me. She's been living in Cawnpore since the time of the Mutiny and I suspect she has quite a story to tell but she's very secretive. It's almost impossible to get her to talk,' said Jenny, gathering up equipment and medicines for her medical bag, unaware of the sharp interest in Sadie's eyes.

More at home in the city now, Jenny did not have to wait for the messenger girl to show her the way as she pedalled off into the warren of streets that made up the bazaar district. She had not been there since the really hot weather began and the smell of rotting vegetables, spices and urine in the alleys was stomach turning. To her horror she saw several rats lying dead in open sewage gutters, but the area in front of the big cloth shop was sanded, watered and swept clean. As usual its proprietor was sitting on a mound of pristine pillows fanning himself.

When he saw Jenny a smile of pure relief lit up his face. 'Welcome, Doctor. Let me take you to my mother. We're all worried about her because she's behaving very oddly. We're afraid that she's dying.'

Jenny frowned, surprised at this sudden degeneration in her patient. 'Perhaps it's only the weather,' she suggested, remembering what the Begum had told her about the effect hot weather had on European women.

He ushered her through the shop, talking all the time. 'No. It's not that. Her mind is very disturbed. She eats nothing, stays awake though she's exhausted and weeps a great deal. She's fighting off sleep because she has nightmares and says she's frightened to die in the middle of one in case it goes on for eternity.'

The very idea of such a thing made Jenny frown even more. 'We must talk her out of that,' she said firmly.

The Begum looked up when they entered her dim room. 'So you're back,' she said to Jenny, but did not sound too displeased.

The doctor's eyes scanned the thin old face and noted how haggard it had become in only a short time. 'I'm surprised to hear that you've been giving your family a lot of worry,' she said, sitting down.

The old woman's eyebrows lifted and she asked, 'In what way exactly?' The tone of her voice made her sound like an offended duchess.

'By starving yourself.'

'It's my decision not to eat, and if that's my way of dying, it's my business entirely.'

'After a life like yours it seems rather cowardly.'

'What do you mean? You don't know anything about my life.'

'I can tell it's been eventful. You've never walked away from a challenge before, have you?'

The Begum sighed. 'It has been eventful. That's the trouble. That's why I can't sleep.'

'Are you totally sleepless?' asked Jenny.

'I fight it off because I don't want to sleep.'

'Why? It would soothe you. You must sleep.'

'It doesn't soothe me. When I sleep, I dream.'

'What about?'

'The past. My past. I've been cursed by too many adventures.'

'Would you change that if you could?' Jenny felt encouraged to ask the question by her patient's sudden increase in vivacity.

The Begum went silent for a few moments

144

but eventually said, 'To be honest with you, I wouldn't. Apart from some things, terrible things that I still dream about.'

Jenny leaned over and wiped a sheen of sweat off the old woman's face. 'Would it help to tell me about them?' she suggested.

The other women standing in the room shifted uneasily as the Begum's eyes ranged over them. 'Leave us,' she said in Hindi and, one by one, they shuffled out.

When they had gone, Jenny held a cup of coconut milk to the Begum's dry lips. She sipped at it, and sighed, before she said, 'This is all your fault, you know.'

'What do you mean?' Jenny was surprised.

'The first time you came to see me I thought you were Lucy. I thought you'd come back for your necklace.' She lifted the gold chain from her neck and showed it to the doctor.

'You were confused. When someone's coming out of a coma they don't know what's happening,' Jenny said.

'No, I wasn't confused. It was your eyes. They're very blue, like Lucy's. I remember the way she looked at me that last time when I had to let go of her hand. Your blue eyes started me dreaming and since then the dreams have been very bad.'

'I'm sorry. But it might help to tell me about Lucy. Who was she?'

'My sister, my only sister. I was with her

when she was being killed. She was holding on to me but I let go of her hand and ran away. I should have stayed and not let her die alone.' The Begum's voice cracked.

Jenny patted her arm and asked softly, 'Don't distress yourself too much. Are you sure you want to talk about this?'

'Oh yes, yes, now that I've started I want to tell you what happened. Don't stop me.'

'All right. Where was Lucy killed?' Jenny asked.

'Here, in Cawnpore. In the Bibighar. You've heard of the Bibighar, haven't you?' The tone was challenging.

'I have, you know I have.' Jenny's reply was short.

The Begum went on, 'Lucy and I were in the Bibighar together. Our mother was with us, too. She died first, before the killing, thank God. I thought I'd forgotten the details but I've been dreaming about it for days, every time I go to sleep.' The expression on her face seemed to crumble as she spoke and she began to shiver.

Jenny was genuinely distressed for her and gently took the Begum's shaking hands, holding them in hers. 'Don't talk about it if it upsets you,' she said.

'I have to now that I've started. I can't keep it in any longer. Even my son doesn't know the whole story – he knows we were in the Bibighar but not about what happened on the last day.'

'You were very fond of your sister?' asked Jenny, chafing the old hands. The wrinkled skin felt like paper.

'I loved her. She was older than me and we were always together till she married. We had a brother but he died when I was eight and Lucy was nearly eleven. She was so pretty! Every man who saw her fell in love with her.

'Our father was Colonel of the 24th Foot and all his young officers would have died for Lucy, but she picked Matthew and married him when she was eighteen. It was a good choice. He was a fine man, but the mutineers killed him in Meerut. Lucy saw it happening, she was lying beside him in their bed when his throat was cut. She began to lose her reason then but things got worse later on in the Bibighar. They really loved each other, you see...'

'What a terrible story,' said Jenny and the Begum shot her an angry look as she said, 'Bad enough, but not as terrible as what happened afterwards.'

'If she was in Meerut, how did you all end up in the Bibighar together?' Jenny asked.

'Because our parents were in Cawnpore, and Lucy escaped from Meerut with her baby to join them, just as I did. Everyone thought Cawnpore would be safe. They came flocking in from all over the place. Only some very cautious people kept on going down river to Calcutta. I wish we'd done that.'

'What happened to Lucy's baby?' whispered Jenny.

'Bobby was two years old. It was only because of him that she managed to get to Cawnpore. She was determined to save him. Without him, she might never have left Meerut.' The Begum's eyes were blank, looking into the distant past.

'Did Bobby die too?' Jenny asked softly. This story had her gripped.

The Begum turned her head to look at her. 'I don't know. I wish I did. I told his ayah to smuggle him out of Cawnpore when Lucy really lost her mind. He had a sporting chance of survival if the ayah took him away. I told her to try to get to Delhi where my husband was with his regiment. I hoped he'd send poor little Bobby home, and I couldn't think of anyone else who might take him...They were all dead and I didn't know where Matthew's people were – south of England somewhere I think. I never saw Bobby again. There was an occasion when I could have found out if he got to Delhi – but I didn't. That's something else I feel guilty about.'

The true horror of the Bibighar was becoming real to Jenny as she listened. The marble angel did seem to be an inadequate, sentimental symbol now.

She whispered, 'So you never found out if the little boy was safely handed over? Perhaps your husband was killed too.'

The Begum shook her head. 'Oh he survived all right – I saw him again, but I never spoke to him.'

'Why not?'

'There was too much to lose by that time. I didn't want my old life back, and if I'd spoken to him, other people would have suffered. Anyway I couldn't stand him. Even being in the Bibighar was preferable to living with him.'

Jenny could only say, 'Oh!' The Begum sat up in her nest of cushions and surveyed her with a sardonic look. 'You're a married woman. Were you happy with your man?' she asked.

'I adored him,' said Jenny simply.

'Yes, it's possible to feel like that, I know. People who do are very fortunate. Their memories may be sad but not bitter. I married when I had no knowledge of the world. So innocent! My father tried to talk me out of choosing Dickie but I was determined. What a terrible mistake!'

'But you got another chance,' said Jenny boldly. Vikram Pande must have come from somewhere.'

'Yes, I did. That was why I didn't want to go back. By that time I knew that all men were not like Dickie, who was a horrible

149

creature. He beat me and made me do things that I loathed. I once had to fight him off with a croquet mallet. I hit him full on the face and broke his nose. He told other people he'd had a riding accident!' she laughed derisively but went on, 'When we were in the company of his fellow officers he laughed at me and called me names. It wouldn't have been so bad if he'd taken a native mistress like some of them did, but he liked to sleep with young boys from the bazaar. He had them brought to our bungalow! I couldn't tell my parents, because though my father didn't like him, he had no idea of how bad he really was.'

'Why did you marry a man like that?' asked Jenny. The Begum struck her as a sensible woman who would work things out for herself, even when she was young.

'He was very handsome and I was a young fool who wanted to be married. Lucy was so happy with Matthew and I thought my wedding day would be the happiest day of my life – what a fool! We met when he came to Cawnpore on leave. His colonel didn't tell father what a cad he was, though I'm sure he knew. When he packed me off back to Cawnpore because there was trouble in Barrackpore, I was too delighted to be leaving to be afraid.'

The effort of saying all this sapped her. She looked drawn, and sweat was beading on her face again. Jenny wiped it off before giving her more coconut milk to drink and said, 'I think you should lie down now. All this talking is wearing you out.'

Obediently she did lie down flat, but grasped Jenny's hand in an agitated way as she said, 'Please don't stop me now. I've got to tell you. It's the only way to clear my mind.'

Jenny nodded, hoping for the Begum's sake that the story would not be too long and upsetting.

She went on, 'Until the fifteenth of July, the last day in the Bibighar, I didn't tell her that I'd sent Bobby away. Then it happened—'

Tears began to flow, pouring down the old woman's cheeks.

'All right, all right,' whispered Jenny, her own lips quivering.

'The Nana Sahib's mother told the sepoys to kill us but they wouldn't, so she and Dolly Mullins brought in a gang of butchers – from the bazaar probably or perhaps from the palace kitchens. They started chopping us down.'

The Begum was openly sobbing now and Jenny's own eyes were full. She wished she could stop this terrible recital but it was impossible. In a strangled voice, the Begum said, 'It was like being in hell, and I'm reliving it every night in my dreams.'

'I'm very, very sorry,' said Jenny simply. There were no words to convey the sym-

151

pathy and pity she felt but it did not matter what she said because the Begum was not listening to her.

'They were savages. They killed children clinging to their mothers. I remember the screams as they cut them down. They slashed the women, young and old. Some of the poor souls couldn't believe what was happening and ran around in all directions, trying to hide, but it was useless. Their blood marked the floor and the walls – some splashed on to my face. It was warm!'

She put up a hand as if to wipe it off her cheeks but went on talking.

'Lucy wouldn't come with me. She sat down on the paving stones and gave herself up. The one who cut her throat was only a boy. Dolly Mullins pushed him at her. He wasn't a mutineer. He wasn't a sepoy. Not one sepoy touched a woman or a child in the Bibighar but they've been blamed for it. I'll never forget the face of the boy who killed my sister. And I didn't forget Dolly Mullins either!'

Tears were cascading down her face and she was shaking so violently that her teeth began to chatter. Jenny stood up and said very firmly, 'That's enough. No more, no more. This is upsetting you and it's upsetting me. You'll make yourself ill if you go on.'

She went across to the door and opened it to call for the Begum's daughter-in-law who came running and gasped in horror at the sight of the weeping patient. The cloth merchant followed her into the room and looked at Jenny accusingly as if she was the cause of his mother's collapse, but she took charge of the situation and said, 'Bring hot towels for her face, bring a blanket to wrap her in. I'll give her something to calm her down and I want her to go to sleep. Someone must stay with her at all times and if she starts crying out, waken her but do it gently. She badly wants to talk about her sister in the Bibighar. You must all listen, even if she tells the same story over and over again. Telling it will clear her mind.'

By the time the Begum was settled in sleep, it was dark and once more Vikram Pande sent Jenny back to the hospital in a tonga. As he helped her into it, he said, 'I'm sorry for thinking you upset my mother. I know now you didn't. You've been very good. She's never talked to anyone outside the family before about being in the Bibighar, and she rarely talks even to me about her sister. She must trust you.'

An indescribable sorrow was weighing Jenny down. She looked into Vikram Pande's concerned face from the high seat of the tonga and said, 'Your mother has more to tell. She has been bottling up terrible memories for years. If she wants to talk to me again, send a message and I will come.'

153

June 15th, 1919

In the early morning Fred Allen stood at the white-painted rails of a P&O steamer staring down into the silver waters of the Red Sea. He'd risen from his bunk while it was still dark, and gone up on deck in the hope of escaping the dreams that haunted him whenever he drifted into sleep.

In less than a week's time he'd reach Bombay, and three days after that he'd be back in Cawnpore. Perhaps work would cure him. Perhaps his mind would clear and the terrible internal shuddering that seemed to churn him up all the time would be stilled.

He was trying to light a cigarette with his shaking hand cupped over the match when a pleasant young fellow, whom he'd overheard saying he was going out to work in a bank in Delhi, walked up behind him and said cheerfully, 'Good morning!'

Allen jumped, turned his head and fought to stop himself from shouting at the stranger. Instead he managed to grimace in an attempt at a smile.

'Good morning, old chap, Karachi next

154

stop,' said the youth, who looked as if he was barely eighteen.

'Yes, so they tell me,' said Allen.

'Where are you bound for?' asked the youngster.

Allen said, 'Bombay first and then Cawnpore.' He wished the bloody fool would go away and leave him in peace to watch the soothing hypnotic flow of the ship's wake. It calmed him when he was at his most tense.

'In the mills there, are you?'

'No, I'm a doctor in a mission hospital.'

The word 'mission' always sobered people because it made them think he was very straight-laced and religious. The young man's face assumed a pious expression and he said, 'My word, that's worthwhile work.'

'It is, I suppose,' said Allen.

'Back from the Front, are you?' The inevitable question and one he always dreaded.

'Yes.' Inside he was shrieking, *Go away, go away. I don't want to talk about it.*

'That must have been tough,' said the other, in a concerned voice.

'It was.' *Don't ask about it, just don't ask...*

'How long were you there?' It was becoming obvious that this youth was idealistic and misguided enough to wish he could have served in the army, but he was obviously only just out of school.

'Nearly three years,' Allen said shortly, but he was thinking, *Lucky man, you escaped going into hell.*

'And you got through all right?'

Allen's patience snapped. He turned and faced the questioner, leaning back against the rail, with both hands gripping it tightly. 'I wasn't shot, if that's what you mean – but I did go mad. I'm not responsible for my actions. Please go away and bother somebody else,' he said.

For the rest of the voyage, the young man avoided him, but being well brought-up, always nodded politely if they came face to face. His embarrassment amused Allen.

He was one of the last off the ship in Bombay because he liked to lean over the rail and watch the other passengers disembarking. Newcomers were obviously dumbstruck by the noise, smells and incredible din; blasé old hands showed their familiarity with the country by throwing their weight about and shouting out orders in ungrammatical Hindi. The only verbs they ever used were imperatives – 'Go!', 'Come!', 'Be quick!' or 'Take care!' and 'Hurry up!'

When he did go ashore, he took a horse-drawn gharri to Green's Hotel and settled down on his balcony with a bottle of whisky to watch the sun setting over the bay beyond the Gateway to India. Tonight he meant to get drunk. Tomorrow he planned to board the train to Cawnpore at Victoria terminus.

★ ★ ★

At noon on the day after Allen's ship docked in Bombay, Mary Mullins hobbled out of the open door of her bedroom and propped her aching bones on to a rocking chair over-looking an overgrown garden. She and her daughter Sadie lived in three rooms in the end wing of what had been a fine bungalow in pre-Mutiny days but was now an island of broken-down grandeur among hundreds of ramshackle hovels inhabited by mill workers.

There was still a strip of garden between the house and the main road, and every now and again, especially after rain, Mary's soul was delighted to see a perfect rose peeping out of a thicket of thorns or a camellia bush unexpectedly bursting into flower. In the middle of a patch of dry earth before the house a tall frangipani bush reached for the sky, its smooth grey bark gleaming nakedly and clusters of cream-coloured flowers at the ends of its fat twigs filling the air with a heady scent. Many people were made nauseous by the smell of frangipani, but not Mary. She was proud of that tree because its presence in a garden meant that at one time English people lived in her house. Indians never planted frangipani in their gardens.

She leaned back in her chair and closed her eyes. Reading used to be her greatest plea-sure but in the last few years an opaque film of bluish grey had started to creep across the pupils of her eyes and it was now almost impossible to follow the lines on a page. When she told Sadie about the interference with her vision, her daughter turned her face to the light and examined her eyes. 'You've got cataracts, mother,' she announced in a matter-of-fact tone.

'What can be done?' asked Mary and Sadie shook her head.

'Nothing.'

Life had taught them to be pragmatists, so she didn't make a fuss. When Sadie returned at night from her work in the hospital, if not too tired, she would sit with her mother and read the novels of Charles Dickens aloud. They were particularly fond of his descriptions of London, imagining that the capital city was still like that.

'I've always wanted to go to London. My grandfather came from there,' Mary said at the end of every reading.

She was slowly rocking, staring into the garden, which now looked to her out of focus and wreathed with mist, when she heard Sadie ringing her bicycle bell as a signal that she was turning off the road. She got up and hobbled into the kitchen, where she began haranguing the sweeper for not cleaning the floors properly.

'I'm here,' she called out as her daughter entered their end of the house. She wished she could see Sadie properly because she was proud of her daughter, her youngest and only surviving child, who had been beautiful as a girl and was still handsome at twenty-nine. It was a pity that she never married, but she was a good nurse and seemed to be appreciated by the hospital where she worked.

Everyone who knew the family said that Sadie looked like her grandmother Dolly, who'd also been a beauty. Hanging on the wall of their sitting room was a portrait of Dolly, drawn by some long-dead admirer, and they did look alike, but unfortunately Sadie's complexion was much darker, as was her father's. Not even Dolly was sure of the identity of his father so he'd taken his mother's surname. Recently Dolly Mullins had been elevated to the status of a freedom fighter, especially since the awful business in Amritsar.

'Fred's coming back,' was the first thing Sadie told her mother when she burst into the kitchen. Mary stopped talking and stared at her daughter. Though she was unable to make out the expression on Sadie's face, she knew by the way the girl was standing that she was delighted beyond measure. She had not been so carefree for a long time.

'When?' she asked.

'He sent Dr Mason a telegram from Bombay. It said he was on the P&O boat that arrived yesterday. He should be here the day after tomorrow,' Sadie said in a jubilant voice.

'Has he written to you?' asked Mary and Sadie shook her head. 'No, but he wrote to Dr Mason some time ago and said he was coming back soon but didn't give a date – then the telegram arrived. Isn't it wonderful?'

'I thought he was wounded in the fighting in France.'

'So he was. We heard last year that he was in hospital in a place called Hastings, and then he moved to a convalescent home in Derbyshire, but he must be well again or they wouldn't be sending him back.'

Mary flicked her duster at the sweeper to send him on his way. When he sidled off into the garden, she told her daughter, 'Don't build up your hopes too much. He's never been in touch with you since he left. He was kind to you when he was here but that's probably all there is to it. Don't be disappointed.'

Sadie was ebullient however. 'I'll be so pleased to see him, and I know he'll be pleased to see me again. It'll be as if he's never been away.'

She had been in love with Fred Allen for two years before he went off to the war, and was sustained by romantic longings and a conviction that he loved her back ever since because, on the day he left in 1916, he

160

suddenly handed her enough money to buy the little house where she now lived with her mother.

When he had given her a thick wad of currency notes, she had gazed at him in astonishment.

'What's this for?' she asked.

'It's some money I've saved. I'd like you to have it. Buy a bigger place for you and your mother to live in,' he said.

Their friendship began because, on the pretext of getting him to look at her mother's eyes, she took him to see Mary when they lived in one room in the middle of the bazaar. He charmed them and never behaved as if he despised their poverty, but sat with his long legs stuck out, chatting to her mother as if he was in a middle-class drawing room. After that they began going for walks together, and eating in small tea houses and native eating places that he preferred to European-style hotels. As their closeness grew, she longed for him to make an overt sexual approach to her but he never did, and she wondered if there was something odd about him because her previous experiences with men had been of having to fight them off rather than encourage them.

'I can't take your money,' she said stiffly.

'That's a pity, because I don't know what to do with it if you don't. I'll have to donate it to a church or something,' he said.

161

'Don't you want to spend it yourself?'

He shook his head. 'Not particularly, and I've got more than enough to see me through anyway.'

'Haven't you a family?' she asked. He shook his head again.

'Take it, Sadie,' he said. He didn't tell her that he was convinced he would be killed in the war he was off to fight, and the plight of the two Eurasian women living in that miserable room had wakened his sympathies, especially since Sadie was so touching in her neediness and, also, a first-class nurse.

Not without protest, she'd taken the money and dreamed about him ever since.

'I can hardly wait to see him,' she told her mother who shook her head. 'He'll be different. Men who come back from a war are often changed by it.'

Sadie brushed off these misgivings. 'What do you know about it? You've never known anyone who fought in a war.'

Mary hobbled out of the kitchen and sat down in a wicker chair. 'I know about men though,' she said.

Jenny was sick when Allen arrived. She'd been running a fever for three days before she collapsed and took to her bed, where she lay sweating and dreaming strange dreams that were difficult to distinguish from reality. Molly worried about her but Harry knew

162

she was only going through the Indian initiation illness that affected all newcomers sooner or later – once she'd worked that climactic infection out of her system, she'd be fine. He told her to drink lots of liquid and sleep the fever off.

'Allen's back tomorrow or the next day, so don't worry about work,' he said when he looked in on her in her sick bed.

Two days later, she felt a little better, got up, dressed and tottered through to the Masons' dining room where she found them eating breakfast. Molly gave a little squeal at the sight of her. 'Oh Jenny dear, you're so pale. And so thin! Are you sure you should be out of bed? Do sit down and I'll pour you some tea.'

Jenny sat, but her head was swimming. 'I have to get up sometime,' she said feebly.

Harry looked concerned. 'Don't force yourself. Allen arrived back late last night and he's offered to do your clinic this morning,' he told her.

She bristled. She didn't want anyone else to take over her work.

Harry saw her defensiveness and said, 'He's a bit rusty still, but he'll be back in the swing by the time Molly and I go off on leave the week after next.'

'You go so soon?' Jenny asked. Time had flown by recently.

Molly nodded eagerly. 'We sent a telegram

to Calcutta and there's a cabin on the next mail boat out. Isn't that wonderful!' she said.

'Do you feel able to come through to the hospital for a few minutes to meet Allen?' Harry asked.

She didn't feel like it but stood up and said, 'Of course.'

Her first sight of the newcomer was a tall, scarecrow figure with short, bristly hair who was pulling on a white coat in the doctors' office. He's awfully Irish looking, was her first thought. His face was very thin, with sunken eyes, a deep upper lip and high cheekbones. It was difficult to put an age on him, for he could be anything between thirty and forty, but he obviously belonged to the old school because there was no mistake about his attitude towards women doctors.

There was a hostility in his glance when he looked at her that he made no effort to conceal. A typical middle-class suffragette type, was his first impression, for what he saw was a determined looking, upright, fine-skinned woman with light coloured hair and eyes, an English rose on the verge of fading.

Affable Harry said, 'Now Jenny, meet Fred!'

She smiled and held out her hand which he took without a smile and said, 'Allen.'

Put out at his formality, she replied, 'Jenny Garland.'

In fact Garland was her maiden name

164

which she retained for professional work. Her time as Mrs Hope had been so short, and the marriage took place so close to her graduation, that many of her colleagues and teachers at university only knew her as Garland, and that was the name on her professional papers.

Harry Mason sensed the tension between the two, who were obviously taking stock of each other, and felt disappointment and disquiet at how things might go during his absence. He hoped Allen would not be too obstructive with Jenny.

'Come on, let's have a cup of coffee together before work starts,' he cried in false bonhomie, but Jenny shook her head. 'Sorry, Harry, but I still feel weak at the knees. I think I'll have to go and lie down again.' She saw a sceptical look in Allen's eye when she said this and wished she could take the words back, for she didn't want him to think of her as a feeble woman.

As she left the office, she brushed past Sadie, who had just arrived for work, and was watching the three of them through the half open door. The eagerness on the girl's normally reserved face surprised her.

Unlike Jenny, Allen did not live in the Masons' bungalow but had his own small apartment at the back of the main hospital. When Jenny went back to the bungalow because she was still shaking with fever, he too returned to his room to fetch a textbook he needed but really to collect himself, to be alone for a little while before plunging back into the old routine.

His hands were shaking and his heart pounding as he sat down on his bed, and surveyed his meagre possessions. The walls of his room were distempered white and the legs of the curtain-shrouded bed stood in saucers of water to stop ants and bed bugs ruining his sleep. By the bed head was a writing table bearing a paraffin lamp and the bearer had already ranged a line of his books along a narrow shelf above it. Then came a cane-seated chair on which lay his folded pyjamas; an almost empty wardrobe; a chest of drawers with a mirror on top; a shoe rack holding three pairs of shoes; a peg on the back of the door for his solar topee; and, beneath the bed, a battered leather suitcase, containing personal papers and his service revolver.

'It's just the same. This is what I went off to fight for, but I'm different now. I've lost my faith, and all my optimism,' he said aloud, surveying the bleak surroundings.

He threw himself backwards on to the bed and stared up at a ceiling that was crossed by a thick supporting wooden beam. A big grey-ish-green gecko that looked like a miniature dinosaur used to hunt along that beam and he wondered if it was still alive. What was the lifespan of a gecko? He had no idea. He crossed his arms and put them over his eyes, longing to sleep but afraid to do so.

In his self-imposed darkness he seemed to drift weightlessly, till, outside the curtains of the bed, he heard a sound, and, thinking it was his bearer, said without removing his arms from his eyes, 'Leave me for a moment, please.'

'It's me,' said a woman's voice and he sat up to see Sadie standing beside him. Her heart-shaped face looked stricken with pity and her lips were trembling. She was still pretty, with coal black hair that shone with a blue sheen when the light caught it, but her skin seemed to have darkened. It was now the colour of dark coffee and no longer like the petals of a fading magnolia.

'You look very tired, but welcome back,' she said.

Defensively he pulled himself up against the hard pillows. 'Thanks,' he replied. He hoped she wouldn't try to touch him. He hated anybody touching him now.

She stood holding the edge of the mosquito net and looking at him as he told her, 'I was only testing the mattress. I'm getting up now.'

She dropped the curtain as he swung his legs to the floor on the other side. 'How's your mother?' he asked.

'She's well but almost blind. Both of her

eyes have developed cataracts,' she said.

He walked across to the mirror on the chest of drawers and began to comb his uncontrollable hair. 'I'm sorry to hear that,' he said.

'Nothing can be done for her,' said Sadie.

'No.'

'She's very happy in the house I bought with your money,' she went on.

'I'm glad to hear you bought a house,' he said, putting the comb down and deliberately avoiding her eyes.

'You must come to see it. We'll give you dinner. Perhaps you might even move in with us. This is such a comfortless place and we have plenty of room for you.' Her voice was strained because she was finding the formality between them hard to understand. He used to be so kind and warm towards her.

He turned and looked at her without smiling. 'No, that won't be possible,' he said.

'But it's your house really. You paid for it.'

'I gave it to you. It's entirely yours. You have no obligation towards me,' he said, as if he was talking to a stranger.

She backed away. 'But will you come to see mother?'

'Yes, I'll come, but Sadie, I'm not the same. I've been ill. I lost my mind for a while.'

'You'll get better,' she whispered.

'I doubt it. I went mad, you see,' he said in a bleak voice.

Mary was in the garden sniffing her roses when Sadie arrived home in the late afternoon and flung herself on to a verandah chair. 'Is he back? Did you see him?' Mary asked eagerly.

'Yes, I saw him.'

'Has he changed?'

'Not so much to look at. He's thinner but he never was fat.'

'Has he been wounded? Does it show?'

'No, he still has all his legs and arms, but you were right when you said war changes men. He says he went mad. That might have been why he was in hospital.' Sadie's voice was dull.

'Mad?' queried Mary. She looked frightened. To her, madness meant irrationality and danger. Mad men ran amok and hurt people.

'Not mad exactly. He told me he'd lost his mind,' snapped Sadie.

'That's not mad. He might mean he only lost his memory for a while or something.' Mary sounded relieved.

'I don't think so. I think he means *mad*. He's behaving very strangely anyway and he looks – he looks wild.'

'Oh dear, but I did warn you, didn't I? You'll probably have to stop hoping.'

Sadie was irascible. 'I'm not hoping. I haven't hoped for anything for years and years. I go on from day to day, that's all.'

Her mother groped her way across the floor and hugged her. 'It'll be all right. At least we have this house and you have a good job.'

Sadie sighed. 'The trouble is I love Fred. I really love him. He needs to be loved though he might not know it. He needs to be helped. It's as if he lost part of himself in that war, left it behind on the battlefield.'

'I warned you,' said Mary again, even more sadly.

Angry and confused, Sadie felt she had to get out of the house and away from her mother before she ate supper, so she went for a walk to think about Fred. The road ran along the bank of the Ganges and she soon found herself on a pleasant promenade where expatriate families liked to walk or ride in the evening. Some of them hired old-fashioned horse-drawn carriages that trotted along, giving the passengers good views of ornamental gardens and the stalking herons and cormorants in the water.

She followed the dawdling crowds till she found herself at the ornamental gates of the Remembrance Garden. She'd never been inside it, never seen the famous marble angel. Her father wouldn't take her because he said the British only mourned their own dead, and didn't give a thought to the hundreds of others – including his mother – who were killed on the rebelling side. Tonight however she wanted to see the mourning angel. She wanted to find out if it could give consolation.

When she turned to go in at the gate, however, a shabby guard came out of his little sentry box and waved her away.

'But I want to go in to see the angel,' she protested.

'It's not for your kind. This garden is only for white people,' he said rudely.

Cawnpore, June 22nd, 1919

The arrival of Allen did not go unnoticed for long by Robert Ross who first saw him on a Sunday morning ploughing his way up and down the swimming pool at the Gymkhana Club.

'Who's that?' Ross asked, eyeing the lanky shape with flailing arms that seemed to be trying to beat some aquatic record.

'He's an odd fish. An Irishman just back from the fighting in France. He's a doctor in that Mission hospital on the other side of the bazaar. Definitely not the friendly sort, I'm afraid,' said his friend, a mill manager.

Alarm bells rang in Ross's head. 'Is he married?' he asked.

'Not him. He used to be friendly with a little chi-chi nurse before he joined up, though, so I don't think he's one of *those*.'

'Which part of Ireland is he from?'

'I've no idea, but you could cut his brogue with a knife.'

When Allen came out of the pool and sat down in one of the cane chairs to drink a beer, Ross appeared beside him, exuding bonhomie. 'I hear you were in France. It must be a relief to be back in Cawnpore,' he said.

'Why?' asked Allen, looking up.

'Well, after the fighting. France sounds like hell on earth.'

'It was. You were lucky if you managed to miss it.'

Ross flushed. He hated to be reminded that he didn't go to fight. 'I'd have gone like a shot but I'm in the police and they needed me here in India.'

'Oh yes, to round up a few *goondas*, I expect.' Allen sipped his beer and did not invite the stranger to sit down with him, but Ross did so anyway.

'I had a job to do, serving my country here,' he said defensively.

'Serving your country. Which one is that?' asked Allen, running his eye over the other man's dark hair and strongly defined features.

'England, of course.' They were touching on dangerous ground now because though he claimed pure British blood, and boasted about his indigo planter grandfather, Ross had Indian blood. Both his grandfather and grandmother were part native, though that was well hidden and Ross had been educated in England, as was his father.

'Really?' said Allen, in a tone that clearly doubted the answer.

'And which part of Ireland are *you* from?' asked Ross, hiding his anger and going on to the offensive.

'Cork.'

'That's Fenian country, isn't it?'

'It is but I've had enough shooting and killing to last me for a lifetime. Excuse me, I've work to do,' said Allen, laying down his glass and rising to his considerable height.

He had made an enemy, however, and the unimaginative Ross's animus against him was based on several things – his rudeness, his justified suspicion about Ross's ancestry, the fact that he came from a part of southern Ireland where disaffection against the English was running high, but most of all because he worked in the same hospital as Jenny and might manage to worm his way into her affections – though that seemed unlikely judging by his surly manner.

Ross decided to watch him anyway in case he sympathised with the Fenians. A case could be made to link those sympathies with the anti-English movement in India. He remembered the case of half-Irish Dolly Mullins, and could almost make out a case against Allen without any evidence at all.

The fact that another bachelor had entered Jenny's circle of acquaintances, however, spurred him on in his courtship for he did not intend to miss out there and watch his prize being snatched up by someone else.

Though he had been half-hearted in his pursuit of her before, Allen's appearance sharpened his ardour and she seemed more desirable than ever. Instead of dining at the club, he decided to call on her without warning and invite her to go for another drive to cheer her up after her recent illness.

Till now their occasional evening drives never took them very far, usually to the river bank where they parked by the fishermen's temple and watched men hauling up their nets under the eyes of the ever watchful birds who pounced on the wriggling silver catch before the men could get at them. Ross never told Jenny that the temple behind them marked the site of the Satichaura Ghat massacre of 1857, and they only gossiped or talked about generalities, avoiding the subjects of Dyer and Gandhi on which he knew they did not agree.

When he drew up his car outside the Masons' bungalow that evening, Molly and Harry were bustling about packing up their trunks in preparation for going home on leave. Jenny, still wan faced, was trying to help.

He went in and greeted the Masons before suggesting that Jenny might like to take a drive. Dark rain clouds on the horizon presaged the coming of the monsoon and the land looked as if it was heavy and brooding. It would be cooler, he said, when the rain

175

began to fall but, in the meantime, a drive in fresh air might do her good.

She looked doubtful but Harry was all for the idea. 'Go,' he urged her. 'You need to get out.'

Ross added an inducement. 'I'll take you to see a famous temple about ten miles from the city. Have you ever been inside a Hindu temple? It's very interesting,' he said. That temptation made her agree because she was becoming aware that she had seen or knew very little of the real India. All she had experienced was the European life that surrounded the Masons while another teeming world seethed outside, unknown to anyone without curiosity and a sense of adventure.

As they bowled along in Ross's car, the feeling of speed and freedom made her suddenly so exhilarated that she began laughing and chattering as she had never done with him before, and a barrier between them dropped. She was a young woman, and he was an attractive man. Perhaps it *is* possible to love again, she thought, though not as violently and uncritically as the first time of course.

She glanced sideways at his distinguished profile and strong, sinewy hands on the steering wheel, and accepted that he was physically attractive, though too hidebound in his ideas. But did that matter? In her situation, was it not better to look for a suitable companion instead of an ideal lover? Her mother's lonely life in Edinburgh was an intimidating example of what could happen to a woman left on her own, living on memories and loving in retrospect.

When they arrived at the temple it was crowded with pilgrims of every age, and to her surprise, he showed an unexpected reverence and tact, not scoffing, throwing his weight about or elbowing in as she might have expected, but standing back and watching with a strange expression of reverence on his face. It was as if something deep inside him responded to the tinkling bells, the smell of incense, the bland expressions of the carved gods and the overall sense of sanctity.

She stood behind him, using him as a buffer, because the size and fervency of the crowd scared her. It made her realise that India was teeming with people who had no wish or reason to kowtow to the whites. The British made no impact on their world and never would. Ross's description of a bloodthirsty mob bursting into the Bibighar and creating carnage came into her mind. Even to be overrun by a peaceful crowd like the one surrounding her now would be terrifying.

Because he was considerate about her recent illness, they did not stay long and as they were driving back to the city, she suddenly asked him, 'You were telling me about the Bibighar the other day, and I was wondering if any of the captives escaped?'

He shook his head. 'No. Not a single soul. The massacre was complete. When Havelock's men got into the building two days later there was no one left alive. Some of the prisoners had kept notes or scrawled messages and records on the walls about the people who died before the final slaughter and most were accounted for though the bodies in the well were all in pieces – it was a terrible thing, terrible.'

'What about a child or a baby? Could a small child have escaped?' Jenny asked.

'Not without help from an adult. A small baby could have been smuggled out I suppose. But who would take it?'

'An ayah?' she suggested.

'That's possible. She'd have to colour its skin though, and she'd probably keep the child, especially if it was a boy. If it survived it might have gone on living in some remote village till it died without ever knowing its true story. Why do you ask?' he asked.

'Because I have a patient in the bazaar who is English and she says she escaped from the Bibighar while the killing was actually going on,' Jenny told him.

He took his eyes off the road and looked hard at her, his interest clearly showing. 'Your patient has to be fantasising. How old

178

is she?'

'Eighty.'

'Senile?' he asked sharply.

'Not at all. Very much in possession of her faculties.'

'Then she's probably a ranker's wife who took off with an Indian before the killing started. Some of them did that. They still do. The natives have a great appeal to women of a certain class.'

'She's not a ranker's widow. She's definitely a lady. In fact she says her father was a Colonel in the Company army.'

He laughed. 'All tarts say they come from good families,' he said and added, 'But if she was a well-born woman, surely she'd have tried to contact her family after the trouble died down, wouldn't she? She'd not go on living in Cawnpore bazaar. Mind you, I have heard about one young woman who escaped while the people were being loaded into the boats at Satichaura Ghat. She was saved by an Indian who made her marry him, and after six months she escaped from him too. She tried to go back to her own people but they wouldn't accept her because she'd let herself down by marrying an Indian. My grandmother knew her and said she went to Calcutta where she made a living as a piano teacher. She was very bitter apparently.'

Jenny frowned. 'No wonder she was bitter.

What a terrible attitude for her family to adopt.'

He looked surprised. 'Hardly surprising really. She shamed them. They thought she should have chosen to be killed like the women in the Bibighar rather than marry a native.'

Jenny realised that this was another topic on which their opinions differed, and she changed the subject. 'The woman I know in the bazaar doesn't seem to have wanted to escape. In fact I get the feeling that she has spent her life hiding from her own people.'

'She's either spinning you a yarn or she has something to hide,' said Ross and, though she was not convinced, Jenny agreed. 'I suppose you're right.'

'Doctor Jenny. Where is Doctor Jenny?' a distraught girl asked Fred Allen who was alone in the hospital dispensary on the afternoon Jenny was at the temple with Ross.

He was surprised and pleased to realise that his ability to understand Hindi had not deserted him during the terrible months in the trenches and answered her in her own tongue. 'She's out. What do you want with her?' he asked.

'My lady the Begum is very sick. Dr Jenny must come to see her again. She saved her last time,' sobbed the girl.

'The Begum?' he queried.

The girl nodded, and pleaded, 'If you are also a doctor, please come, please come.'

He took a tonga, sitting up bare-headed in the back because he would not wear a solar topi, which he considered to be an English affectation. It was beginning to rain and he liked the feeling of it on his face because it reminded him of Ireland.

At the bazaar, a tall man was waiting by the silk shop to take him into a hidden compound where he found an old woman in a diabetic coma. When she came round, she spoke to him in perfect English, and, like Jenny, he was sufficiently intrigued to stay and talk to her for longer than was absolutely necessary.

When she felt better, she stared at him and asked, 'Where's Dr Jenny?'

'Do you mean Dr Garland? She's been ill and went out for a drive to make her feel better. I came in her place. I'm Dr Allen,' he said.

'*What* did you call her?' said the patient in a sharp voice.

'Her name. Dr Garland. That's what I call her.'

'You mean Dr Jenny, don't you?'

He nodded. 'Yes. Jenny Garland.'

She repeated the surname and asked, 'Garland, like a bouquet of flowers?'

'I suppose so. I don't know how she spells it but I suppose it's the same as a bouquet,' he told her.

The patient leaned back against her pillows and smiled wanly. 'How strange,' she said and closed her eyes. With them still closed, she said to him, 'Ask her to come back to see me, please.'

Next morning Jenny felt well enough to go back to work, and was greeted by Allen who said, 'I was called out yesterday to one of your patients who seemed disappointed that you were unavailable. She wants you to go to see her again. I don't think she thought I knew what I was doing.'

He was only joking she realised when she saw a faint twinkle in his eyes, so she smiled and said, 'That must be the Begum. She doesn't think anyone knows what they're doing except her. Has she had another collapse?'

'Yes, they called her the Begum, though I doubt if she deserves the title. She's an Englishwoman, unless I'm very much mistaken.'

'Good for you. She is, and she's my special favourite though she can be very rude. Is she all right?'

He shrugged. 'She's not going to be around much longer, I'm afraid. Her heart's giving up.'

Jenny looked stricken. 'I was afraid of that, too. And she won't keep to the diet, though

I tell her over and over again.'

'I suspect she's not a woman who'll do what she's told if it doesn't suit her. She probably knows as well as you or I that she hasn't much time left,' he said.

'I don't want her to die till I've found out more about her. She's my mystery woman,' said Jenny.

'In what way?' he asked.

'She told me she escaped from the Bibighar but Robert Ross thinks she's a fantasist because there's no record of anyone ever escaping from there.'

He frowned. 'If you want my opinion, I'd prefer her story to anything Ross said. Like you, I prefer mysteries.'

And he doesn't like Robert, thought Jenny. She was unsure whether that should put Ross up in her estimation or not.

Throughout her long life, except for the time in the Bibighar, the Begum had always bathed and changed her clothes when evening came. Jenny arrived while she was being waited on like a princess by the women of her household, and as they fussed around her, Jenny sat by the well, watching the servants bustle about their business. When the smell of cooking the evening meal filled the air, she was finally allowed to go in to see her patient.

The Begum was in the big bed, lying

against piled-up pillows, and looking more peaceful than the last time they met.

'I heard you had to call out Dr Allen yesterday. Are you feeling better now?' Jenny asked.

The old woman smiled rather feebly. 'A little better but I'm tired, though I'm not suffering, Doctor. I think my mind is more at peace, at least I hope so. But what about you? He said you'd been sick.'

'I'm better too. I've only looked in to make sure you're all right.'

'Don't you trust the man doctor?' asked the Begum mischievously.

'Of course I do, but you're my patient and I'm interested in you. I want you to go on telling me what happened when you got out of the Bibighar.' Jenny knew that her approach was very outright, but she was unable to contain her curiosity. Was Ross right, she wondered? Was the Begum a fantasist?

The old woman frowned and shook her head. 'I wish I could stop remembering. It was awful. I didn't leave my sister till I knew there was no hope of her surviving.'

'I'm sure of that. But how did *you* escape? According to the records no one else did,' Jenny said.

The Begum smiled. 'So you have been checking up, have you? The records are wrong because I escaped. I was saved by a man who was watching out for me. He was a

184

soldier in my father's regiment, who knew me before I was married.'

'Did you know he was in the Bibighar?' Jenny asked.

'Yes, but only on the morning of the killing when he spoke to me, then he came in with the murderers and took me away. I don't know how he did it really. I fainted when Lucy was being killed. When I came to, he was lifting me on to a horse. No one stopped him. I suppose they thought he was helping himself to a woman.'

'What was his name?' asked Jenny.

'Dowlah Ram.' The Begum's voice was filled with pride and love when she said it.

'How did he manage to spirit you away?' was Jenny's next question, thinking that even when free of the Bibighar, an Indian man with a white woman would have attracted attention.

'Oh my dear, it's such a long story.'

'But you stayed with him?'

'Yes, at first only to save myself, but later because I wanted to. I made myself an outcast, Dr Jenny, a pariah to my own people and I couldn't have gone back if I wanted to – which I didn't.' The old woman sounded triumphant.

They were interrupted by the arrival of the Begum's daughter-in-law carrying a tray of food that she set down by the bed. It was obviously not a good time for the doctor to visit, so Jenny rose and said, 'You are going to eat now. I'll call in again, but if you want me, let me know and I'll come at once.'

The Begum shook her head and put up a detaining hand, 'Before you go, there's something I want to ask you. What is your name?'

Surprised, Jenny frowned. 'Dr Jenny, of course.'

'I know that. I mean your surname.'

'My husband's name was Hope so I'm Mrs Hope, but I use my maiden name for work. Then I'm Dr Garland. I'm Mrs Hope and Dr Garland,' said Jenny pointing at her own chest and laughing.

The Begum went very still and she asked, 'Are you sure?'

Surprised Jenny said, 'Of course I'm sure.'

'They're nice names but quite unusual, especially Garland – like a bunch of flowers,' said the Begum.

'I've got used to them. Eat your supper and then have a good sleep,' laughed Jenny, making for the door.

Later the old woman lay against her pillows and stared out at her beloved purple sky through the window. Once again the young doctor had started her mind racing but now the memories were not horrific. Now she was strangely jubilant.

Nor was she sorry that she'd told the girl the name of her beloved man. They'd spent

186

years in hiding, afraid of repercussions, but now it did not matter any longer. He was dead and could not be harmed, she was dying and beyond reproach.

'Dowlah Ram,' she said aloud, patting the side of the big bed where he used to sleep. 'Dowlah Ram, I love you,' she told his empty space.

On the Run, 1857

When Emily came to she was hanging over a man's shoulder, staring at the ground, with her hair falling over her face. He was running fast, loping along with giant strides, and gasping, 'Keep – silent, missee. Keep – silent.'

One of her arms was swinging loose over his back and she looked down it, remembering a rag doll that she used to play with in that other life – so long ago, it seemed. Her regard was dispassionate, as if the arm belonged to someone else. The pale skin between the elbow and the wrist was smeared with drying blood, Lucy's blood, she realised with a stab of pain and horror.

Guilt filled her. That arm had been held by the sister she abandoned to be hacked to death by a grinning fiend, who was urged on by the hateful Dolly Mullins. Oh, Lucy, Lucy, Lucy, I'm sorry. Forgive me, she thought, but grief clouded her perception and she did not know where she was or what was happening.

The man carrying her suddenly skidded,

scattering stones as he went, half turning and almost losing his balance. Beneath her she saw running water. Unceremoniously he threw her into a small dug-out boat tied up by the river bank and leaped in after her, grabbing a paddle from the gunwhale. Like someone in a nightmare, unable to move, she lay on the floor and watched him pushing off into the water.

Soon they were in the middle of the river, running fast downstream with the current. Weakly she tried to sit up but he pushed her back with his foot and snapped, 'Stay down. If they see you they'll shoot at us.'

Now she recognised him. It was the man who spoke to her early in the morning before the killing started, their gate guard from the regiment her father commanded before she married.

What did anything matter! If she was about to die, she no longer cared. Huddling down in foul-smelling bilge water at the bottom of the boat she wondered when and how he would kill her, for she accepted the certainty of death and would fight no longer if this was her last morning on earth.

How ironic that today was her eighteenth birthday for she did not feel young – she felt like a very old woman who had gone through many purgatories. Bright mornings in India used to delight her and today the breeze coming off the water smelt sweet and clean;

and the sky over her head was a beautiful shade of azure blue like the Madonna's cloak in Italian paintings she'd studied at school, but she took no pleasure in any of it. All she could think of were the screams of the dying in the Bibighar and the sight of the heaped-up, dead and bloodied bodies. She hoped Lucy's death was mercifully quick, and that her soul was now soaring upwards into the vast sky above, not wandering confused in that hellish place.

Not till they were well clear of the city, where the river ran past fields of tall maize and soaring palm trees, did her captor allow her to sit up. She was silent, refusing to speak to him, as, leaning over the side of the little boat, she slowly dipped her bloodied bare right arm into the clear water, and washed it clean with her other hand, cupping the palm to fill it with water that felt comforting on her skin. It had flowed down from the icy Himalayas and brought a benison of coolness with it.

Lucy's blood, a mist of red, floated away into the water and disappeared. It was the last link with her sister, and she stared down into the river's opaque depths for a while, trying to follow the traces, wondering where they would go. Then she straightened up to look across at him and ask, 'What's your name?'

Though she knew him by sight, she had

never known what he was called, apart from his rank, 'subadhar'. He had a princely look, for his physique was impressive and his carriage stately, a tall, strong, handsome man with smooth brown skin and large, lustrous, slightly slanted eyes that gave him the look of a startled deer. The hair clustering in little curls at the nape of his neck, and his drooping moustache were jet black. Golden earrings glinted in his ears. He must have stolen that junior officer's jacket because it was Company red and white, with gilt buttons and white pipe clayed trimmings on the collar and cuffs. Beneath it he wore white breeches and heavy boots. He looked clean and punctilious.

She remembered that he was always smartly turned out when he commanded the guards on the gate of their family bungalow. Not for him the pan chewing favoured by other soldiers, who so stained their mouths with chewing betel nut that they looked as if they were spitting blood. His lips were fawn coloured and his teeth gleaming white.

'My name is Dowlah Ram,' he said shortly, continuing to paddle fiercely.

'Why did you take me away?' she asked.

He was preoccupied by the swiftness of the river which was running fast with long stretches of rippling eddies, but in a few moments he paused in his paddling and said simply, 'I did not want them to kill you.'

'Are you going to kill me yourself – or rape me?' she demanded

He shook his head. 'No. I'm not a brute. I respect you because I have known you and your family for a long time. You are my colonel's daughter, I owe you loyalty.'

'But you let them kill Lucy and you knew her too.'

'I couldn't save you both. I would if it had been possible, but you were the important one. I especially wanted to save you because I remember you going out riding in the morning with your sister. You rode a grey mare with a long white tail and looked like a queen. I always liked to be there to watch you pass. After the rising, I heard that you were in the Bibighar, so I stayed back to look for you.'

She stared hard at him and said in her most commanding voice, 'But you're only a *sepoy* and I'm the daughter and the wife of Englishmen. I'll never be your woman, so what are you going to do with me?'

There was not much hope of a reassuring reply, for as far as she'd heard, Indian mutineers were rampaging through the country killing and raping every white woman who came their way. Why should this one be any different?

He shrugged, indifferent to her high-handedness. 'I do want to keep you but if you won't stay with me, I'll take you to a place from where you can make your way back to your own people. At least you'll be alive and you can tell them that we're not all murderers. I've a horse waiting in a village not far downstream, because we must ride out of the Ganges valley. It's full of mutineers who'll kill you even if I don't.'

'You've been planning this for a long time?' she asked in surprise.

'Since I first heard you'd survived the killing on the Satichaura Ghat and were in the Bibighar. I'd have saved all your family if I could get a cart, but that was too difficult. Then I was told your mother had died and your sister was losing her mind, so I knew there was little chance of getting her out. I tried to tell you about my plan this morning, but the killing started, and I had to act quickly. I went in with the butchers, took you and ran.'

How could this awful thing have happened? she wondered for the hundredth time, and shook her head as she said, 'My father always said you were a good soldier, Dowlah Ram, yet you rose against him. You broke your oath of obedience.'

'Yes, I did,' he agreed, bending with the paddle.

'Why? An oath is sacred.'

'Your father was a reasonable man but many other officers denigrated us, looked down on us, and called us insulting names

193

like "nigger". They greased the cartridges with pig fat and cow fat and made us wear leather helmets which is against our beliefs. We objected but no one paid any attention. They were trying to turn us all into Christians,' he told her.

She knew that pig fat was unclean to Muslims and cows were sacred to Hindus and that stories about the defilement of the cartridges, which outraged both religions, were spread through the military lines by plotters to rouse the native troops. They chose their time well too, because the Company army was demoralised by rumours of defeats and large death tolls among the British forces in the Crimea. After a hundred years of ruling India, it seemed that British dominance was doomed to end as the soothsayers were also predicting.

It was undeniable that stupidity and insensitivity among the officers fomented the unrest, because, as he said, many bullied their native soldiers unmercifully and never listened to complaints; others, more trusting, simply refused to believe that their men would rise against them. Even when specifically warned, they closed their eyes and went on as if nothing was happening.

Emily remembered her own father sending away a spy who brought information from the bazaar about the Nana Sahib's double dealing. 'He'll never betray us. He admires us too much,' he said. Yet the Nana Sahib, preening and unctuous as he seemed, nurtured hatred against the people who were condescending to him. Her father and his family had paid a terrible price for naïvety, and they were not the only ones.

Her husband Dickie had been equally blind. Though warned by his servants that an insurrection was brewing in the military lines, he took no notice till the Sunday morning when he and Emily returned from church in Barrackpore to find the heads of their informing servants stuck on the railings of their bungalow garden.

To do him justice, Dickie acted fast. He did not wait to be slaughtered but rode off to Delhi to join the British garrison and sent her to Cawnpore. Even the sight of the bloodied heads did not squash her spirit then. She'd been full of confidence that nothing could harm her.

No longer! She would never be the same again. Her youth, her optimism, and her hopes for the future were all gone. It seemed unlikely that she would survive to see tomorrow and she did not greatly care.

To give herself time to think, she closed her eyes and pretended to sleep as they floated down the river. Neither of them spoke again till she was jolted sideways when the little boat's prow thudded into the earth of the bank and Dowlah Ram jumped ashore, grabbing her arm to pull her after him.

By this time it was late afternoon. Soon the sun would set and the air would be full of the smell of cooking fires from a village not far off beneath a grove of mango trees. To her amazement, and shame, she felt hungry.

'Lie down and hide in the grass while I go to fetch the horse. I don't know if the people in the village are friendly to whites so they mustn't see you,' he told her as he hauled her up the bank.

She had thought of running away from him at the first opportunity but caution prevailed and she lay flat in muddy earth, with her head turned so that she could watch him loping off across a wide field. She could hear the noise of the river running at her back and considered giving up and rolling down into it. Would drowning be a better death than rape or stabbing? Though he said he would not hurt her, she had seen and heard of so many broken promises that anything was possible and she had no trust left.

Turning over, she looked down into the fast-running water. Here the river Ganges was so wide that she could not see the other side from where she lay. Though there had been no rain for a long time, it was also very deep with treacherous whirlpools, but drowning was said to be quick and merciful. Her body would be carried away and washed up downstream, in Calcutta perhaps. The people who found her would not know who she was, and none of them would care.

On the other hand, if she rode off with Dowlah Ram, she could play the Indian game with him, pretend to go along with his plans and look for a chance of escape. Perhaps they'd meet Havelock's force, the one that poor Mrs Maguire said was on its way to relieve Cawnpore. If she did, she could make herself known to them somehow.

She had a basically optimistic nature and when the cliché about there being hope while there was life came into her head, she was surprised to realise that she still wanted to go on living, though there was no one she cared about – except perhaps Bobby – left in the world.

The dying sun beat down on her back as she lay drifting in a kind of half world where anxieties floated free. She was almost in a trance when he knelt beside her again and said, 'I've brought the horse. Get up on it.'

Her spirit was coming back fast so she frowned and snapped. 'I don't know what you want from me but you aren't going to get it. I've no money to give you.'

As he helped her to her feet, he nodded towards Lucy's necklet, which was still round her neck and tucked between her breasts in the bodice of her chemise. 'You've got gold,' he said mockingly.

'Do you want it?' she asked, pulling it out.

'No, but someone else might. Don't wear it openly. Hide it where it can't be seen.'

She looked down at her tattered clothes, and, for the first time, became aware of her semi-nakedness. There was nowhere to hide anything. She didn't even have shoes.

'I can't hide it,' she said.

'Give it to me then and I'll put it in my boot,' he told her. She handed it over, thinking, Well, that's that. He's got my necklace now. Let's hope it's all he wants from me.

The horse he brought was a big chestnut stallion with sharp, forward-pointing ears and big, alert eyes, a fine, well-nourished animal, the sort that could go for long distances without flagging. Like his jacket, he's probably stolen it from some murdered officer, she thought.

In front and behind the saddle, two bundles were tied and he quickly opened one, pulling out a length of ochre-coloured sari cloth, the sort worn by the poorest working women, which he passed to her and said, 'Put this on. Pull one end over your head and hide your face in my back if we pass anyone. Do you know how to put on a sari?'

'Of course,' she said, and tied the length of cloth around her waist, wrapping it over her hips and across her breast. The back bundle made a pannier seat for her to sit side-saddle style behind him, but before she mounted, she pointed down and said, 'I've no shoes and, look, my feet are very white. If you're trying to make me look Indian, they'll give me away.'

He made a tutting sound. This was something he'd forgotten. Kneeling down he scooped mud from the river bank and smeared her feet and ankles. It would dry like a crust on her, she knew.

'What about my arms?' she said, and he smeared her hands and lower arms too.

'We'll get you some skin dye as soon as we can, but first we must get away from here. There's many mutineers roaming around and they'll kill you outright if they know you're white,' he told her as he took her foot in his cupped hands and threw her on to the horse's back before leaping up himself. Though feeling distaste at his physical proximity and garlicky smell, she put her muddied arms round his waist and clung to him as he dug his heels into the animal's ribs. It snorted and reared before setting off at a gallop.

They headed west. By the time darkness fell, they'd covered thirty miles in the direction of the river Jumna. When she climbed down from the sweating horse, her legs were shaking and she felt so feeble and enervated that she was unable to stand and slid to the ground. He picked her up and carried her into a thicket of shrubs where he laid her down on the ground, telling her to stay there while he went foraging for food from a cluster of huts whose lights could be seen on the top of a little hill to the south.

For the first time since escaping from the Bibighar she began to weep, overcome by terrible grief. She wished she was able to pray but all faith had left her. If there was a God, why had He permitted so many awful things to happen? Why did He allow little children to be massacred when they had done no wrong? She was still weeping, but more quietly, when he returned with a bag of food for the horse and an earthenware pot of dhal stew for them.

They ate with their hands, hungrily scooping cold, gritty dhal out of the pot. Eventually she wiped her mouth with the back of her hand and asked him, 'How did you get this?'

'I told them I was on the run from a platoon of British soldiers and they gave it to me. They say there is a lot of fighting going on between here and Jhansi.'

'Is that where we are going – to Jhansi?' she asked.

'Yes, it's my native place. After Cawnpore fell some of my comrades went back there to join the Rani's army. I only stayed because I knew you were in the Bibighar and would need help.'

Emily felt a tremor of fear at the thought of

riding with him into the rebel stronghold of Jhansi where the ruling Rani was said to be fiercely anti-British. 'How will you get me into Jhansi?' she asked.

'I'll say you are my wife.'

She folded her arms round her chest and drew up her knees defensively. This was the danger time. If he planned to attack her, he'd do it now. He saw her reaction and asked, 'Are you cold? I can't risk lighting a fire because someone might see it.'

'By *someone* do you mean Indians or the English?' she asked.

'Either. One lot is dangerous for me and the other is dangerous for you. We will only be safe when I am among friends. Then you must decide what to do.'

He threw her a blanket from the bundle in the front of the saddle. 'That will keep you warm,' he said.

Gratefully, she pulled it over her shoulders. 'Have you a blanket for yourself?' she asked.

'No, but I am used to sleeping in the open. Sleep now because we have a long way to go tomorrow.'

She lay down on her side, resigned to whatever would happen. There was nothing she could do about it because he was far stronger than she was. But he made no move towards her, and, though she fought against sleep, exhaustion swept over her and she was soon unconscious.

A few hours later she jolted awake. Somewhere in the undergrowth an animal was howling but, in her half-wakened state, she thought it was one of the weeping women in the Bibighar. When she looked around, memories came slowly back though for a few moments she had no idea where she was or how she got there.

A silver moon was casting strange, mystical shadows all around her and across the clearing she made out the figure of the man called Dowlah Ram, still sitting with his back propped against a tree trunk and his head hanging down in a defenceless way while he slept.

Like her he was unprotected. If she'd had a knife she could kill him, or she could saddle the horse and ride away before he woke. She could leave him. But the realisation struck her that she needed him. Thanks to him she was still alive. He had saved her and, in spite of her suspicions, he'd not touched her – not yet anyway – so she'd go on making use of him till he took her to some place where she might find friends. As soon as possible she'd get a knife or some kind of a weapon to protect herself with as well.

When she woke again it was morning, and a yellow mango and a ripe papaya were lying beside her on the ground, but there was no sign of Dowlah Ram. She sat up and ate the fruit greedily, inelegantly spitting out round, black papaya seeds, and not caring that juice from the soft mango was running down her arms and making them sticky.

She began to lick the sweet juice off the back of her wrists but suddenly remembered that the last stain they'd borne was Lucy's blood, and stopped in horror. Instead she took off her sari and, in her underwear, ran down to the river's edge. The feel of smooth pebbles beneath her bare feet, and the river lapping gently at her ankles was delicious as she walked into it, and went on walking till she was waist deep in water. Squatting down, she rubbed at her arms with her sticky hands, wishing she had a cake of soap.

The sun was beating down and it was very hot. To sit in flowing cool water was bliss. Her flimsy petticoat skirt floated like a water lily round her and, face upwards, she leaned back into the water, closing her eyes against the blazing sun. Through the closed lids she saw a kaleidoscope of colour, floating yellow orbs, strange purple and scarlet blotches.

Her pleasure was suddenly interrupted by a loud splashing noise and she felt herself being roughly pulled out of the water. 'Don't do that. Why should you kill yourself? I'm not going to harm you,' shouted Dowlah Ram as he hauled her on to the bank.

Soaking, she sat on the grass and glared at him. 'What do you think you're doing? I was only washing myself. I'm desperate for a bath. I smell of the Bibighar.'

'I thought you were trying to kill yourself,' he said angrily.

'That's the last thing I intend to do,' she snapped, and was surprised to realise that she spoke the truth. After coming through hell, she was not going to throw her life away now.

He held out a hand and pulled her up to her feet. 'There's no time for bathing. I'll find you somewhere better soon. You do smell a bit. We have to go now,' he said.

She bristled when he said she smelt. Why should she bother about being polite to him? 'At least I don't smell of garlic like you do,' she snapped, and then noticed that he was no longer wearing the red-and-white jacket. Above his white breeches, he had on a tattered shirt that had once been white but was now a dirty grey.

'What have you done with your fine jacket?' she asked.

'I exchanged it for this shirt with a man in the village.'

'Huh! You got the worst of the bargain,' she said.

'You're not very well dressed yourself and you're soaking wet,' he said, staring at her. She looked down to see that her flimsy chemise and underpants were clinging to her like a skin. Her nipples and dark bush of pubic hair were clearly visible through the thin cheesecloth material. She blushed and crossed her arms in front of herself.

He looked away and said, 'Put on the sari I gave you, at least it's still dry.'

She stalked off behind a bush and wrapped herself up in the sari. For a bodice she had only her soaking chemise to wear but the sun would dry it out soon. Her wet drawers were rolled in a bundle and handed to him. He tied them to the saddle of the waiting horse, then came back and rubbed more mud into her bare arms and legs. She flinched, partly because his touch upset her and partly because she hated to be made dirty again.

'Pick up anything you've dropped. We mustn't leave any clues behind,' he told her, searching the ground for traces of their stay, including the remains of the mango and papaya which he dropped into the river.

They rode north in silence for about an hour and then hid in a patch of jungle on a hillside where they slept away the hottest hours of the day. When evening approached, they were off again, following rough paths, and skirting primitive villages where people turned to stare as they went by. To avoid being seen too closely, she hid her face in his back and was surprised to realise that his musky smell was not so unpleasant now. Perhaps she was just getting used to it.

He was adept at finding food, sometimes bartering for it in villages, using the gilt buttons and military insignia that he'd had the foresight to remove before he swapped his jacket. Occasionally he was given things to eat for nothing when he found people who sympathised with a runaway mutineer on his way to join the forces of the Rani of Jhansi.

From local people he also picked up items of news and they told him that the country they were about to enter was fairly quiet because British troops, and the Indian soldiers that remained loyal to them, were either advancing on Cawnpore on the northeast, or concentrating on clearing mutineers out of the Jabalpur area which was at least a hundred miles away to the south. Emily's heart sank when she heard this because it meant that there was little chance of meeting a British patrol to rescue her.

By the time five days passed in what seemed like aimless travelling, she lost her sense of direction but he obviously knew the country well. Sometimes it seemed to her they were doubling back on themselves and she wondered if he was deliberately delaying their journey, but when she asked where they were, he explained that he was following a circuitous route to avoid crossing bigger tracks that might be used by patrols or raiding parties.

The country was in turmoil and people on the roads were in danger of being murdered for as little as their boots by dacoits who were making the best of current lawlessness. The ritual stranglers, the Thugs, worshippers of the cruel goddess Kali, were also out in force, preying on unwary travellers. The land was given over to lawlessness and it was every man for himself.

On the sixth night, around midnight, in brilliant moonlight, they approached a fairly sizeable village and he turned the horse off the path to ride up to a thatched house that stood on its own in the middle of a cleared patch of land. Dismounting, he gave a sharp whistle which made a guardian pi-dog come rushing round from the back of the house barking wildly, but he grabbed it by the scruff of the neck and held his hand around its snapping mouth.

While it struggled in his grip the low door was unbarred and a man brandishing a rifle looked out. Dowlah Ram hissed something to him and the man grinned, opened the door wider, put down the rifle and spread out his arms. 'Come in, brother,' he cried.

Emily, every bone in her body aching, slithered down from the horse and followed the men into a dim, smoke-smelling room where several people lay sleeping on the floor, wrapped up in pieces of cloth like winding sheets.

Dowlah Ram and the owner of the house were delightedly clapping each other on the back and laughing. They were about the same height and their masculine bulk seemed to fill all the unoccupied space in the middle of the floor. A woman lying by the wall raised her head and reprimanded them in a language Emily did not understand. Dowlah Ram answered, apologising to judge by his tone, and the man of the house said something, too.

The woman stood up and walked across to where Emily was waiting by the door. Gently she pulled her arm and guided her to the back of the room and a door that led to a lean-to where there were several wooden buckets full of water standing on the floor – and, thank God, thought Emily, a rough cake of soap. Still pulling her unexpected guest with one hand, the woman lifted a bucket and led the way into a back courtyard. Without asking Emily to take off her clothes, she unceremoniously poured water over her head and soaked her before vigorously rubbing her with the soap.

She soaped her arms and legs, neck and shoulders and briskly rubbed the suds into her breast and back through the thin sari cloth.

The water was cold and at first Emily gasped but soon began to enjoy the feeling that the dirt of weeks, and some of the horrible memories that went with the dirt, was pouring off her. She grabbed the soap from the woman's hand and soaped between her legs and beneath her breasts, then rubbed it into her hair and stood still while more water was poured over her to wash the grey suds away.

A feeling of liberation filled her as she watched the dirty water swirling round her feet and soaking into the ground. Clean at last, and wearing one of her hostess's saris – a blue one this time – she went back into the main house where the men were sitting round a guttering oil crosier and eating. She was given a helping of rice, served on a folded banana leaf, and ate it with one hand as they did. It tasted delicious.

The other sleepers had woken up by this time and she was aware of curious eyes staring at her while she ate. Though an old woman croaked questions at Dowlah Ram which she guessed were about her, none of them addressed her directly. Whenever she raised her head and looked at any of the women, they would giggle in embarrassment with hands held over their mouths and look away. After she finished eating, overcome by terrible tiredness which she could fight off no longer, she lay down on the floor beside the woman who washed her and fell into a sound sleep.

Dowlah Ram shook her awake next morning and said, 'Sit up. Go with Lila and she'll rub this into you.' In his hand he was holding a small glass vial.

'What is it?' she asked suspiciously.

'Walnut juice, a skin dye. It's best that none of the people we pass know that you're a *feringhee*.'

She looked at him blearily and asked, 'So who am I?'

For a moment he was nonplussed. 'What do you mean?' he asked.

'Who did you tell your friends I am?'

'Oh, I see. I told them the truth. They know I took you out of the Bibighar. The man's my old comrade Rajesh and he won't betray me. Even if I hadn't told him, he'd know who you are anyway because he was serving in Barrackpore when you lived there with your husband. He remembers you.'

She sat up. 'Does he know what happened to my husband?'

'I don't think so. When the rising in Barrackpore fizzled out, he came back here, to his home. It was better than staying and being shot for attempted mutiny. Does what happened to your husband worry you very much?'

'Not at all. I couldn't care less if Dickie's dead,' she said vehemently, but didn't tell him about Bobby, who was her major concern and the only reason she wanted to know if Dickie was still alive. It was best to keep Bobby to herself. After all Dowlah Ram was a mutineer, with a mutineer friend, and their contacts could be widespread. Her long-held trust in the Indian soldiers, among whom she had spent so much of her life, was badly affected by recent experiences.

Not till much later did she realise how the slow pace of life in that remote house embraced her, calmed her and restored some of her peace of mind. As the days passed, little by little she stopped thinking continually about the horrors of the Bibighar, stopped sweating in nightmares every time she slept, and mourned Lucy without a terrible agony of remorse, only deep sadness. She also stopped starting up in terror every time there was an unexpected noise or the guard dog barked.

She learned to communicate with the other women who treated her with great gentleness for Dowlah Ram had told them her story, and asked them not to question her too much for fear of reopening her mental wounds. Her closest friend was Lila, the wife of Dowlah Ram's friend, Rajesh. It was Lila who washed her on that night of her arrival and, next day, took her back into the bathing place to dye her skin with the vial of walnut juice, giggling all the time as she did it. Emily would only let her colour the parts that showed and, when the job was finished, she looked like a piebald, but fortunately there was no mirror for her to look into.

After the dyeing was over she was dressed

in another sari – a green one with a narrow golden border – and all the women came to watch as Lila combed and oiled her hair, which was beginning to grow again. Soon it would be long enough to coil at her neck in the same way as they wore theirs.

'Ah, you look like a Begum!' exclaimed Lila when she finished, and that was how she got the name which Dowlah Ram was to call her by for the rest of his life.

'My Begum,' he always said.

Rajesh came from a family of small landowners and his fields were worked by peasants living in huts round about. From time to time he and Dowlah Ram went away for unspecified hunting and news-gathering trips that could last for days at a time and she was left behind with the women of the household who spent their days in a leisurely way, spinning flax on simple wooden wheels, weaving on small looms, gossiping, cooking, and looking after a gaggle of children of different ages. Though she spent several months in the house she was never exactly sure which child belonged to which mother. They all seemed to be loved by everyone.

Dowlah Ram still treated her with courtesy, but they never spent time together and rarely talked because she spent her time with the women. When he was absent from the household, she could have tried to run away, but, she asked herself, where would she go?

She had no idea where she was exactly, and he always took the horse. He also still had her necklace, which she could have used to buy another horse, and she suspected he did not give it back to her because he was afraid she'd use it to finance an escape. In fact, she did not run away because she was too afraid to risk travelling without him.

By the time the temperature dropped and October came, she was partly recovered, growing restive and ready to leave. On a cool evening, as they sat round a bonfire listening to an old woman telling stories about the gods, she leaned over to him and whispered, 'What are you going to do with me? Are we going to stay here for ever?'

He drew her aside and asked, 'What do you want me to do with you?'

'I want to go back to my own people. I can't stay here for the rest of my life.'

'But there's still fighting going on and you're safe here.'

'I know, but I'm still a *feringhee*. I don't belong here. I haven't told you this before but I sent my sister's little boy out of the Bibighar with his ayah and I want to find out if he's still alive.'

He nodded while he listened, then asked, 'I knew she had a child. Where did the ayah take him?'

'I don't know, but I told her to go to Delhi and try to find my husband. If he was still alive, he'd look after Bobby, and send him home.'

'So you want to find your husband after all? I thought you said you didn't care if he was alive or dead.'

'I don't care about him, but I do care about Bobby. I know he would have been murdered, too, if I hadn't sent him away, but I feel responsible because that might not have been a good decision either. If he had to die perhaps it would have been better to die with his mother. For my sister's sake, and my own peace of mind, I must find out what happened to him.'

He sighed and held out his hands to the fire. 'The cold weather is coming. It will be easier to travel soon and Jhansi is only four or five days' ride away now. The British garrison was murdered several months ago but things have quietened down since, and the Rani is negotiating again with the British. She's not come out against them so there's no fighting. If I take you there, it should be possible to contact Englishmen who are in contact with the Rani and you can give yourself up into their care. Is that what you want?'

'Yes,' she said.

They left the thatched house next morning. Lila and the other friendly women were weeping as they waved her off.

Cawnpore, July 1919

The working atmosphere of the Mission hospital changed after the arrival of Allen and the departure of the Masons. The camaraderie that Jenny enjoyed with Harry was replaced by a feeling of tension that grew worse every day.

No longer was she called on for advice on difficult cases, and she was relegated to the women's clinic, which immediately became more crowded than usual because some of the patients who'd still preferred to be treated by a man while Mason was there, rapidly switched loyalties when faced by grim looking Allen.

What made Jenny most resentful was that Allen treated her as if she were a nurse and not a doctor on the same standing as himself. When he was doing some minor surgery one morning, he pointed to his used instruments and said curtly, 'Boil those up for me, please.'

Though she often helped the nurses to sterilise instruments, she resented his highhandedness, flushed in annoyance and

215

called to Sadie, 'Nurse Mullins, Dr Allen would like his instruments sterilised, please.'

When he looked at her, she saw the surprise in his eyes, but turned her back and walked away. During a mid-morning lull, she joined the nurses who were taking the chance to have a cup of tea, and her seething resentment made her burst out with a question, 'Was Dr Allen always so unpleasant?'

Sadie protested, 'He's not really unpleasant, but he is a little more touchy now than he was before he went off to the war. He'll settle down. He's actually a kind person underneath.'

Flora agreed. 'Yes, when people are really in pain or trouble, he's very good to them. He used to take any amount of trouble, visiting sick people in their huts, though he was told not to do it because Marshall did that too, and he caught the plague as a result.'

Jenny felt ashamed to be gossiping about a colleague with the staff, so she smiled and said, 'Oh, all right. I'll get used to his ways, I expect.'

Neither Jenny nor anyone else could have guessed what an effort it was for Fred Allen to cope with life and a return to hospital routine. Most of the time he operated by habit, doing the same things in the same way as he had done for years, before everything was turned upside-down. Only when Jenny reprimanded him was he aware that he was treating her with scant respect, and resolved to remember that there were women doctors now.

His hidden terrors still haunted him. Every time he unwrapped a dressing, he was transported in his mind back to the scenes of horror he'd experienced in France. He flinched and had to steel himself against revulsion when he remembered looking down at men with bloody stumps where legs and arms should have been, or whose guts spilled out when the blankets over them were removed. The smell of death was always in his nostrils, his skin itched as if with scabies. Sometimes the nausea that overtook him was so bad that he had to walk outside and light up one of the many cigarettes he smoked every day. He was beginning to be afraid that he was incapable of working as a doctor any longer and worried about what else he could do.

The idea that appealed most was to become a half-naked holy man, stride off into the blue haze of India and simply disappear. The idea of owning nothing did not scare him. He was very conscious of Sadie's questioning eyes forever on him, and increasingly those of the woman doctor too. He guessed she thought him a boor and a slacker who was indifferent to his patients, but made no attempt to explain himself to her. In fact, he hardly talked to her at all.

For her part Jenny regretted the change in her circumstances. She missed the Masons and there was no time now for banter and chat with the nurses, because Flora and Sadie bustled around being businesslike but unusually silent while Allen gloomed in silence. Jenny sometimes wondered if he was a secret drinker. Depressed at the prospect of spending her nights and eating her meals alone in the medical superintendent's bungalow, she was always glad when Robert Ross turned up to invite her out, as he did more and more as the days passed.

One evening they sat parked by the promenade overlooking the river, and she stared out at the tranquil view before she said, 'I'll miss this city when I leave.'

He turned towards her, surprised and alarmed. 'But you can't be leaving yet. You've not been here very long,' he said.

'I'm on a year's trial which runs out soon after Dr Mason gets back. I could go earlier if I wanted to, but I'll wait till then because I can't let him and the hospital down,' she replied.

He wondered if she was deliberately leading him on, trying to find out if his intentions towards her were serious. 'Why do you want to leave us? I thought you were happy in the hospital,' he said.

'I was, but the new man Allen has changed everything. He resents me for some reason.

218

He's very rude and hardly speaks to me at all. There are times when I think I ought to pack up and quit.'

Ross frowned and the muscles along his jaw tightened. It had not been his intention to propose to her yet, but she was so suitable for him that he was reluctant to let her go. Something had to be done to keep her in Cawnpore.

'I met him in the club and he was pretty rude to me, too. What's wrong with the fellow?' he asked.

'I don't know. It's as if he's made a black cloud settle over the whole hospital though. I was beginning to get over the loss of James and I don't want to go back to feeling miserable all the time. I want to start over again.'

'Perhaps he won't stay. I'll make enquiries about him. It always helps to know your enemy,' said Ross, still holding back from commitment.

Next day he came back at lunchtime and took Jenny off to his club. 'I've been asking around about Allen,' he told her when they were settled on cane chairs in the verandah staring out at grey monsoon skies.

She raised her eyebrows expectantly. 'And?'

'And – before he went off to the war, he seems to have had some sort of liaison with one of your nurses, Sadie Mullins. He gave her enough money to buy a house in

Nawabganj, about a mile up-river from old Cawnpore.'

'But he doesn't live there. He lives behind the hospital.'

He leaned back in his chair, making the wickerwork creak with his weight. 'She must have been his mistress then, Jenny. You don't go around buying houses for mere acquaintances. Perhaps she's the one that's causing the trouble with him.'

Though Jenny was fairly worldly wise, a connection between Allen and Sadie had never occurred to her. 'Goodness. That's a surprise!' she exclaimed.

He laughed. 'I don't think goodness has much to do with it. Are they still together, do you think?'

She shook her head. 'As far as I can see they seem to be very stiff and formal with each other.'

'Then he's trying to shake her off but these girls don't give up easily, especially when they've got their claws into a white man. She's getting older too and he's probably looking around. I hope he doesn't set his sights on you.' This idea had persisted in his head since their last conversation and he had decided to try to pin Jenny down.

What she said next reassured him slightly. 'I don't like him so there's no chance of that,' she announced firmly.

'Good, but that's not all. One of Philip

Villiers' colleagues went off to the war with Allen and he's just got back to Delhi. When I said I was interested in him, Philip phoned his friend up to ask about the chap, and apparently he was some sort of a hero. He got mentioned in despatches for hauling wounded men out of shell holes and saved lots of lives before he was invalided out and sent home.'

'Didn't they give him a medal?' asked Jenny bleakly. Talking about the war made her miserable. She felt as if James was there beside her, bloodied and corpse-like.

'They were thinking about it apparently, but he spoiled his chances by punching a visiting general who turned up on an inspection. He felled the man and began yelling that the war would soon be over if generals had to go over the top in the mornings with the men from the trenches. That was when they reckoned he'd cracked up and sent him home for treatment. The diagnosis was shell-shock but he was lucky not to be shot. He discharged himself from hospital eventually and wanted to go back to the Front but the authorities refused permission because they thought he was still unstable. Then the war ended and he rejoined the Edinburgh Medical Mission.'

'The trenches must have been terrible,' she mused, not listening to Ross really but still thinking about James. Only recently had information about the hell of the war in France started to leak out and she found every new revelation, every poem, every newspaper article, every anguished letter to the press, horrifying. How did her husband cope with such obscene conditions? Was he on the verge of cracking up like Allen before he was killed?

'Terrible for all of them,' said Ross briskly. 'But I'm afraid that our friend Allen might have been some sort of agent provocateur among the ranks – he's Irish you see, and from Cork, which is a hotbed of dissent. He punched a general after all. He should have been court-martialled for that.'

She stared at him, uncomprehending. His lack of sympathy appalled her.

'And Sadie Mullins has Irish ancestry, too,' he went on.

'What has that to do with it?' she asked.

'Her grandmother Dolly Mullins, the one who was shot after the Mutiny, was half Irish. There was a lot of hatred against the British then, and that could have turned her mind. Allen's Irish and probably anti-English as well. That might have been the bond between them. That might have been why he gave her money.' His policeman's mind was racing away into hypotheses and suspicions.

Jenny protested, 'But he was fighting on the British side. And anyway, isn't it only the

222

Irish Roman Catholics who hate the British? Allen can't be a Catholic or he wouldn't be working in our hospital. The Edinburgh Medical Missionary Society is allied with the Church of Scotland, and that's a very Presbyterian organisation. They'd never employ a Catholic.'

'Does he go to church here?' Ross asked.

Jenny shook her head. Allen avoided church services, she'd noticed.

'I suspect that he's hiding something. I'll go on asking questions,' said Ross, very pleased with himself, especially when she complimented him by saying, 'How clever of you to find this all out so quickly.'

In fact she was only speaking by a habit of politeness, but gratified by what he took to be her admiration, he beamed and decided to continue ferreting away on Jenny's behalf. He had risen through the police service because he was punctilious, unimaginative and hard working, prepared to grizzle away at problems till he found an answer. Nor was he too discriminating about how he extracted information. If force was needed, Ross would supply it.

He remembered that, as well as wondering about Allen, Jenny wanted to know about the people in the Bibighar, and set about providing her with all the information he could find. Within a few days, he had five yellowing sheets of paper covered with crabbed handwriting and official stamps, dating back to the late 1850s, in a tattered manila folder on his desk. It listed the evidence against Dorothy Mullins and was delivered to him by special messenger from Lucknow.

The papers related that several unnamed witnesses told the court that they knew Mullins in Meerut before the Mutiny broke out there. She was a well-known bazaar prostitute who talked violently against the British and, during the highly charged weeks before the sepoys rose, worked her soldier clients up to murder, even before the first killings began.

On May 10th, 1857 she was seen in the forefront of the murderous crowd running through the streets, crying for the blood of the British. On that first night of the killing, one of her clients, a Rajput sergeant, brought her the severed head of a colonel which she stuck on a post by her door. It was the opinion of the witnesses that Mullins was not sane, but no one could suggest any reason why she was so violently against white people, especially since she was Eurasian herself, and looked and dressed like an Englishwoman.

The next sighting of her after Meerut was in Cawnpore, where, six weeks later, she was seen cheering on the Marathi soldiers of the Nana Sahib's army while it besieged the

British garrison in the cantonment. At that time she attached herself to the retinue of the Nana Sahib's mother, a woman as rabidly anti-British as herself. These two viragos urged the normally lethargic Nana Sahib into action, and were suspected of planting in his mind the idea of enticing the garrison to surrender on the promise of a safe passage down the Ganges, a promise that was immediately broken and massacre ensued.

Cawnpore was finally retaken on July 17th, and, after the shocking testimony of a scene of massacre in the Bibighar, sweeping revenge was taken on Indian men, innocent or guilty, but in the hunt Dolly Mullins was forgotten.

No one would have known or cared what happened to her if a letter had not been delivered to the headquarters of Sir Hugh Rose, the captor of Jhansi, in November 1858. It told him that Mullins, a particularly wicked woman, who incited the killing of women and children in the Bibighar, was living in Cawnpore city in the third hut in the street of the shoemakers, beside the Subedar's Tank. She was a murderess who ought to be hunted down and punished for her wickedness, said the letter writer.

Rose, distracted by military concerns at the time, delayed doing anything about the letter because he thought it was one of the many malicious anonymous accusations that were flying about everywhere at the time. Eventually the letter was found by one of Rose's adjutants who had been in Meerut and knew Dolly Mullins. He was Captain Richard Maynard, an officer burning with hatred against the rebels because he had lost several members of his family, including his young wife, in the Mutiny. Maynard was on a mission to punish every Indian, whether or not they had taken part in any killings or not, and for months he rode through the Punjab like an avenging archangel, hanging indiscriminately, shooting men from cannon mouths and burning villages where runaway mutineers might be hiding. To make an example of Dorothy Mullins was a great coup as far as he was concerned.

The mechanics of retribution were quickly set in motion. Under the command of the vengeful Maynard, a detachment of sepoys rode into the street of the shoemakers before dawn on a chilly December morning. They drew up their horses around the third hut, lances pointing inwards, while Maynard used the steel tip of his weapon to break down the fragile door.

The terrified family came rushing out, and stood gibbering with fright in the pale light. A gaunt man raised his arms to the sky and cried to the stern-faced officer on the horse, 'Oh great lord, what do you want with us? We are poor people.'

'I want Dorothy Mullins. Bring her out,' said Maynard.

There was no argument. One of the women ran back inside and returned hauling a fighting, screaming woman in a dirty sari with long, tangled hair. In spite of the sari, she could not hide that she was Eurasian for when Maynard whipped the clothes from her with the tip of his lance, her skin was waxen pale.

In an attitude of supplication, she threw herself down on the ground between the front hooves of Maynard's horse and he looked down to ask her, 'What is your name?'

In Hindi she said it was Shamila.

'Your real name,' he persisted, but she would not speak. So he ordered one of his men to tie her up and carry her across the pommel of his saddle back to headquarters. Then the troop burned down the shoe-maker's house, which started a fire that consumed the whole row.

Maynard's captive, still mute, was taken under escort to Lucknow forty miles away. When they arrived, a panel of three men was set up to judge her.

Even if she had not been Dorothy Mullins they would have hanged her. For a white woman to be hiding in a street of untouchable Indians was sufficient proof of some sort of culpability. As it turned out, when she saw there was no hope of release, she turned on them. Eyes flashing, she screamed abuse and years of pent-up hatred against the British poured from her.

'Yes, I'm Dorothy Mullins and I hate you all! Sitting there in your fine uniforms like jackanapes, thinking you're better than us. I wish you'd all been slaughtered in the rising. You have no right to be in this country. Every white person who died deserved what they got as far as I'm concerned. I'd do it again, but to more of you next time,' she yelled.

They listened stony faced and none of them asked why she hated the British so much. Their minds were made up. The trial lasted five minutes and they passed a sentence of death. There had been no open hearing and no jury

The next paper in the sheaf was a transcript of the verdict which condemned her to hanging for treason. The sentence was carried out at seven o'clock next morning, December 18th, 1857. Because no one claimed her body, it was buried in an unmarked grave among dead paupers and criminals alongside the wall of Lucknow jail.

When Ross lifted up the last page in the file, he saw it was a copy of the letter sent to Sir Hugh Rose. Extremely fluent and correct and containing none of the flowery, flattering phrases that Indian writers, especially of anonymous letters, always used, it read so straightforward and matter of fact, it could have been written by an Englishman – no, an Englishwoman, he corrected himself after he read it.

Addressing Sir Hugh by his correct title, Major General, and listing his decorations, it said that the writer had heard that Dolly Mullins was living in Cawnpore because she was seen there buying food in the bazaar.

From personal experience, the writer knew that Mullins had taken part in the massacre at the Bibighar, and had her followed to the street of shoemakers, a low-class district inhabited by untouchables, and not the sort of place where even a poor white would live except when trying to evade discovery.

The unsigned letter went on:

In the interests of justice and rightful retribution it is essential that this woman is made to pay for her past misdeeds. I myself saw her inciting the killers, and building up their blood lust, on that apocalyptic day and it was only through a miracle that I have lived to make this testimony against her. I was shut up in the Bibighar with my mother and sister and was the only one of my family to escape. With my own eyes I saw Dorothy Mullins urging on the man who stabbed my sister Lucy to death and will never

229

forget it. All I want now is for this wicked woman to be made to answer for her crimes. Because I have no wish to return to my old life, I will not tell you my name or my present location but I assure you that what I say is true.

Ross read the letter several times, nodding his head whenever he came upon a word like 'retribution', 'apocalyptic' and 'blood lust' which made the letter seem genuine, because it was obviously written by someone well educated, for whom English was a first language.

He frowned as he remembered that as far as was officially known all the captives were slaughtered – but, according to Dr Jenny, one woman survived. And she was the mother of the man who owned the Celestial Silks shop in the bazaar.

He sat at his desk with his head in his hands, thinking how strange it was that Jenny's two questions should be so closely entwined. She wanted to find out about Dolly Mullins, and was also curious about the woman who said she'd escaped from the Bibighar. The letter in his hand linked them.

The next thing he had to do was find out the names of the victims of the Bibighar.

That was not too difficult. A list was still in the Cawnpore files. He sent for it and soon found what he wanted. There were several people with the same surname, but most of them were in pairs, or were mothers with small children. He needed a group of three, and at the bottom of the list he found what he thought was a possibility – Mrs Mary Crawford, wife of Colonel Crawford who was killed at the Satichaura Ghat, died in the Bibighar with her two adult daughters, Emily and Lucy, and Lucy's child, Robert, aged two. The person who wrote the letter about Dorothy Mullins to Hugh Rose referred to her mother and a sister called Lucy. Because so many of the bodies were horribly mutilated, it was not possible to positively identify every one, but it was taken as certain that all the people who had been in the Bibighar never came out again. But Emily must have escaped.

What was also surprising about the story was that Emily Crawford was the wife of Captain Richard Maynard of the Company army, and it was Maynard who presided over the panel that condemned Dolly Mullins to death.

Highly pleased with himself, Ross retied the file and, leaving it on his desk, hurried out of the office to tell Jenny what he had discovered. In his haste he forgot to put a hair over it, but he saw no reason why any of the clerks should be particularly interested in the information it held.

He drove fast to the hospital and sought

out Jenny, glad to find her on her own in her little office where she was writing up her notes.

'I've found out the name of your mystery patient in the bazaar,' he triumphantly told her.

She looked at him in astonishment. 'Have you? What is it?'

'Next time you see her, tell her you know she is Emily Maynard, wife of Captain Richard Maynard of the 24th Lancers.'

Cawnpore, July 1919

Fat, jolly, given to giggling in an infectious way, Balraj, the police office clerk, had no trouble making friends. People brightened when they saw him approach, even if they did not know him, because he looked so genial.

Through a cousin, a police sergeant in Cawnpore, he'd found a position in the headquarters' clerical department and was appointed to a place in the office of the new man who everybody knew had been sent from Calcutta to infiltrate anti-English agitator groups.

Balraj knew a great deal more about Ross than Ross knew about him. He knew that though Ross passed as an Englishman, adopted every English attitude, spoke with the right accent and played the right games, he was actually tainted by what he himself would have described as 'a touch of the tar brush'.

Like Ross, Balraj was not what he seemed. Though he acted the fool, splashed careless ink blots on his work, allowed his work

233

mates to make fun of him and seemed to care for nothing except his food, he was actually a link in the chain of plotters that stretched from Amritsar to Cochin.

The other clerks in Ross's office knew about Balraj's hidden agenda, but he was not fully aware of theirs. They knew that whenever the policeman went out, Balraj went into his office and read his papers. The Muslim, Akbar, openly sympathised with him in his hatred of the British, but the two other men seemed to prefer a quiet life. They assured him however that they had no wish to betray him to the authorities. If they did, they knew they would suffer, so it was best to say nothing and see nothing.

Jadhav, the Marathi, was the most reticent of them. He knew about Ross's trick of putting a hair on his papers, for he was not the first man he'd worked for who did that, but said nothing to Balraj about it. Let him find out for himself, he thought, and even better, let Ross think Balraj was the only man of suspect loyalties among them.

After the shooting at Amritsar, a group of dissident Sikhs, including Lal Singh, drifted into Cawnpore and met up from time to time in a particular tea house in the bazaar. Balraj knew about their meeting place but never joined them. His task was to set up a communication system to allow him to pass on any information he found in Ross's office, and to hear about their plans in return by the same circuitous method.

Originally it was hoped they would start an armed riot on June 6th, which was the sixty-second anniversary of the rebellion by native soldiers in Cawnpore; and the start of the siege of Major General Sir Hugh Wheeler's British garrison there.

However, the date had to be postponed because armaments that were meant to be sent to Cawnpore from the north never arrived, and the plans had to be put in abeyance. Because the consignment was expected to arrive very soon, however, it was important to find a safe place to keep them, away from prying eyes and yet centrally available for would-be rioters to pick them up. The proud and handsome Lal Singh, who knew an importer of cloth in Amritsar, was advised by him to call on another silk merchant in Cawnpore to find out if he knew of any good places for storing the arms.

The other silk merchant was Vikram Pande.

They sat together in Celestial Silks, conversing and exchanging news of mutual acquaintances, till the lamps in the stalls all around were dimmed and shop assistants ran about putting wooden shutters across shop fronts. When Vikram Pande's yawning assistants fussed around, waiting for the signal to shut up shop, he realised how late it was, stood up and invited Lal Singh to accompany him into his hidden compound for supper.

The Sikh did not protest for this was exactly what he wanted. When they entered the shadowy compound, where dim lights flickered through the open windows and doors of the rooms, he stared around and said, 'This is a big property, my friend.'

Vikram Pande agreed. 'Yes, it is. It is my family home and we store the silks for the shop here as well.'

'You have a cellar?'

'Yes, a fine cellar, large, very dry and good for storing.'

'You are fortunate. Silk must breathe.'

'It breathes well here.'

The two men went into a room where women waited to serve them food, and when they finished eating, Lal Singh broached the subject uppermost in his mind. 'Have you read about the killings in Amritsar? My brother was one of the victims,' he said.

Vikram Pande shook his head in sympathy. 'Ah, that was bad. It was unjustified murder. That man Dyer ought to be punished.'

'There are people who have a mind to do that, and to punish the governor O'Dwyer as well. They won't forget.' Nor did they. Within a few years O'Dwyer was to be murdered, although he had retired to England.

236

'But Mohandas Gandhi says we should endure without retaliation. Only then will we win,' said Vikram Pande.

'That is not the Sikh way,' said Lal Singh bitterly. Then he looked hard at his friend and asked, 'Is it your way? Your father was out in 1857, was he not? Did he believe in not fighting back?'

'He thought all killing is bad.'

'So do I, but there are times when it is necessary to kill.'

There was silence between the men then because both of them knew that the real point of their meeting was about to be revealed.

Lal Singh spoke first. 'There are plans to start a rising here in Cawnpore soon.'

Vikram Pande frowned. 'It would be bad if there was much killing.'

'That won't be necessary. There will only be token killings – men like Villiers, the ICS man, some of his assistants, and white policemen, especially the new man Ross who is infiltrating our contacts in the bazaar, as well as some army officers perhaps – but no innocent people, no women and no children. We will not repeat the slaughter of the Bibighar. We want the British to take notice of us, to recognise that we have the right to share in the ruling of our own country. If we show we have teeth, they will climb down.'

'How do you intend to show your teeth?'

asked Vikram Pande.

'In the middle of a certain night, we will attack their houses and shoot them down as Dyer shot my brother.'

'What night?'

'It is not yet fixed because we must first find a safe place to hide our armaments.'

'Where are they now?'

'Waiting to be brought into the city. They could be carried in packed into bales of hay, or perhaps into packs of cloth...' The Sikh's voice trailed off and Vikram Pande slowly shook his head. 'You want me to store them for you? That would be dangerous because I have my family living here and my mother is old and very sick.'

'You are a patriot like your father, aren't you?'

'My father grew tired of the killing when he saw it achieved nothing.'

'It did not then, not at that time perhaps, but we are stronger now. We're not ignorant sepoys any more,' said Lal Singh.

'I agree with you that the British are overbearing, and that we ought to rule our own country, but I am not in favour of bloodshed.' Vikram Pande's tone was firm.

Lal Singh leaned forward with his dark eyes blazing. 'They started the killing. When Dyer gave his order to shoot, and gunned down my brother, they started it.'

Vikram Pande sat silent for a while and

then said, 'That's true.'

'Let me see your cellar,' said the Sikh, pressing his advantage. They got up and walked across the courtyard to a wooden door on the opposite side from the Begum's room. She was sitting up in bed having her hair brushed when she saw the light from their lanterns shining on the white wall and heard the mutter of their voices.

Meanwhile, Balraj, sparked off by Ross's information about Dolly Mullins, began finding out about her family and it did not take him long to track down Sadie and follow her to her house in Nawabganj.

She is a very neatly shaped woman, he thought as his tonga followed her through the streets from the hospital. She cycled quickly, covering the mile and a half from her work place in only fifteen minutes, which was very fast considering that she had to negotiate crowds of people who came out from their homes to wander around as evening fell. When he saw her wheeling her bicycle into her garden, he paid off the tonga wallah and, clutching a bunch of multi-coloured zinnias, loitered in the street for about ten minutes, before he went in and knocked on her door.

When she saw the beaming Bengali on her doorstep, she raised her arched eyebrows disdainfully and asked, 'What you are wanting?' In conversation with natives, she adopted local idioms.

He pushed the flowers into her hands and said politely, 'I need a few words with Miss Mullins.'

'I am Miss Mullins. Go away.'

'No, no I am not going away. I have some information that will interest you, Miss Mullins. It is about your grandmother.'

She said nothing, only stared at him. For years she had not given Dolly a thought, but in the last few weeks, she had been cropping up continually.

'Let me in, Miss Mullins,' said this stranger, who looked completely inoffensive with eyes that sparkled with bonhomie.

She held the door against him, and looked over her shoulder at her mother who was sitting fanning herself on the verandah. Mary was listening to the exchange and she said, 'Tell him to say what he has to say on the doorstep, Sadie.'

'You heard my mother,' snapped Sadie to Balraj.

'No, no,' he said, completely unabashed, 'This is private business and it will interest only you. It should not be shouted out for the neighbours to hear.'

Sadie's neighbours were a very inquisitive Goanese family towards whom the Mullins behaved with disdain. Not knowing what Balraj was about to say, she reluctantly opened the door and let him in.

Tripping lightly in spite of his bulk, he skipped into the house, his sharp little eyes taking everything in. 'You have a very nice place here. How much are you paying for it?' he asked.

Sadie bristled. Indians always asked the price of everything. 'That's none of your business,' she said.

'It is Dr Allen's business, am I right? Is he coming here to live with you?'

She folded her arms as if in self-protection and felt scared. How had he found out about Allen giving her money, she wondered? There was nothing wrong about it, of course, but it was a private matter. What she did not know was that Balraj's contacts in the city included a bank clerk who had paid out a considerable sum in notes to Allen before he sailed for Europe, and received them back in the same paper wrapper when she deposited the money in her newly opened bank account the day after.

When Balraj started making enquiries among his varied acquaintances about Dolly Mullins' descendants, the bank clerk remembered that transaction, and also that Sadie withdrew the money again within a month and used it to buy a house. The deduction he made was that Sadie had been Allen's mistress and was being paid off. Nothing was too small or apparently too inconsequential for native gossips to remember.

'What is this about?' Sadie snapped, but Balraj was making a tour of her sitting room, peering at the pictures. There was a photograph of a family group of her parents with her as a girl, and he paused before it. 'That is your father?' he asked, pointing at the man.

'Yes – but what?' But before she could complete her question, he whirled round and said, 'How old was he when his mother was taken away from the shoemaker's house to be hung?'

Mary appeared in the doorway, blinking in the light. 'He was seven,' she said.

'Did he know what happened to her?' asked Balraj.

'Not for a long time. He had a hard childhood. The shoemakers brought him up, but they were very poor and he begged on the streets. Then some friends of his mother heard about him and paid for him to go to school for a little while. When he was thirteen they got him a place as an apprentice tool maker in the Elgin Mills.'

'What did he think about his mother?'

'He loved her. He used to weep when he talked about her.'

Sadie stood silent, staring from her mother to this inquisitive stranger. Mary walked farther into the room and sat down, gesturing to Sadie and saying, 'Bring tea.'

Balraj sat opposite her, and smiled even

wider. He'd wormed his way in. Behind Mary the drawing of a woman hung on the wall and he got up to look at it.

'That's Dolly,' said Mary.

'A handsome woman. Your daughter looks like her,' he said, and they started chatting while Sadie resentfully banged pots together in the kitchen as she heated water for the tea.

'Now tell us what you have come here for,' said Mary when the tea arrived.

He leaned towards her, plump hands clasped and hanging between his white-clad knees. One of his legs jiggled as if he was suffering from a palsy. 'I have news for you,' he said.

They sat silent, staring at him.

'There is a new police inspector in Cawnpore who is very interested in Dolly. He sent off to Lucknow for the details of her trial and execution,' he told them.

'Why should he bother? It's all so long ago,' said Mary.

'I don't know except that he is a very nosy fellow, always asking, asking.'

'How do you know about him sending off for information about Dolly?' asked Sadie.

His beam became even broader. 'Because I am his clerk. I read his papers.'

'So?'

'He has found out that your grandmother was betrayed by an Englishwoman who escaped from the Bibighar. If that woman had not written a letter to say where she was hiding, she would never have been captured and her son would never have been orphaned.'

Sadie shivered, 'But no one escaped from the Bibighar,' she said.

'One did, and she is still alive, an Englishwoman living in the bazaar.'

A spark of awareness showed in Sadie's eyes. 'An Englishwoman?' she asked, and Dr Jenny's patient came immediately into her mind.

He nodded. 'Do you know her?' he asked.

'I have heard of an old Englishwoman in the bazaar. The woman doctor in our hospital goes out to treat her.'

'You mean the woman doctor that Ross, my policeman, is courting?'

'Yes, he comes to take her out in his car.'

'Her patient in the bazaar told the authorities about Dolly Mullins. Because of her, your father grew up in poverty. For your father's sake, you should hate that woman.'

Sadie and Mary looked at each other. Both of them remembered the bitterness of Dolly's son when he talked about his mother, whom he had loved with a fierce devotion.

'Why did they hang Dolly?' Sadie asked.

'Because she supported the Indians. They wanted to make an example of her. They'd do it again if the same thing happened. Look at the way they are behaving now – shooting innocent people, denying us any rights, disdaining our intelligence and treating us like dogs.' Balraj's cheerfulness left him and his latent resentments blazed out. His vehemence daunted the two women.

Sadie nodded. Since Allen's return she had started to believe that if she was not Eurasian, he would have taken up with her again, perhaps even married her. She watched him beadily, missing nothing he did, always fearful that he would start warming towards Dr Jenny, whose only advantage was that she was pure-bred British. Her suspicions were eroding her confidence and warping her mind.

'Are you sure about this?' she snapped.

'I have seen it in writing. I have seen a copy of the letter the Englishwoman wrote to Sir Hugh Rose telling him where to find Dorothy Mullins. I have seen her death certificate, and the account of her trial. It was a travesty. She did not have a chance to ask for mercy. They hanged her within a day.'

'Poor woman. That was what my husband feared,' said Mary in a low voice.

Balraj never took his eyes off Sadie. 'You can avenge her if you are brave enough,' he said.

'How?'

'We need a place for passing on messages and this house would be perfect.'

'Who are *we*?'

'My friends and I who are planning a demonstration against the English.'

Sadie shook her head. 'My mother is old. We cannot risk getting into trouble.'

'I promise there will be no trouble for you. All you have to do is accept messages and when someone comes, pass them on.'

'But I work every day. I am not always here,' said Sadie.

'Your mother is,' Balraj replied.

'She is almost blind. She can't take notes,' Sadie protested.

'Nothing will ever be written down. There must be no evidence left behind. All she needs to do is remember what is said. The information will be brought and taken away by fruit sellers or hawkers, men who plump up old cushions, fortune tellers, knife sharpeners, people like that. Sometimes you can pass the information on at the hospital. A patient will give you a password and you'll know it's safe to tell what you know. No one, not even your neighbours, will notice anything unusual.'

Sadie looked at Mary. 'I don't think it is safe for my mother,' she said.

Balraj pressed on. 'It will only be for a week or two. It'll all be over soon. You will have done something to honour Dolly Mullins. She would be proud of you.'

Mary leaned forward in her chair and said

246

to her daughter, 'I'm not afraid, Sadie. Let's do it.'

Sadie looked up at the picture of her grandmother. In the drawing, Dolly's face was proud. She stood up for what she believed, and died for it before she reached the age of forty. Poor Dolly!

'All right, but all we'll do is pass on messages. Expect nothing more from us,' she said.

When Balraj slipped out into the black night, he did not notice a man waiting under a tree by the road side. Ali Bey had followed him, and by chatting to passers-by, had found out that his quarry was paying a visit to the house of Dolly Mullins' granddaughter.

He tracked Balraj back to his room in a mill chawl and next evening, when the clerk went to eat supper in a little cafe nearby the dark-browed man at the next table fell into conversation with him. They became quite friendly, especially when they discovered that they both knew Robert Ross and neither had a very high opinion of him.

Every now and again India's monsoon comes in grudgingly, as if it is reluctant to satisfy the thirsty land. In the summer of 1919 intermittent rain was interspersed with days of grilling heat that made life almost insupportable. A constant stream of water was poured down the chick blinds outside the verandahs of the hospital and the Masons' bungalow, but even round-the-clock efforts of hosepipe-tending gardeners failed to relieve the baking heat inside.

Jenny, who was still feeling feeble after her bout of fever, had to change her sweat-soaked dress three times a day and found herself moving around like an old woman. The only time when it was bearable to go out was either in the very early morning or at sundown when a merciful breeze came in from the river.

When evening was approaching on a very hot day, a message came asking her to call on the Begum. Like someone in a dream, she bicycled from the hospital to the bazaar, for, though she did not feel like going out, she responded at once, mindful of Allen's gloomy assessment of the old woman's life expectancy. For some reason, the Begum was important to her. She was becoming Jenny's wise woman, her guru.

The silk shop was still open when she reached it, though darkness had swept over the city. Its lights blazed out, the most brilliant in the whole street, and people crowded inside, fingering the silks and haggling about prices.

The proprietor gave her a folded hand gesture of respect when he saw her and said, 'It is good of you to come. We heard from the other doctor that you were sick but every day my mother has asked me to send for you. The servant girl has been going to your hospital but you've not been there, but today she found you. My mother is most anxious to speak with you. She has been in a strange mood recently.'

'What do you mean by strange?' Jenny asked.

'She is weakening but still seems excited, as if she is waiting for something to happen,' he said.

'I hope it's something good,' said Jenny as he hurried her through to his mother's room, before returning to the commercial bustle with apologies for not being able to stay. He seemed anxious and overwrought.

The Begum, looking like a great lady, was sitting in a low reclining chair with a table beside her. On the table top was an open notebook.

When Jenny was shown in, she smiled, and said, 'Welcome, Dr Bunch of Flowers, I'm glad to see you. I want to talk to you.'

Jenny laughed and sat down beside her, asking, 'Is it about your illness? Is that worrying you?'

'No, I'm not foolish enough to think I can live for ever. I know I must die soon but it doesn't frighten me. I want you to talk to me about all sorts of things – divert me.'

'I'd prefer it if you talked to me. Your life

must have been so interesting and you haven't told me nearly enough about it. Why are you keeping so many secrets? I want to know what happened after you escaped from the Bibighar,' said Jenny.

'All right, we'll exchange stories. I'll ask you a question, and after that it will be your turn to ask me one.'

Jenny smiled and sat down on a stool beside the chair. 'That seems fair, providing you don't tire yourself out. You start.'

The Begum's eyes seemed more intensely blue than usual as she stared at Jenny. Imperious and overbearing she may be, but she was formidably intelligent and unafraid to speak her mind. She must have been impressive as a young woman.

'Let's start with you,' she said. 'I know your husband was killed in the war and you've come to India to do good works, but that's about all except that you have two very nice-sounding surnames – Hope and Garland.'

Jenny nodded. 'That's right, but you knew that already. Now it's my turn to do some quizzing. You've never told me your real name but I've found it out anyway. You were Mrs Emily Maynard, weren't you?'

The Begum looked surprised but smiled nonetheless. 'Emily Maynard! No one has called me that for years. In fact I'm still Emily Maynard because I ran away from Dickie, and don't even know if he's still alive

– nor do I care. I loathed the man. How did you find that out?'

Jenny replied, 'A policeman I know searched through the names of the people in the Bibighar for me and found an Emily Maynard who had a sister called Lucy. That was you, wasn't it? I remember you called me Lucy the first time I came to see you.'

'So you've been checking up on me.'

'Only after you said you escaped from the Bibighar. Everyone kept telling me your story couldn't be true, that it was impossible, but I believed what you said – and it turned out I was right, wasn't I?' said Jenny.

'I assure you I did escape. It's a long story but before I tell it, I want to know about you. Garland is a delightfully pretty name. Are there many of you? Is there a flourish of Garlands? How many are there in your family?'

'There's only me and my mother. I have no brothers or sisters because my father was never in good health. He died when I was small,' said Jenny.

The Begum was obviously interested. 'So your father is dead. That's sad. He must have died young. What was his name?'

'He was called Robert Garland.'

The old woman put a hand over her eyes as if to hide her feelings and said, *'Robert.* And he's dead.' Her voice quavered.

'Are you all right?' asked Jenny, concerned by this unexpected reaction.

The Begum nodded. 'I'm perfectly well. I just think it's sad. Do you miss your father? How old was he when he died?'

'He was forty-five.'

'Too young! When did that happen?' She sounded very sad. Jenny frowned slightly because she had long ago stopped grieving for her father. 'I'll have to work it out. I was seven when he died and I'm twenty-six now, so it happened in 1900. My mother's the same age as he was and she's sixty-four now, so they must both have been born in 1855.'

There was a note of returning vivacity in the Begum's voice as she asked, 'Did he have any brothers or sisters?'

Jenny shook her head. 'No, he was an only child like me, but my mother has a brother with two sons, both older than I am.'

'It sounds as if the Garland family is shrinking rapidly,' the Begum said, obviously not very interested in Jenny's mother's family.

'I suppose it is. I'm the only one in my branch, though there's probably some others around, but I've never heard of them.'

'What did your father die of?' asked the Begum, monopolising the questioning again.

'Tuberculosis, though in his time they called it galloping consumption. In fact his doctors said he shouldn't marry at all, but when he met my mother, he fell head over heels for her and she adored him. Her father tried to stop the marriage because my father's health meant he might not live very long, but they succeeded because they were both old enough to marry without parental consent. It was very romantic really.'

'The power of love. I hope they were happy,' said the Begum.

'I think they were. They had twelve years of marriage, and still, when she talks about him, she lights up somehow.' Jenny's eyes became abstracted as she thought about her mother who lived engrossed with her memories to the exclusion of everything else, including her daughter. Jenny had always felt like the odd man out in the family.

'What did your father look like? Tell me about him,' was the Begum's next question. She leaned forward eagerly when she asked it.

Jenny frowned, surprised at this cross-questioning. 'I was too young when he died to have a lot of consecutive memories, but I remember him sitting by the fire reading Kipling's *Jungle Book* to me.' She closed her eyes and summoned up the memory. 'He was tall, and very thin, and had yellow hair, the colour of butter. It gleamed in the firelight.' Her voice was sad because, even as a child, she'd been aware of constant apprehension, when every cough from her father brought her mother rushing in to examine his handkerchief for spots of blood.

'What was he good at? Was he a mathematician, or an artist? Was he clever? What did he do for a living?' the Begum asked. Her voice was intense, as if she really needed to know the answers.

'He was often ill, even as a boy, so he never went to school but was tutored at his grandparents' house in the south of England, Brighton, I think. They brought him up. He studied philosophy at Oxford, but never took a degree. After they died he went on holiday to the Highlands because his doctor thought Scottish air would improve his health and that's when he met my mother. He didn't have to work because he was left enough money to live on, but only just. Then an uncle left us a little more later on and that's what paid for my medical training. Why do you want to know all this? It's not terribly unusual or very interesting,' Jenny said.

The Begum nodded solemnly. 'I'm interested because I once knew people called Garland and I wondered if he was related to them. He may have been a member of their family.'

Jenny brightened. 'Did you know them in India? His parents died in this country when he was very small so he couldn't remember either of them. He was only a baby when he was sent home to his grandparents.' She had a sudden flash of memory of her wan-looking father lying out in the garden in a reclining chair not unlike the Begum's, but in cloudy Edinburgh weather. A blazing Indian sun might have kept him alive a little longer.

'Next time I write home I'll ask my mother to tell me anything she knows about his family and we can compare notes. It would be interesting to find out if the people you knew were his parents,' she told the Begum, who was sitting forward eagerly and saying, 'It would indeed be interesting. Coincidences like that do happen, you know. I was very fond of the Garlands. Why don't you send your mother a telegram and ask your father's parents' names?'

'A telegram? Is it so urgent?' Jenny asked in surprise.

The Begum smiled ruefully. 'Only because my time is running out, as you well know, Dr Jenny, and I'm a very curious woman who doesn't like having to wait for anything. Please send a telegram.'

In the dim light of the room, her lips looked blue and her voice quavered when she spoke, which made Jenny give her a searching look and say, 'You mustn't tire yourself. With us it's always the same, you know. When it's my turn to ask the questions, you are too tired to talk. You should go to bed now and I'll come back tomorrow. Then *I'll* ask the questions.'

Next afternoon, on her way back to see the Begum, she stopped at the Central Post

Office and filled out a reply pre-paid telegraph form. She knew if she left it to her mother to decide when to reply, parsimony would rule and it would be sent in a letter. 'Telegraph by return the names of father's parents stop there is an old lady here who might know them stop love Jenny.'

The Begum was gloomily looking out at the rain when the doctor arrived and told her, 'I've sent a telegram about the Garlands to my mother. She should reply very soon.'

'I'm glad. I'll keep to our bargain and talk about Emily Maynard. Will I tell you how she got away from the Bibighar?'

'Please,' said Jenny, settling herself among the cushions like an enchanted listener.

'I was carried out of that awful place by a sepoy called Dowlah Ram. He ran off with me slung over his shoulder. The killers thought he was helping himself to a woman, which I suppose he was in a way. He ran across the bridge that carries the road to Lucknow over the Ganges and threw me into a boat. That was when I came round from my faint...'

'He must have loved you to make off with you like that,' said Jenny.

'He said he did but I didn't believe him for a long time because he didn't really know me. He told me he'd fallen in love with me even before I married Dickie. I always told him that was a very rash thing to do.' And she laughed, her voice ringing out with a girlish sort of glee and making her look young again.

'It is possible to fall in love like that,' sighed Jenny. 'I fell in love with James the first day I saw him doing ward rounds in the Royal Infirmary. I said to myself that he was the man I was going to marry – and I did.'

'A *coup de foudre*! It does happen and the people who experience it are very lucky,' said the Begum.

'I don't think it can happen to you twice,' said Jenny.

'Perhaps not, but it sets a standard. It takes bravery to pursue the person you love and Dowlah Ram was very brave. I would not be here now if he wasn't,' the Begum said.

'Did you love him back?' Jenny asked.

The Begum frowned. 'At first? Of course not! Love an Indian? It was unthinkable. I never even considered it. I admit I'd seen him on guard duty outside our house and noticed how handsome and proud looking he was – but I didn't think of him as a man, if you know what I mean. That came later ... when everything changed.'

Jenny sighed. 'I suppose important changes do happen in one's life. I'm going through one myself at the moment. When I first arrived here, I was bitterly unhappy and thought I'd never feel carefree again, but, over the last few weeks, I've changed – at least I'm changing. I'm going to be forced to take a big decision soon – whether to go home or stay here – and I won't know what to do till the day comes.' She was thinking about Robert Ross because she knew very well that he was on the verge of proposing to her, and was unsure what she would say when he did.

The Begum nodded. 'Don't worry about it. Keep an open mind, and when it comes time to decide, you won't have any doubts. I didn't, but if you'd asked me a day before, I'd have said I had no idea what I wanted. It will do us both good to talk, Dr Jenny. I have questions to ask and things I want to say and I'm sure you do too.'

Jenny looked at the old woman. 'Yes, I have. Can I start us off? How did you come to marry your Indian?'

The Begum laughed, 'My dear, I never married him! I've told you I'm still Mrs Maynard, haven't I? But Dowlah Ram was the only man in the world for me, the only one I've ever loved and it didn't matter a jot if we couldn't marry. I lived with him for sixty years but never married him. I didn't know if it was even possible because I was married already and had no idea if Dickie Maynard was dead, and I wasn't going to go out of my way to find out. Knowing Dickie's capacity for making my life difficult, he's probably alive to this day. He'd be eighty-

seven now, and as horrible as ever, I'm sure.'
She laughed and went on, 'I'd better start by
telling you my story. Let's go back to the
beginning...'

Even now, after all those years, she could
not talk about the Bibighar without shaking,
so she did not dwell on the subject too
much, except to tell Jenny about how Dowlah Ram broke in with the butchers and
carried her away.

'Where did you go after you got into the
boat? He must have kept you hidden,' Jenny
wanted to know.

'He had a horse waiting at a village down
river and we set out for Jhansi, which was
where he came from originally. But there
was a lot of trouble going on and it took us a
long time to get there, though we could
easily have done the journey in a week at
normal times. We had to hide from dacoits
who wanted to kill us for anything we were
carrying, from other mutineers who would
have killed a white woman on sight, and
from the British who would have shot him
down.

'It was very exciting at times and I didn't
make it easy for him because I was always
thinking about ways of escaping and never
stopped being rude to him. Now I'm ashamed of the way I behaved. I was totally ungrateful to him for having saved me and
ordered him around like my father ordered

his sepoys.'

Jenny laughed. 'I can imagine it,' she said.

The Begum shot her a hard glance. 'But I changed of course,' she said.

'What changed you?' Jenny asked.

'I suppose his good nature wore me down. It was almost impossible to anger him. And he was very gentlemanly. He never made any sexual approaches to me though I used to catch him looking at me with such longing ...I thought he was sure to rape me eventually but he didn't even touch me if he could help it. Eventually I began to think that I repelled him or something. I suppose he was using a very sophisticated strategy on me. And it worked. I felt insulted, especially as I began to want him. I first noticed that when I realised that I liked the way he smelt.' She laughed again, her eyes shining like a girl's.

'Smelt?' Jenny was interested. She had a keen nose herself and was very interested in the techniques of diagnoses which relied on patients' smell. One of the ways she originally knew the Begum suffered from diabetes was because of the sweet smell of her breath and urine.

'Yes, the smell of his body. That can be very exciting, you know. Babies smell new and sweet and that's lovely. Dickie smelt like sour custard pudding and he repelled me. Dowlah Ram smelt of spice and garlic – I didn't like it at first, but soon, when we were riding along, I found myself wanting to put my face against his back and breathe him in. Very animal, isn't it?'

'Delightfully animal I think,' said Jenny, remembering the feeling of wanting to breathe in James who smelt of soap and disinfectant with an undernote of something else, something very primitive. The memory made her ache.

The Begum's voice was dreamy as she went on. 'I can't impress on you enough what a magnificent man he was. I have never seen one who was more handsome either.'

'Your son Vikram Pande is also very handsome,' said Jenny.

'Yes, he is, but not as handsome as Dowlah Ram, but then he's not his real son. Actually, he's the child of his brother and we adopted him as an infant when his mother died. I love him as much as I would have loved my own child though, and I think he loves me,' the Begum said.

'What happened to his real father?' Jenny asked.

'I'll tell you about that later. It almost broke my Dowlah Ram's heart,' said the Begum shortly.

They were interrupted in their conversation at that point by the Begum's daughter-in-law coming in with a tray of sweetmeats and cool drinks. When Jenny looked disapprovingly at the sweets, she rapidly took them away again.

The Begum's eyes followed the departing tray of sweets with regret and when she saw Jenny watching her, she smiled. 'I love sweetmeats. I yearn for them and lapse occasionally, but I'm old and it doesn't matter much any longer. In fact I think it would be a good way to go,' she said.

'Don't eat too many sweets if you want to live long enough to finish telling me your life story,' Jenny told her, only half joking.

'Where was I in the story?' the Begum asked.

'You were on your way to Jhansi.'

'We stayed for a while in a village, I've no idea where it was, but Dowlah Ram's friend there gave him some money, and when I said I wanted to go back to my own people, we set out again for Jhansi because the Rani, who ruled that place, was neutral then and negotiating with the British. Dowlah Ram said he would pass me over to them if that was what I wanted.'

Jenny nodded to encourage the story to go on, but the Begum fell silent and her eyes filled with tears. 'That was when the sadness began,' she said.

'For you?'

'No, for him. That was when everything changed.'

Jhansi, 1857

It took them nearly a week to reach Jhansi because, although the terrible heat was lessening and the days were pleasantly cool, Dowlah Ram still preferred travelling by night. He heard from people met on the way that the British were gradually subduing the mutineers and taking their anger out on any Indians they met.

They spoke easily, like friends, during this second leg of their journey, but on the third day, he suddenly cried out, 'Look!' and drew on the reins, stopping the horse as he pointed across at a high plume of smoke rising from a clump of trees in the valley beneath them.

Emily, craning to look over his shoulder, heard him muttering under his breath as he drove his heels into the horse's flanks, making it plunge downhill. As they neared the smoke, they could smell the stench of burning thatch, for it was coming from a little village where all the huts were burning. Women and children were huddled in a field, weeping and wailing. When they saw

263

the approaching strangers, they scattered like frightened animals.

Dowlah Ram cantered into the village, and drew up in horror when he saw that several men and boys were swinging by their necks from the branches of a big banyan tree between the burning houses. A few dogs and three dead cows, with their bellies slit and innards spilling out, lay on the ground.

He jumped out of the saddle and stared at the corpses. Then he raised his clenched fists above his head and started swearing in Hindi.

A bent old woman, braver than the others, came limping out of the undergrowth and shouted to him, 'Go away, stranger.'

He waved a hand at the bodies in the trees and asked, 'Who did this?'

'The *feringhees*. They rode in this morning, killed our animals and torched the huts. Then they rounded up the men and boys and shot or stabbed them too.'

Dowlah Ram looked wild eyed. 'Why?'

'Because one of our men was a runaway mutineer. He was still wearing his sepoy's clothes. That's him over there...' The old woman pointed to a man swinging from a farthermost branch.

'So they killed them all?'

She nodded. 'As a warning, they said.'

'Where did they go?' he asked.

She pointed to the north. 'There.'

'How many of them?'

'Ten, maybe twelve...We did not stay to count.' Other women were coming out now too and stood behind her, wiping their eyes on the ends of their saris and sobbing as they looked at their dead husbands and children.

'Go away. You can't stay here,' one young woman shouted. 'You are a sepoy, too. I can tell by your boots. If you stay, they'll come back and kill us all.'

Emily, on the pannier, huddled down and pulled the end of her sari over her face. If they realised she was a white woman, they could tear her limb from limb, and judging by the expression on Dowlah Ram's face, he may stand back and let them do it.

'Yes, go away,' said the old woman.

Still cursing, Dowlah Ram put his foot in the stirrup and remounted. As he was turning his horse round, the old woman shouted, 'If you're going to Jhansi, tell the Rani to avenge us.'

It was difficult for Emily to keep her seat as the horse plunged through rough country because Dowlah Ram was riding like a man chased by the devil. Desperately she clung to him, twisting the hem of his shirt in her hands as she wrapped her arms around his waist, but he seemed to have forgotten she was there.

Very conscious that she, too, was a *feringhee*, she said nothing. If he intended to revenge himself on her after all this time, he would do it soon, she thought.

Still silent and grim looking, he found a place by a deserted little shrine to camp when evening approached and busied himself gathering wood for their cooking fire. When he got it going, he produced a small bag of rice from the pannier and boiled it up in a billycan. She watched, too scared to speak, as he scooped some of the rice on to a large leaf and handed it to her. She stared at the food, feeling nausea rise within her, for the memory of the hanged men in the trees filled her mind.

All her thoughts were terrible that night. When she closed her eyes, she was transported back to the Bibighar; and her head rang again with Lucy's anguished screams as the killers fell on her. She hated Indians for what they did, but now she had to balance that hatred with the shame she felt when she saw the terrible harvest on the banyan tree.

Was it right to retaliate with killing for killing? She wished she could speak about her confusion, but the stony look on Dowlah Ram's face told her not to broach the subject. He, too, was lying by the fire, and turned on his side away from her. The gulf between them seemed unbridgeable. As she looked across at him she knew she had to be the one to speak. 'I'm very sorry,' she said.

He said nothing.

Nor did he speak to her next day, but everyone they met on the road told him more terrible stories of the cruelty of the British raiding party. Not only were they killing the men, but in some places, the soldiers had broken away from their officers and raped several women. When she heard that, Emily shrank. Even in the Bibighar, and in the cantonments before that, in spite of rumours to the contrary, none of her fellow captives had been sexually attacked.

Her suspicions and hostile attitude to Dowlah Ram changed after they left the burning village. Though she did not at first realise it, to her he was no longer an Indian – no longer a servant and someone of a different colour. He had become a man with feelings and loyalties, a man worthy of her respect.

In sympathetic silence she rode behind him with her head and face covered, only showing her dyed hands and feet when absolutely necessary. Other travellers disregarded her because, as far as they were concerned, she was simply a possession of his, a woman less important than his horse.

On the evening of the fourth day, she spoke for the first time and gently asked him, 'Where are we?'

'Near Jhansi. We will reach the city tomorrow,' he told her.

'What will you do with me then?'

'I will ask the Rani to send you to the British.'

'Will she do that?'

'I think she will. I know people in her court.'

'Are you a native of Jhansi?'

'I was born there. We pass my family home on the way.'

She fell silent again. Though she was tongue-tied, she badly wanted to thank him for saving her life. She wanted to say that she knew she would be dead but for him and, in spite of the grief she felt for her lost family, life was surprisingly sweet. Every morning she woke, she gazed at the sky and the trees with a feeling of wonder mixed with guilt. Every time she tasted any food, no matter how cold or stale, or drank fresh, cold water, she was filled with more delight than she had ever felt sipping fine wine. She recognised that a miracle gave her life.

As she rode along she composed in her mind the words she would say to him when they parted – for now she trusted his word. She had to find the right thing to say to thank him properly for what he had done; and she would also make him a gift of the gold necklace that he still carried inside his boot.

The country around Jhansi city was a dried-up waste of scrub and desert. On the fifth morning, as they crossed another ridge of hills, she saw a walled city far off on the horizon and gasped in admiration. It was an impregnable and sinister looking fortress, a huge citadel in the middle of empty red desert, standing proud on a rocky outcrop, and surrounded by massive walls like a city out of the Bible; Jericho, perhaps.

A flag flew from a tower in the middle of the citadel, and before the city gate was a collection of ruined buildings laid out in the unmistakable pattern of a British army cantonment. Dowlah Ram stopped the horse, pointed ahead and turned to tell her, 'Jhansi.'

'Journey's end,' she whispered. Her confusion of feelings surprised her. Now she did not know if she wanted to ride into the sinister city or not. What would happen when she did?

'We must wait for dark before we go in,' he said.

'Don't they close the gates at night?' she asked.

'Only against enemies, but I'm known there. They'll let me in,' he replied.

'So we'll wait,' she said.

'I'll take you to my family house and we'll stay there till nightfall,' he said, turning the horse round back down the ridge where they branched off into a dry-looking field where a herd of emaciated goats grazed on meagre stalks of yellowed grass and weeds.

But there was some greenery ahead too. A mud-walled house behind a high fence was tucked away in a hollow, shaded by a few trees and beside a big well. She felt excitement radiating from Dowlah Ram's back when he caught the first glimpse of his home. In his urgency to get there, he made the horse canter, although it was jaded and he was usually very solicitous about not tiring it too much.

As usual their arrival brought out barking dogs and anxious people who stood shading their eyes to see who was approaching. One old man carried an ancient blunderbuss that he pointed towards them but when Dowlah Ram called out, the blunderbuss was lowered, and they all started running towards him, hands out and faces alight. The son of the house had come home.

Standing tall in the middle of a cluster of people, all of whom were trying to touch him, he lost his grimness and embraced them, as excited as a boy. Leading the horse, with Emily still on its back, he and his welcoming committee walked towards the compound gate but before he reached it, an old man in a white dhoti and a loosely tied scarlet turban appeared in the gap and called out his name.

'Father!' cried Dowlah Ram and ran towards him. They embraced, hugging each other, and Emily saw the old man bend his head as if he was weeping while he talked earnestly to his son. Then, with a yell of anguish, once again Dowlah Ram raised his fists to the sky as he had done in the burning village, but this time his anguish was even greater. His eyes were shut and she felt a chill of fear sweep through her as she watched.

After what seemed like a long time, he came back to the horse and said shortly to her, 'Go with the women.'

He did not seem to be able to look directly at her and she slid from the saddle, almost waiting for a blow. Instead he turned away and walked back to the old man who was still standing with his head lowered and shoulders shaking.

It was obvious that the women of the household did not know what to do with her and she felt like a prisoner when they took her to a small empty room where there was only a string bed in the middle of the floor. She stood looking at them, wanting to ask questions but afraid to do so. Instead she awkwardly asked for water so she could wash herself.

A small brass bowl and a bucket of cold water drawn from the well appeared beside her and she dipped the end of her sari into it to wipe her face while the hostile-eyed women looked on. One young woman, who was heavily pregnant, suddenly started to wail and was led away by the others. Though Emily was very hungry, she did not presume to ask for food from people who obviously resented her presence. Instead she lay down on the string bed and closed her eyes. God knows what's going to happen now, she thought.

She must have slept because the sun was setting when a noise woke her and she opened her eyes to see Dowlah Ram standing beside her.

'My father tells me that the *feringhees* have been here, too, but they did not harm our house because they were anxious not to antagonise the Rani and we are of her family. They are encamped now in the old cantonment before the city walls. I'll take you to near their camp tomorrow and you can walk in. Even they will not shoot a woman on her own.' His voice was cold and very formal.

'What's happened? Why is everyone so sad?' she whispered.

His face was hard and he did not meet her eye. Looking over her shoulder at the blank wall, he said, 'My family has suffered a great loss. My brother has been shot.'

'By the British?' she whispered.

He nodded. 'Yes. He was a sepoy like me and my father. The *feringhees* shot him for taking part in the mutiny at Delhi. They caught him with several others and executed them all.'

'I'm sorry,' she whispered.

'Don't bother being sorry. My people killed your family; your people have killed my brother. Now we are equal. There should be no more killing but I'm afraid it's not finished yet.'

'I am very sorry and I want to thank you for saving my life,' she said, standing up and holding out her hand.

He did not take it. He was looking at her as if she was unclean, and she flushed.

'I don't know how to thank you. I'll tell my people that you saved me,' she stammered.

'I don't care what you say about me.'

'But I care. We are friends. It's not my fault what the British are doing now.'

'I don't blame you, but my heart is broken. My brother has been shot – but not only that. They made my father shoot him.'

'What?' she whispered in disbelief.

'My father stayed loyal. He did not mutiny and stayed with the Company army in Delhi. He kept to his oath. When my brother and his friends were captured, his officer told my father to form a firing squad to shoot them though they were only running away, and hadn't killed anyone, but they were mutineers and had to be shot, he said. My father told him that one of the condemned men was his son. The officer said that to prove his loyalty and fulfil his oath of obedience, my father *had* to shoot his own son.'

There were tears in his eyes as he told this terrible story. Forgetting everything except pity and sympathy, she stepped close to him and whispered, 'That's a terrible story. Surely it's not true?' Even the most brash officer she'd ever met – even Dickie –would surely not do such a sadistic thing.

'It's true! Of course it's true. Why would I lie about a thing like that? My father shot his own son and then he deserted. That is why we are all in mourning. My mother is asking me if I have lost my mind, saving a white woman's life, while her people kill my brother.' His face was so contorted with rage and grief that he was almost unrecognisable.

She sobbed. 'Oh, please tell them I am so sorry. I hate all this cruelty. It's like a nightmare.' Not caring that he might thrust her away, she stepped up close to him and put her arms round him, hugging him tight to her. She was tall and their faces were almost on the same level.

'I am sorry, sorry, sorry,' she repeated over and over again, holding him to her.

At first his body was rigid, and she felt the muscles of his shoulders knotted beneath her hands, but she went on hugging him even tighter, and gradually he relaxed, before bending his head on to her shoulder. She put up her right hand and stroked his long, silky hair that he wore in a kind of pigtail. It was beautiful hair.

As she felt his defences ebbing away, something happened inside Emily too, something she'd never felt before. She turned her face towards his and put her lips on his cheek, crooning gently but wordlessly to him. Tears were squeezing out between the closed lids of his eyes and she wept, too.

But something else was happening to her. Her whole body was on fire and for the first time in her life she felt an uncontrollable desire that was sharpened by her awakened awareness of life and death. It was as if her mind switched off and nothing mattered in the world except that she should go on holding this man close to her, feel his breath on her face, and his strong body beneath her hands. Till that moment she had not realised that it was possible to desire like that. Growing up she was kept in ignorance of such things because desire in a woman was unseemly.

Lucy had once hinted at her enjoyment of being loved by Matthew, but reticence had prevented the sisters discussing it, especially because by that time Emily was physically repelled by Dickie and reluctant to talk about her hatred of him.

When she held Dowlah Ram in her arms for the first time, she abandoned all reticence and fear of physical contact. She wanted him, wanted him, wanted him more than she had ever wanted anything in her life.

275

Recklessly she kissed him hard. His mouth tasted of salt, and his eyes opened in surprise as he kissed her back.

'Oh my Begum,' he said.

She seduced him. Shamelessly she struggled out of her sari before falling on to the floor and pulling him on top of her. The room was in darkness but somewhere in the distance voices called and cooking pots clattered, and she didn't care.

In the middle of their love-making, she heard a voice moaning in delight and was astonished to realise she was the one making the noise. There was nothing in the world but the two of them, loving in the darkness on the hard floor but she wouldn't have been happier if they'd been in a feather bed.

The whole thing was a miracle, a new birth. Sleeping with Dickie was always horrible, because he'd plunge into her, not caring if it hurt, and in a few moments it was all over. Dowlah Ram was so different that loving him was not the same act. It was sweet and gentle and urgent and magnificent – ending in an explosion of light that made her cry out. She was transported with delight and never wanted it to stop.

The coming of dawn brought an end to their love-making, however, and she dropped off to sleep with her head on his stomach and his arms around her. In the full glare of morning she woke up alone. There was a woollen shawl draped over her and for a moment she lay still, remembering.

Had it really happened? Where was he? Had she taken leave of her senses? She sat up and rapidly dressed herself in the discarded sari. Someone was walking along the path outside the room. Her eyes were fixed on the door when it opened and he stepped inside. He had obviously been bathing because his hair was wet and plastered close to his head, and he was wearing fresh white clothes. Her heart jumped again at the sight of him, but she said nothing, only stared.

'Do you want to bathe?' he asked.

She nodded.

'My sister will show you where to go and give you some clean clothes.'

She stood up and said, 'Thank you.' They were being very formal.

'My father thinks it best if I take you to the encampment now. He's afraid that something bad will happen if an Englishwoman is found here,' he said.

She nodded.

'Do you want to go?' he asked.

She looked at him, hoping he'd ask her to stay, but last night was probably just his reward for saving her as far as he was concerned. Why should he encumber himself with a white woman when Indian girls were so much more beautiful?

'I ought to go so that I can find out what

happened to my sister's son. I want to know if the ayah managed to save him,' she stammered.

'So you want to go back to the *feringhees*?'

'I don't know...' For the first time in her life she was lost for words.

He held out his hand towards her and she saw that her gold necklet was coiled up in his palm. 'You will need this,' he said.

So he wanted her to go.

She shook her head. 'No, you must keep that. For your trouble.'

He laughed bitterly. 'For my trouble. Thank you, memsahib. When you have washed and eaten I will ride out to Jhansi with you.'

Cawnpore, August 1919

Little by little, as time passed, Fred Allen's broken mind was beginning to heal. He realised that his despair was lifting on the morning he felt a sudden surge of happiness as he stepped out of his room and stood on the verandah to light his first cigarette of the day.

A strong smell of damp earth came from the garden because there had been a fall of rain during the night. He put down the cigarette and breathed in deeply, relieved to find that the smell of earth no longer took him back to the mud of Flanders. Instead he felt a heightened sense of delight in the world around him. Every green leaf, every blade of grass, every silver globe of rainwater on the petals of the roses seemed larger than life and significant. The entire world delighted him. It was like being drunk or drugged.

Thank God I'm alive, was the joyous thought that jumped into his mind.

Not so long ago the realisation that he was not dead would have filled him with guilt because he was agonised by the memory of his friends and colleagues who gave their lives, while he, unaccountably and without any conscious effort on his part, continued to live. *I should have died too, I should have died last night* ... said his inner voice after every bombardment he endured in the trenches. But, thank God, on this sunny morning in Cawnpore that inner voice was quiet, and he hoped that its silence was not temporary.

He knew he would never forget Flanders. The terrible memories would stay in the back of his mind and haunt his dreams for ever, but he was beginning to appreciate that there was still life ahead for him and he'd be a fool not to make the best of it. As he walked to work he felt like a man who had been shown a vision.

At the hospital's main door, he saw Sadie hurrying up the path from the outpatients' department. As she ran, she skipped over big puddles in a way that made him smile because it reminded him of the Beatrix Potter story about Jeremy Fisher that he'd bought in a London bookshop when he was at his lowest ebb after coming out of hospital. He read it over and over again, temporarily soothed by its cheerful innocence, and it stayed vividly in his mind.

He called out cheerfully, 'Hello, Sadie! Good weather for ducks.'

She stopped skipping, looked up, and her face broke into a smile, delighted because he looked like the old Fred. She ran towards him, but, to her disappointment, he was already turning away and going into the surgical ward.

Jenny, hair tousled and face tired because she was called out of sleep when a woman in complicated childbirth was brought in at dawn, was bending over a bed near the door. On it lay a young woman who looked on the point of death.

Allen went up behind Jenny and looked over her shoulder.

The woman on the bed was waxen faced, in deep shock and having difficulty breathing. Flora, looking worried, was standing by the bedside ready to assist. 'What's happened to her?' he asked, nodding at the comatose patient.

As always with him, Jenny stiffened defensively as she straightened up and replied, 'She was brought in this morning because she was knocked down by a car and as a result she went into premature labour. The baby, a boy, was a breach delivery. We couldn't save it. She's lost a lot of blood and it's touch and go but I think she'll make it.'

To her surprise she felt Allen put a friendly hand on her shoulder and heard him say, 'If anyone can save her, you can. Do you need any help?'

Astonished, she stared at him and said, 'Thank you, but she's in shock and it's really a matter of whether she fights hard enough to live. Her husband's waiting outside. Could you talk to him for me please and ask him her name?'

Allen looked back at the door where a little group of people waited. 'Which one is he?' he asked.

'He's the one with very dark eyebrows that look as if there's no break in them. He's a policeman.'

Allen walked back to where Ali Bey stood. 'Are you the husband of the woman who was run over?' he asked.

'Yes, sir, I am. Will she live?' Ali Bey looked stricken.

'Dr Garland thinks she has a good chance, but the baby is dead I'm afraid. The doctor wants to know your wife's name and what happened to her.'

Ali Bey frowned and lowered his head. 'She is called Yamin. One of the new police drivers knocked her down when she was going to the well for water early this morning. He was coming into the compound too fast and he says he did not see her in the dark. We put her into the car at once and brought her here. Do you think *you* could treat her, sir? I can pay and I would prefer her to be looked after by a real doctor, not by a woman.'

Allen's voice hardened. 'I can assure you that Dr Garland is a real doctor and very competent. Your wife is in good hands.' As he spoke, he realised he was telling the truth. Jenny Garland *was* a first-class doctor. Awareness of her competence and patience had been gradually growing on him, almost unnoticed, over the past few weeks.

When he went back to the bedside, he said, 'Her name is Yamin,' but he did not interfere or offer advice. He did not need to because he was impressed by how efficiently she moved, obviously taking care to cause as little pain as possible.

When Flora went off to prepare an opiate, he watched with admiration as Jenny started to talk very softly to the sick woman. 'Come on now, Yamin, open your eyes, you're going to be all right. This'll hurt a bit for a while but you'll get better. I'll help you. Don't give up. Help me, Yamin.'

She was talking English, but the sympathy and reassurance in her voice was unmistakable, and she was rewarded by a fluttering of the patient's eyelids. Eventually the dark eyes opened and stared at the faces round the bed in terror. It was obvious that the woman had no idea where she was or what had happened to her.

Jenny took her hand and made more encouraging noises to lessen her fear and as Allen watched, he felt a huge wave of sympathy flow out of him for the girl on the bed, and also for the girl in the white coat. He wanted them to win their battle against death.

At last, when the patient was drugged and more peaceful, they looked at each other, and smiled like survivors of a battle. She said, 'Thank you for your help,' and he knew she was also thanking him for not interfering.

He grinned, suddenly looking much younger than she'd ever seen him before. 'You did it all. It was a pleasure to watch a real professional at work. You've been breathing life into her,' he said.

She flushed scarlet as she replied, 'I think she'll live, at least I hope so.'

Sadie, who had come into the ward during the last few minutes, watched the interchange between the two doctors with disquiet.

To the relief of everyone, Ali Bey's wife survived the night and was on the road to a slow recovery by the afternoon of the following day. On ward rounds in the afternoon she was able to clutch Jenny's hand and speak a few words.

'What is she saying?' Jenny asked Sadie and the reply was, 'She is asking about her baby.'

'Tell her it was a little boy but it died. I'm very sorry.'

Yamin was silent for a few moments when she heard this but after staring at the wall for

284

a few moments, she spoke again and once more Jenny looked to Sadie as interpreter. 'She already has two children, both girls, and she wants to know if what happened means she can have no more babies. She wants a boy, you see. She's afraid she'll lose her husband if she doesn't bear a son.'

Jenny grimaced and replied, 'As far as I can tell there's no reason why she can't have more children. She aborted the baby because of the shock of the accident, that's all, and her injuries are not internal, only a broken leg.'

When this information was passed on, Yamin managed a faint smile and reached for Jenny's hand which she laid against her own cheek in a gesture of thanks.

Meanwhile Allen took himself off to the club for a swim. After he completed his usual twenty lengths, he climbed out of the pool and sat in a cane chair drinking a glass of beer, in peace, he hoped; but was disappointed to see Ross, the policeman, bearing down on him.

Ross, who was also in swimming gear with a large towel hanging round his neck, sat down beside him and said, 'I understand I have your hospital to thank for saving the life of my sergeant's wife.'

Allen, reluctant to engage in conversation, raised his eyebrows and said, 'Really?'

'Yes, Ali Bey's wife was run down by one of

our cars yesterday. He says she would have died if he hadn't taken her to your hospital. I'm very grateful because he's a first-class man and we're very busy at the moment. His wife's death would have been a terrible distraction for him.'

'I imagine it would,' said Allen drily.

'Anyway, old man, thanks a lot.'

Allen bristled. Being addressed as 'old man' by Ross, whom he did not like, rankled with him. 'I'm afraid you're barking up the wrong tree, Inspector. I had nothing to do with the treatment of your sergeant's wife. It was Dr Garland who looked after her. She definitely saved the woman's life,' he said.

Ross stared. 'Do you mean Jenny? Ali Bey seemed to think the doctor was some sort of a genius and I assumed it was a man.'

'Yes, I mean Dr Jenny, that's what most of the patients call her I believe. Tell your sergeant that all the credit is due to her. She's the best doctor in our hospital, perhaps even the best in the whole of Cawnpore. He was lucky she was there when his wife was brought in. I couldn't have breathed life back into her like Jenny did.'

He was laying it on a bit thick, he knew, but the chauvinism of Ali Bey and Ross annoyed him and he was taking up the cudgels on his colleague's behalf.

'That's a surprise,' said Ross again.

'Well, you're wrong to be surprised. The

patient was in deep shock and she was willed to live,' said Allen, rising to his feet and going off to change.

Ross stared after the departing back with disquiet. The man had been like a skinny scarecrow when he first returned from France, but he'd filled out in the last few weeks and seemed years younger and nothing like so melancholic. In fact he was beginning to look almost normal, and not like an ex-patient of a mental hospital. What was worse though was the way he talked about Jenny. There was a note of real admiration in his voice when he spoke her name. Her Christian name too – what presumption!

Once again, after a period of relaxing because she seemed to dislike Allen, he began worrying in case the newcomer wormed his way into Jenny's affections before he declared his intentions towards her. It would be awful to miss out to Allen, so he must propose marriage to her at the first opportunity, though he did not feel ready for settling down yet. A bachelor life suited him, for he had more than one local mistress.

That evening, however, he dressed with extra care and drove to the Masons' bungalow without telephoning first. Jenny was having a bath when the bearer called through the door, 'Ross sahib is here to see you, Dr Jenny.'

Sitting in a hip bath with a book and a pail

of hot water beside her, and intending to stay there for as long as possible, she cursed at this interruption, but called back, 'Invite him in and give him a *chota peg*. I'll be out in a few minutes.'

Ross was in the sitting room, his silk-socked right ankle elegantly propped up on his left knee, when she walked in, wearing a scarlet silk kimono printed with a design of peonies. He jumped to his feet and produced a huge bunch of tuberoses from beneath his chair. 'Congratulations. I've just heard how you saved the life of the wife of my best sergeant,' he told her.

She smiled and sparkled at the compliment. Though he preferred dark-haired women, especially local girls, she really was quite good looking, especially in that red robe.

'Would you like to go out for a drive? The rain has stopped and there's some sort of festival going on beside the river,' he said.

She shook her head. 'I'm not in the mood for festivals. I'm tired. It's been a hectic day. Harry's away, and Dr Allen and I have been worked off our feet.' She still did not refer to Allen by his first name though he had used hers, noted Ross, slightly reassured.

But it was best to secure his hold on her. He coaxed, 'Come on, Jenny, it's only half-past six. It will do you good to relax for a couple of hours. If you don't want to go to the festival, I'll take you into the city, to one of the big hotels. We'll have a champagne cocktail – or an iced coffee if you prefer – and I'll buy you dinner too if you'll let me. That's sure to cheer you up and I promise we won't be late. You can be Cinderella and I'll bring you back before midnight.'

She smiled. The idea of champagne cocktails suddenly appealed to her, for she was growing tired of a missionary's spartan life. 'All right. I'll come. Wait while I go to change, but I can't be late back. We're operating tomorrow,' she said.

As he drove into town, he said in a casual tone, 'How are you and that fellow Allen getting along now that Mason's gone home? Is he still annoying you?'

'It was very difficult at first, but we seem to have reached some sort of understanding. He's actually quite a nice man underneath, I think,' she said, remembering Allen's support when she was working with Yamin.

He frowned. 'You could have fooled me. He's totally anti-social in the club. Those Irishmen often have chips on their shoulders, you know.'

She laughed. 'So do the Scots – and I'm one of them. At least I'm half one.'

'Since it's only half, I'll allow you to pass then,' joked Ross.

By the time they had two champagne cocktails each, Jenny felt young and giggly as

289

she sat across the table from him and dispassionately, with a clinician's eye, admired his fine physique. As well as handsome, he was flattering, courteous, and gentlemanly –what more could she want?

Any previous disquiet she'd felt about him seemed based on nothing at all as the champagne made her more tolerant and cheerful. Cocktails led to dinner and when dessert was cleared away, he leaned across the table to take her hand. 'I've got something very important to ask you, Dr Jenny,' he said.

She stared at him, suddenly sobered. I don't want to hear this, she thought.

'What is it?' she asked in a defensive voice.

He sensed her change of mood, changed his mind, leaned back in his seat and grinned. 'Would you like a cigarette?'

She let her breath out in a sort of gasp, but whether it was in relief or chagrin even she did not know. Is he playing games with me? she wondered.

'Actually I would like a cigarette,' she told him.

He produced a gold case and lighter from his pocket, gave her a cigarette and leaned over to light it. When he did this, his hand lightly touched hers, almost stroked it, but she could not tell whether it was by accident or design. The touch made her nerves tingle. It was a long time since a man had touched her like that, and she was surprised to realise she wanted it to happen again.

As the smoke rose from their cigarettes, he watched her closely before he said in a soft voice, 'I think you and I make a good pair. Would it be very presumptuous if I asked you to marry me, Dr Jenny?' It did not occur to him for one minute that she would not accept at once.

Very slowly and carefully, she laid the burning cigarette down in a glass ashtray and said, 'When James was killed, I thought I'd never marry again.'

'Do you still think that?'

'I don't know. I don't suppose he'd want me to live like a nun for the rest of my life. He was not a selfish man.'

'I want to marry you,' said Ross.

She lifted the cigarette again and looked at the wreath of smoke rising from it, wondering if it was trying to write her some sort of message.

'I'm very flattered,' she said. That was the way cautious young women were meant to respond to offers of marriage, he knew, and smiled. She was remembering when James asked her, she'd jumped from her seat, threw her arms round him, and carolled, 'Oh yes, yes, yes!' That would not be her response this time.

He was watching her carefully and she was uncomfortably aware of what he did for a living. Every nuance, every reaction would be noted by his policeman's eye.

'I'm very flattered, but, as I said, I haven't given any thought to marrying again,' she told him.

He was obviously surprised. 'What does that mean?'

'It means that I still think of myself as being married to James.'

He nodded. 'I understand, but he is dead and you are still alive, with the rest of your life ahead of you. Marrying me would be a good idea because you'd be able to go on working in the Mission hospital if that was what you wanted...'

Her reluctance spurred him on. Now he was seized by an overwhelming determination to win her. She would be a trophy for him, a victory over Allen and a defiance of all the hints that had been thrown at him over the years by people who thought themselves his social superiors. Even Philip Villiers was not above making the odd reference to Ross's suspect ancestry.

'Please say yes,' he said, looking into her eyes.

She looked away. 'I'll have to think about it,' she said. She wondered if he was in love with her, but he hadn't said so. She was not in love with him, that was certain, but she did not dislike him and perhaps, as the Begum said, love only happened once in a lifetime.

She should now be looking for security and companionship. Her mother's lonely, mourning life among other sad women in Edinburgh was a warning to her. If she married Ross, it would be a pragmatic decision because he would guarantee her a place in local society and she would be able to stay in India. That was a big plus because the country and its people were beginning to claim her heart. Most important of all, she would be able to satisfy her maternal craving and have a baby. He looked as if he would father fine children.

'Take as long as you like,' he said.

She lifted her eyes and looked straight at him. 'Why do you want to marry me?' she asked. She was hoping for some sort of loving declaration from him but she was disappointed.

Taken by surprise, he said, 'Because you are a lovely woman, because everything about you interests and intrigues me. We're past the stage of hearts and flowers, but I think we would suit each other very well. I'd look after you, Jenny. I wouldn't let you down.'

'I'll think about it,' she promised.

'I'm not going to hurry you. Let me know your decision when you're ready, but I hope you are half in favour of the idea already.'

She laughed and sipped from her cocktail glass. 'I might be,' she said.

Cawnpore, 1919, and Jhansi, 1857

When everyone else was asleep, the Begum often rose from her bed and wandered around her room, bringing old treasures out of her trunk and looking at them. Recently, increasing stiffness, blindness and swellings in her legs made these nocturnal expeditions more difficult, but she still woke in the small hours and lay staring through her window into the darkness of the compound round the well, waiting for the first streaks of dawn to paint the sky with colour.

It was during those silent hours that she relived her life, remembering its highs and lows, and mourning with melancholy sweetness for Dowlah Ram. She took the greatest pleasure in remembering Jhansi, for that was the place where she stopped being a European and became an Indian by adoption. That was the place where her new life really began after the Bibighar. As rain teemed down outside, she lay on her bed, closed her eyes and went back through time to the morning she and Dowlah Ram rode out of his uncle's farm and headed for the Rani's walled city.

As if he no longer wanted to have any physical contact with her, he rode alone on the horse and she was carried in state in a palanquin on the shoulders of four grizzle-bearded bearers. The palanquin had frayed silk inner curtains with sequinned hems and curtains of tooled leather. Inside there were four threadbare cushions, a padded mattress and only enough space for her to lie down with her knees drawn up almost to her chin, because she was taller than most Indian women.

When he told her to get into it, she grimaced. 'But it's so small. I'd rather ride with you. Why do I have to travel like that, all squeezed up like a snail in a shell?'

He gestured towards the walled city looming mistily on the horizon. 'It's not far, only four miles, but the road will be busy and when we meet people, especially soldiers, they won't be suspicious if you're in a palanquin. When you're challenged, all you have to do is hold out a hand to make them think that you are an Indian lady in purdah and they'll leave you alone. In the open, someone would soon realise you're a *feringhee*.' That word again.

Her hands and forearms were still dyed brown. The stain took months to wear off. By showing them and nothing else, she could pass muster, she knew, but she wished with all her heart that she could still ride behind him with her face pressed against his back, if only for the last time.

The palanquin bearers went off at a fast trot, balancing her closed-in throne precariously on their shoulders. This way of travelling had been popular among Europeans fifty years ago, and some white women still used them but she had never been in a palanquin before – always preferring to ride, for she was a good horsewoman – but the motion proved to be remarkably reassuring and comfortable. Between a chink in the curtains, she caught occasional glimpses of Dowlah Ram, sitting easily on the horse they had once shared, and now and again a quick sight of the rapidly approaching walled city. She was apprehensive about what would happen if they met an English military party. Would they attack him for travelling with a white woman? She did not want him to be hurt.

Within a very short time, the curtain was pulled aside and his face looked in at her. 'There's Englishmen ahead. The bearers say they're the ones who've been going around burning villages and hanging people so I'll have to leave you now. Introduce yourself to them and explain what happened. Delay them if you can so they don't follow me. Try to give me enough time to get to Jhansi city. May the gods take care of you, my Begum.'

296

His voice softened when he spoke her name.

Unable to speak because of a welling up of tears in her throat, she stared at him. Was this the end? Were they to part like this? Words formed in her mind but she could not say them. Before she dropped the curtain she saw him wheeling the horse round and there was a scattering sound as its hooves threw up a shower of pebbles, then silence.

The bearers began their running trot again, and soon she heard a voice shouting in English, 'Where are you going?' and repeating the question in Hindi.

The leader of her bearer team shouted something back, and she heard the sound of clinking saddlery outside her closed curtains. Sitting up on her knees, she pressed her eye to the biggest chink. An officer of the East India Company army, in the familiar red-and-white uniform, was trotting his horse alongside. 'Stop!' he shouted to her bearers.

They stopped, and she sat very still inside the little compartment, holding her breath.

The officer yelled questions to her palanquin men. 'Where are you going? Who are you carrying?'

She could not hear the replies, but they seemed to partially satisfy him. Remembering Dowlah Ram's advice about showing her arm, she pushed the silk of her sari back to the elbow, and put her right arm through the gap in the curtains. She let her hand hang down limply, and felt the sun warming her skin.

There was silence as the Englishman stared at the dark arm and long-fingered hand. Then she heard his voice asking the palanquin men if there was anyone else in the compartment where she sat.

'No,' was the reply.

Another hand, very white skinned, projecting from a white cloth cuff with a gold button at the wrist, was pushed in beside her, and the fingers spread wide as he explored the dark space. She drew back from the hand because she did not want it to touch her. Staring at it as it groped about, she recognised a ring on the little finger. Already she'd thought she recognised the voice and here was confirmation. It was Dickie's ring, engraved with his family crest. Amazingly, Dowlah Ram had brought her back to her husband.

Did he know that was going to happen? she wondered. In terror she held her breath, though this was the time when she ought to cry out. If she wanted to return to her old life, all she had to do was draw back the curtains and reveal herself. Then there would be a reunion between Emily and Richard Maynard.

But she sat still and watched as her husband's hand was withdrawn and the curtain dropped back into place. When he began interrogating her bearers again, she went back on to her knees to peer out at him. He sat on a big grey horse, his uniform jacket open at the neck and a lance sticking out of his boot. His face was burned brown, and his curly hair shone golden under the brim of his military cap. He was undeniably hand-some, but the sight of him chilled her. She still hated him.

Bad memories came rushing back, mem-ories of her weeping, of them fighting, of his hand striking her across the face, of his voice calling her names. She had no wish to go back to being Mrs Maynard. Especially since she now knew what it was like to be trans-ported by love-making. Especially since she had fallen desperately in love with another man. It was when she saw her husband again that she realised how much she loved her Indian saviour. She was at a major cross-roads of her life and everything depended on what she did now.

The palanquin bearers had obviously been briefed by Dowlah Ram and expected her to come out and reveal herself, but she sat tight, huddled up with her head resting on her crossed arms, desperately hoping that they would not tell Dickie they were carrying a white woman. Providing they stayed silent, even he would not attempt to drag an unpro-tected Indian woman out of her seclusion.

The voices went on but nothing else happened till she heard one of the palanquin men asking an innocuous question, perhaps to give her time to compose herself and appear. 'Are there any dacoits around?' he asked.

Dickie answered, 'No, it's quiet. We've cleaned them all out. Take your woman into Jhansi if that's where you're going.'

She held her breath till the running feet started up again and for what seemed like a long time she sat clutching herself like someone staving off blows. Should she stop them? Should she shout out to let Dickie know she was still alive?

The only reason she'd wanted to see him again was to find out about Bobby. The fact that Dickie had obviously survived the mutiny was reassurance in itself so what would she gain by revealing herself? If the ayah had succeeded in delivering the baby to him, he would make sure it was sent home, for he had a strong sense of obligation to family. Bobby may even be in England by now.

If the ayah had not succeeded, or if she decided to keep Bobby herself, why make contact with Dickie again? There was nothing to gain in that case and she was sure he had as little wish to have her back as she did to be reunited with him. No doubt he justified his rampages around the countryside as

300

the understandable reaction of a man whose beloved wife had been slaughtered, but that was only an excuse. Dickie enjoyed hurting people.

The bearers kept on running and her heart went on thudding fast in panic till she heard another voice shouting at them, but this time it was the keeper of the main gate of Jhansi city. When they stopped, she again let her hand droop out of the palanquin, and again she was allowed to pass. Within minutes the running stopped and she felt herself being lowered to the ground, her curtain was lifted and the chief bearer looked in on her.

'Where do you want to go?' he asked.

'Take me to Dowlah Ram,' she said.

He was in a tea house not far from the gate house. When the palanquin appeared, he walked out and asked the men what happened. She still sat inside and only looked up when he lifted the curtain to put in a hand and help her out.

She took his hand, and put her own over it. 'It was my husband who met us. I did not want to go back to him. I want to be with you,' she told him.

His eyes looked bloodshot as if he had been smoking kif – or perhaps weeping. 'Then you must stay for ever,' he replied and held her to him in a crushing embrace.

Whenever she remembered their reunion in Jhansi, she wept. That was my life, she thought. I have lived eighty years and that was my best moment. Now I am an old woman and when I die, which must be soon, I want to die remembering taking his hand and stepping out into his arms and his world. He was my life, my soul mate.

Her only regret was not finding out about Bobby.

On the night of the rain, she lay in bed, going over her precious memories, savouring them again, but at one o'clock in the morning, she was startled from these thoughts by noises outside in the compound. Feet were going back and forward; and she heard whispering voices, then a banging door, but no one was ever about at this time of night, unless there was an emergency. Was someone ill? What was happening? She was furious that the night was moonless and her eyesight was too bad to make anything out properly.

Clutching a shawl round her shoulders, because she felt the cold much more now than she had ever done in the past, she sat up in bed and stared through the window. A flickering lamp in the blackness was hurriedly put out. Did that mean there were thieves in the compound?

Dowlah Ram's sword had lain underneath the mattress for years and with a supreme effort, she lifted the edge of the feather pallet and grasped its hilt. Armed with it, she limped across to the doorway, opened it and shouted, 'Who are you? Go away! My son is coming. Vikram Pande, help, help.'

The silence that followed was so deep that she knew there were people outside holding their breath and hoping she'd go back to bed, but she had no intention of doing that. Using both hands, she rattled the sword against the half-open door and shouted for her son again.

'I am coming, Mother,' she heard him calling and she almost fell over when he threw the door wide as he came rushing in.

'What are you doing out of bed? And what are you doing with a sword? You could hurt yourself,' he scolded.

'I thought I heard *goondas* in the compound. They're trying to steal from us. They're in your silk store,' she told him.

'No, no, they aren't *goondas*. They are traders from the north bringing me down a load of cloth.'

'At this time of night! Only *goondas* go about at this time.' She was scared and trembling but ready for combat.

His wife also appeared and between them they helped her back into bed. 'They are not *goondas*,' he repeated. 'It's a special order that I am taking in...'

Her old eyes scrutinised his face and she knew he was telling lies. Suddenly her attitude changed. She seemed to stiffen and stared hard at him before she said, 'I hope you're not getting yourself involved in anything dangerous?'

He could not meet her eyes as he asked, 'What do you mean?'

'I was sleepless tonight and I saw things through my window.'

'What things?'

'People coming and going, not our people but other people who do not know their way around here because they knock into walls, and slam doors. I hope for your sake that you're not carrying on some lawless trade.'

'Mother,' he said taking her hand, 'you and Dowlah Ram are my examples in life. Anything I do will be honourable because that is how you taught me.'

She clung to his hand and said, 'Tell me what is going on.'

He sat down on the bed by her side and said, 'I am doing it for the freedom fighters.'

'Doing what?' she whispered.

'Storing their guns.'

'Oh no,' she groaned.

'Mother, you know what happened at Amritsar. You know how Indians are not allowed their freedom. I know you sympathise with their cause. I know my father would too.'

'But no guns, please no guns, no more killing. I know what killing is like. I know the horror of it. It never leaves you.'

304

Vikram Pande shook his dark head. 'The Sikhs are full of hate for the British. They say the only way we can get rid of them is to kill them. They will never go otherwise.'

'So you are storing the guns that will be used to kill them. Here in Cawnpore, where my mother and sister died in the Bibighar. What did that achieve? Nothing I tell you, nothing but more blood lust and more hatred. You must not have any part in it,' she said with fierce conviction.

He looked sad. 'I know what you suffered as a young woman and I know what happened later and how you came to take me as your son. There are things to be forgiven on both sides, but what happened in Amritsar outrages me. I want to help the freedom cause.'

She sighed. 'Amritsar outrages me too, but so did the Bibighar. If that, or anything like it, was to happen again, I would be deeply ashamed if my son was involved in it. Surely what happened in the past will have taught us the benefits of a different approach. Killing is *not* the answer. How many guns are in your shed?'

'Many. Ten bales of silk came down tonight and the guns are packed inside them. More will arrive soon.'

'They must not stay here.'

'But I have promised.'

'Then you must tell them that this property belongs to me and I forbid it. You must accept no more guns and you must get rid of the ones that are here already. Gandhi-ji is preaching a doctrine of passive resistance and I believe, like he does, that it is the only way to achieve your end. It may take time, but it will come. With luck you will live to see it. Your sons certainly will. Killing will not achieve it, for that will only mean more hatred. Believe me, I lived with hatred and took my revenge on the person who wronged me but it was bitter and it did not achieve anything.'

He stared at her. 'I don't know what you mean.'

'I'm not going to explain it to you. It's enough for me to say that you must not become involved in killing. The results could be terrible, not just for you and this family, but for the whole of India. Give Gandhi's ideas a chance. He doesn't believe in killing. And he certainly doesn't want another Mutiny.'

It was not easy for Vikram Pande to go back into the compound and tell the bearded men who were still unloading bales from a bullock cart at the gate that they must load up again and go away.

'But it's almost dawn. We can't move them in light,' they said but their angry protests were useless. He was deaf to them, only saying, 'My mother owns this property and

306

she will accept no more guns. I am sorry, but if you don't go, she is quite capable of telling the authorities. You must move the guns away from here by tomorrow night and I don't want to know where you store them after that.'

Muttering curses, they went and took some of their guns – but certainly not all – with them.

Cawnpore, August 20th, 1919

The Begum was right in her supposition that Dolly Mullins was mad. Transported by illogical hatred, she fomented rebellion and incited killings without any pity or compunction. It was as if some strange malfunction in her brain prompted her to do these terrible things. At the height of her mania, she was outside herself, beyond reason. Her granddaughter Sadie suffered from the same mental defect, but it took longer to manifest itself and, because she sensed it in herself, she fought hard against it.

To all outward appearance, she was mild mannered, deferential, and hard working, but little by little she was being taken over by a burning unfocused hatred, a strange, centralised rage. She was not sure at first what or who it was that she hated, but gradually, very gradually, she was consumed by it.

Always a pretty girl, she very soon realised that white bachelors were eager to pay court to her, and even more eager to bed her, but set against marrying her. In fact, there was once one who was prepared to do so, but the company that employed him sent him home rather than allow him to burden himself with a chi-chi wife.

When the guard at the Remembrance Garden turned her away because she was not English, she felt as if she had been stabbed. Told that people like her were forbidden to wander along its gravel paths, or stand and admire its marble angel, something exploded in Sadie's brain. For years she had battled against the taint of coloured blood and the prejudice it aroused in both Indians and English people alike, so his rejection infuriated her.

Her fury was augmented by a growing disappointment in Fred Allen. When he came back from France, he showed himself as being as bad as all the others. She had built him up in her imagination as a dream lover, especially after he gave her the money, and his new behaviour towards her was a crushing blow.

What she did not realise was that Allen had no amorous intentions towards her at any time. He had no dependants, and when he went to war, he was convinced that he would not survive it. He'd lived frugally during his time in Cawnpore and wanted to give his money to someone who would put it to good use. Sadie, with her gallant way of fighting poverty and discrimination, awakened his compassion.

But he did live, though the war changed and hardened him. He did not regret giving Sadie his money, but was determined that there would be no emotional entanglements of any kind for him because of it. Sensing her feelings towards him, he went out of his way to warn her off. For her part, she felt that his refusal to respond to her as a woman was because he too despised her for having coloured blood and that his previous kindness had only been patronising.

Beadily, with jealousy and anger, she watched the growing relaxation of antagonism between him and Jenny. Though Jenny was unaware of what was going on, Sadie, who missed nothing, saw that, over time, Fred's expression and attitude became less tense if he spoke to the other doctor. When Jenny walked out of the room, his eyes followed her.

But, thought Sadie, if Jenny was a half-caste girl, if her skin was dusky instead of greyish pink, he might still admire her physically but would not consider her his equal, someone of his own sort, someone with whom he could confer, live, and even perhaps marry. Sadie's internal furies built up, consuming her life and poisoning her mind.

On the evening of the day that the Begum sent the gun runners packing, she watched Fred and Jenny smiling at each other as they compared case notes. It was obvious they talked the same language, even though they did not realise it themselves.

She waited till Jenny went home and then slipped into his office to speak to him. They talked of trivialities at first. He enquired after her mother and she tried again to invite him for a meal...'Perhaps on Sunday?' she said hopefully.

It was painfully obvious that he was reluctant to accept, though he vaguely promised that he would come when the pressure of work lessened.

'You and Dr Jenny are having to work very hard to cover for Dr Mason,' said Sadie.

'Yes, but he deserves a holiday. He held the fort here during the war,' Allen replied.

'That's true. But the workload seems to have increased recently. How will you manage when Dr Jenny gets married?' she asked.

He stared at her, obviously surprised. 'Is she getting married? Who to?'

She fiddled with some books on the shelf beside her, and said idly, 'To that policeman Ross. He told someone I know that he'd proposed to her and she'd accepted.'

Allen turned away and started closing his note files. 'That would be a mistake on her part,' he said shortly.

'Why do you think that? Ross is a handsome man,' said Sadie in an innocent tone.

'But he's not the genuine article,' Allen

replied shortly.

'In what way?'

'He's not what he seems. I suspect he's a bully. At least that's my opinion.'

'Perhaps you think he's not what he seems because he's Eurasian? Is that what you have against him?' Her voice was hard.

He turned and stared at her. 'I didn't mean that at all. If he's Eurasian, it's news to me, and anyway, that's his business. I wouldn't care if he was an Australian aborigine if he was a good man. There's something not right about him, that's all.'

But he was speaking to Sadie's departing back. Dolly Mullins' granddaughter had more fuel for the grievances smouldering in her breast. She pedalled home through the darkening streets as if she was being chased. When she wheeled her bike into the garden, through the window she saw her mother in their sitting room with Balraj. He called round a lot nowadays and it had been him who told her that Ross was boasting to the clerks about marrying the lady doctor soon.

She suspected that Balraj's visits to her house were not entirely on behalf of the plotters of rebellion, because he always brightened when she walked in and watched her with gleaming eyes and glistening lips, as if she were a particularly succulent sweetmeat that he coveted.

'You again!' she said rudely when she went

312

into the sitting room. She saw no reason to be polite to him. He might take that as an encouragement. He looked up and for once did not bother to fawn over her. 'I've brought bad news,' he said.

She leaned one hand on the table as she bent sideways to remove her outdoor shoes. 'Yes?' she said.

'That man in the silk shop will not allow any more guns to be stored in his godown. He says his mother refuses permission and she owns the place. The guns there already have to be moved at once. I came to tell your mother that the plans have changed. She's been telling people to pick the guns up at Celestial Silks – but now they're in a boat in the middle of the river because there's no-where else safe. The Sikhs are furious. They wanted to burn down the silk shop, but we've talked them out of it. It would draw too much attention to what is going on, and, if we left him alive, Vikram Pande would go straight to the police and talk.'

Sadie padded barefooted into the middle of the room and stood staring at him. 'Do you mean the rising won't happen now?' she asked.

'Well, the plans have gone wrong. Every-thing will have to be organised again – if possible.' His voice was despondent.

'So much for your rebellion,' she snapped. Her mother looked up in surprise and said,

'But I thought you weren't in favour of them making trouble here in Cawnpore.'

'I'm in favour of anything that gets the British out,' said Sadie.

'I think it's because Vikram Pande's mother is an Englishwoman that he's backed out. You knew that, didn't you? Why didn't you warn the other people in the plot about her?' Mary said to Balraj.

He shrugged hopelessly as he replied, 'She's old. Sadie here told me that she's dying. We didn't think she'd be able to interfere. Anyway we also thought that no one would suspect a house where an Englishwoman lived of being the arms depot. It was a good cover.'

'Not good enough,' said Sadie, then asked, 'What will you do now? Will you take revenge on Vikram Pande for letting you down? Will you kill him?'

'Probably, but not yet. He's an important man and we don't know who else he's told about us. He'd make a bad enemy. If we lie low and do what he says, he won't talk to the authorities – he's enough on the side of freedom for that.'

'There must be some way to revenge yourselves on him,' Sadie said and paused for a moment before she added, 'And I think I know what it is.'

Balraj brightened. 'How? Tell me and I'll tell the others.' He'd take her idea and pass it on as his own, of course, she thought, but anyway there was no way she was going to tell him. This was a plan she would carry out alone.

She shook her head. 'No, it needs someone who won't mess it up. Let me think about it,' she said, and her face lit up in a wicked smile. If the others had ever seen her grandmother – which they had not – they would have recognised Dolly in her at that moment.

Kind-hearted Mary wanted to invite Balraj to share their evening meal, but Sadie snapped, 'No, I don't want company tonight. I'm tired.'

She could not bear the idea of him sitting across from her at the table and devouring her with his eyes as he forked up his food. He was like all men – Indian or European – who thought of her as a diversion, to be taken up when they pleased.

Disconsolate, he left, stepping out into the dark garden with his head down and shoulders hunched. He had not walked far along the street when another man, who had been waiting in the shadow of the wall of a tall building, fell in step beside him. They talked in whispers till they came to a road junction, then Ali Bey passed over some money and Balraj took the right-hand fork while his companion went to the left, heading for a certain tea house in the bazaar.

Lal Singh was alone, sitting in a corner and staring bleakly out at the street. His expression did not change when Ali Bey sat down beside him and said, 'You're from Amritsar.'

It was a statement, not a question.

'So?'

'I recognise you. I saw you once at a political meeting in Calcutta. I share your aims but your plans have gone wrong, I hear.'

'What plans?'

'To store the guns in Celestial Silks. You're taking them to a barge in the river, but that's dangerous. People talk and others listen.'

Lal Singh regarded Ali Bey bleakly. 'Where do you suggest we take the guns?'

'A barge is all right, but not the one everyone thinks. Change the load over to another boat in secret and send it off down river tonight, even if it's not fully loaded. Transfer the guns you've got and cut your losses as far as the others are concerned. There are many places in Calcutta where it can be safely unloaded, and the guns stored. I can tell you where.'

'How do you know so much?'

'Because I'm a policeman and I know Calcutta well.'

Lal Singh laughed. 'I'm not a madman. Why should I listen to a *policeman*?'

'Because I can get you out of this with some of your arms intact. Inspector Ross knows something is going on. He'll be waiting for you. Let him mount an ambush, and seize some of the load, but make sure he only catches the small fry or double dealers like that man Balraj. While his attack is going on, you and the barge could get away. I'm a patriot like you. I want rid of those Englishmen as much as you do. I'll arrange this for you providing you keep your mouth shut and never tell.'

'And what do you want out of it?' asked the Sikh.

'Liberty and revenge on Ross,' said Ali Bey.

Robert Ross was entertaining Daphne and Philip Villiers to dinner in his large bungalow and, after eating, they sat drinking brandy and soda, which was their favourite evening tipple.

Daphne looked around the vast but sparsely furnished drawing room and said scornfully, 'This place is like a barracks. Why don't you hang a few pictures or buy some decent curtains?'

Ross laughed. 'I prefer living in a barracks. I'm used to it. Fripperies don't interest me.'

Philip, who was rapidly becoming drunk because he was less used to alcohol than the other two, said, 'Quite right, too. Bloody ornaments only clutter things up.'

Daphne glared at her nephew and said, 'If you're going to go on courting that missionary girl, you'll have to make your house more welcoming. Has she ever been in here?'

'No, she hasn't, not yet.'

'A girl of strict morals, I presume. She's not the sort to visit bachelors at their private addresses,' sneered Daphne.

Ross, cheered by brandy, grinned. 'That's going to change. I've asked her to marry me.'

The others looked astonished. 'You're getting married!' exclaimed Daphne, slightly piqued now that her plans had come to pass. She used her nephew as an escort on many occasions because her husband hated mixing in smart society and when he married she'd have to find another unattached male.

'Yes! I'm getting married,' said Ross. It didn't matter that what he said was not exactly true yet. He was confident that Jenny would accept him.

Daphne laughed. 'Well, she's not exactly the sort of girl you might have married, but there's not much to choose from at the moment, and it certainly is time you got yourself a wife. People in the club have started asking me if you prefer boys to girls.'

Her nephew flushed. The idea that he was thought to be one of those fellows like that bounder Oscar Wilde, whose disgrace he'd heard whispered about when he was at school, was more than he could stomach.

'They'll stop gossiping when I get married,' he said defensively.

'Then set the date,' said Daphne, getting up and pulling Philip to his feet. She could hardly wait to get home and start ringing up all her friends with this juicy bit of news.

After they left, Ross rang the bell and told his servant to bring another bottle of brandy. He intended to make a night of it. He had consumed a quarter of the second bottle when there was a scratching sound at the glass of one of the windows overlooking the garden. That was Ali Bey's signal. He staggered across to the door on to the verandah and threw it open.

Like a snake, Ali Bey slid into the room.

With an elaborate gesture of folded hands he sarcastically greeted his officer who had trouble focusing his eyes but snapped back, 'You can stop all that salaaming stuff. It doesn't cut any ice with me. What brings you here at this time of night?'

'I've just heard that the man in the bazaar who was storing the guns has backed out. They are having to take them away and find another hiding place,' he said.

'Bloody natives. They can't do anything right, can they?' scoffed Ross.

He's drunk, thought Ali Bey, who strongly disapproved of alcohol. His disillusion with Ross had been niggling away at him for some time, and it grew worse when he was forced to leave Calcutta, a city he loved, and live in

319

Cawnpore which he considered provincial and unexciting. Since the loss of his baby son, his state of mind had grown worse and he was gradually obsessed by the idea that Cawnpore was to be a place of ill omen for him. He had to get away.

But he was tied to Ross and Ross would not leave or allow Ali Bey to go. In Ali Bey's opinion, Ross's eagerness to stay was because of cowardice. Once or twice in Calcutta during the war years they had come within a hair's breadth of disaster in their undercover work, and both of them had been hospitalized. After the last time Ross was stabbed, he seemed to lose heart and petitioned for a new posting.

Ali Bey hated it when other policemen taunted him with being a coward too, and said things like, 'So you've opted for the quiet life, have you? You'll be pensioned off next.' He badly wanted to go back to the bustling city on the Hooghly river, and, most of all, he wanted to be free of the bullying and disdainful Ross. His loyalty was ensured for a superior providing there was mutual respect, but that was now missing.

The shootings in Amritsar were the last straw for Ali Bey. Dyer's actions outraged him as much as it outraged other Indians. As the days passed, he found his prejudice against the British growing, but he was not a murderer of innocent people, and had no wish to start another outright mutiny.

He admired Gandhi and felt the freedom struggle should be an honourable one, but things had come to a head in Cawnpore, and something was about to happen. It was up to him to defuse it as much as possible, but not to prevent it entirely or to betray the most important men behind it. Those thoughts were running confusedly through his head and there was contempt in his eyes as he watched Ross pour himself another brandy and swig it back.

Why doesn't he ask me how I know where the conspirators are taking their arms? he thought.

But Ross was not particularly interested. 'I'm going to get married soon, you know,' he said in a maudlin voice.

He's very drunk, thought Ali Bey, but he replied, 'That is good, sir. A wife is a blessing.'

'The woman I'm going to marry is the one who saved your wife's life,' Ross went on.

Ali Bey nodded. The matter of his wife's accident was another resentment he nursed, because the man who ran her down was Ross's driver, and, though Ali Bey complained about his careless driving, Ross had accepted the other man's excuses. When he requested that the driver be disciplined and demoted, Ross only shrugged and said, 'Oh, come on. He couldn't help it. He's a good man, and he says he's very sorry.'

'It was dark, the roadway was slippery,' the driver said in explanation of the accident. In fact, he had been driving far too fast in an area where women and children wandered about. Yamin didn't have a chance. The worst thing of all of course was that she'd lost his son. Why didn't Ross ask about that?

Two girls had been born to him already and he longed for a boy, for girls were only an expense. A boy was a man's security and proof of his masculinity. To lose his son was like being cursed, and in an unfair, round-about way, he blamed Ross.

'*Sir*, the arms have to be moved out by tomorrow night,' he said, stern faced, reminding Ross that serious business was on hand.

The man in the chair pulled himself together. 'Where are they taking them?' he asked.

'To a barge in the Ganges. The one with a big blue eye painted on its prow.'

'Leave them time to get it fully loaded and then we'll ambush it. Might as well get everything at once,' said Ross, whose eyelids were drooping.

Cawnpore, August 21st, 1919

Jenny's mother, impressed by the fact that her daughter had gone to the expense of sending her a telegram, acted with unusual speed and, after searching through a tin deed box where she kept the family papers, replied within a week, which was quick for her. Mindful of the cost of telegrams, she tried to keep her reply short but did not entirely succeed.

After much pencil sucking, she finally sent:

Father's father Matthew Garland mother Lucy Garland nee Crawford stop Both died India 1857 stop Robert sent to Garland grandparents by uncle Richard, who died in mental asylum in Brighton 1905 stop Love Mother.

When this telegram arrived at the hospital, Jenny read it quickly, then stuck it in her pocket and went on working because there had been an outbreak of what could be typhoid in one of the city slums and dozens of sick people were clamouring for attention.

When darkness fell, everyone was exhausted. As they stood washing their hands and arms in strong antiseptic, she looked across at Allen and saw that his face was so drawn that he looked like a wraith.

'I think you need a drink,' she told him.

He straightened up and said, 'You do too by the look of you.'

'I know where the Masons keep their gin. They wouldn't mind us helping ourselves,' she told him.

They stuck their white coats into a laundry hamper and started to walk across the garden in the direction of the chief's bungalow. Sadie watched them go, and said to Flora, 'We could do with a drink too, couldn't we? But where can *we* get one?'

'Not me. I want to go home, and you should too. We'll probably have to deal with all this again tomorrow,' said Flora.

Jenny only covered a few yards on her way home when she remembered about the telegram, left Allen and came running back, calling out, 'Don't let the dhobi take the laundry away yet.'

Just as the washerman was on the point of hauling off the basket, she fished out her white coat and retrieved a flimsy sheet of paper from its pocket. She stood reading it, committed it to memory, nodded, crumpled it up and threw it into a waste basket, because she didn't want to keep anything that might have been contaminated with germs. To Flora and Sadie she said lightly, 'I've got it off by heart. It'll certainly interest the Begum.'

Sadie's eyes were hard as she watched Jenny depart for the second time. She waited till Flora went home, and, after she left, went into the waste bin, and, regardless of germs, retrieved the telegram form.

A gin and soda relaxed Fred Allen. He sat on a long reclining chair on the Masons' verandah, propped his long legs up on its extended footrest and talked to Jenny in his beguiling, soft Irish accent which became more pronounced as he swigged down his drink.

She was in the mood to be entertained and wanted to talk about things not associated with work. 'I've just had a telegram from my mother and I'm amazed that she sent it, because she normally counts every penny, mine as well as hers,' she said.

'Was it urgent?' he enquired.

'Not really. I sent her a message asking about my father's parents because my English patient in the bazaar, the one I call the Begum, thinks she might have known them long ago. She's interested to find out if they're the same people.'

'And are they?'

'I don't know, but she will when she hears their names. Mother must be intrigued as well. There's nothing she likes better than joining people up, even if she's never set eyes on them.'

He laughed. 'My mother was the same. She and her sisters could talk for hours about who married whom in Ireland. They covered the whole country with their acquaintances and knew their blood lines back for centuries. According to them we were all related to each other.'

'All the world?' Jenny asked in surprise.

'Oh, no, only Ireland, and then only a few special families who came from England or Scotland at the time of Cromwell or even before. A bunch of rogues for the most part, but wonderfully amusing and great judges of horse flesh. That's my background.'

'Are your parents still alive?' she asked. She had no idea how old he was, for sometimes he looked as if he was in his fifties – but at other times he seemed younger than Ross. How could she ask him without seeming rude?

He shook his head. 'No, they're dead. My father was killed on the hunting field when I was studying in Dublin and then my mother started to hit the bottle. She was even more amusing when she was drunk, but it didn't do her liver any good. I miss her. There never was a woman like her for the chat, drunk or sober.'

His last sentence struck Jenny as sounding

delightfully Irish, and she smiled. 'You'd like the Begum,' she said. 'That's another woman who likes the chat. I'm getting very fond of her and could listen to her for hours. Tell me about your mother.'

He grinned. 'What do you want to know? She was mad about horses. There never was a horse foaled that she couldn't ride. When I was a year old she stuck me on a pony for the first time. It felt perfectly normal because she'd gone on riding while she was carrying me, right up to the day before I was delivered. She used to gamble too – she'd bet on anything, horses, donkeys, racing tortoises, raindrops running down the window. She had a splendid, fun-filled life.'

'It sounds as if you really loved her,' said Jenny.

'Yes, I did. I followed her round as if she was a dancing flame. Wherever we went people knew her. Walking up Grafton Street in Dublin with her was like going on a royal procession. She used to wear a fur cape and a big hat with a feather and people shouted across the street to her, "Hey Geraldine! Good to see you."'

Jenny sat forward, entranced by this picture and by the change in him. He was no longer the gloomy spectre that had come back from the war. 'It sounds as if you had a wonderful childhood. Do you have any brothers or sisters?' she asked.

He shook his head. 'Not alive. I had one brother but he was killed when our house was burned down by the Fenians.'

'Good heavens! You must hate those people,' she said.

'Not really. My brother threw his weight around a bit and didn't treat his tenants very well. He was killed because he refused to leave the house when they set fire to it. He was older than me, and inherited what was left over after my mother died, but the house was falling down by then. Burning was the best thing for it, I suppose.

'In spite of what happened I like the Irish. They're grand people, and they keep you entertained. But they want their freedom, and you can't blame them. That's why I can't agree with people here who think Dyer is a hero, and believe Indians should be kept under the British thumb. You can't hold people down for ever. They'll always fight back.'

Jenny nodded. She felt like that too. Ross didn't though. She felt a rush of disquiet when she remembered that she ought to be giving some thought to what she should do about his proposal of marriage.

Allen wouldn't drink a second gin. When he finished his glass, he stood up and said he wanted to go back to his apartment and soak in a bath.

'You should do the same. Swill carbolic

acid about and put Jeyes fluid in the bath water,' he advised.

'Have you ever had typhoid?' she asked.

'Probably,' he laughed, 'but I don't worry about it. Anyway I don't think we have a typhoid epidemic on our hands. My bet is that it's paratyphoid, or maybe even just dysentery and that's not so serious, but bad enough, so don't cut any corners.'

Jenny took his advice and soaked in the bath till the water went cold. Then, wrapped in a towel, she fell into bed without putting on a nightgown and slept for eight hours without moving.

When she woke, she found that her mind was firmly made up about Ross's proposal. Although there were many practical reasons for accepting, she was going to refuse him.

While most people were sleeping, Vikram Pande's godown was still being emptied of its dangerous contents. The Begum was one who stayed awake, watching through her window as shadowy men went to and fro in the darkness.

The weapons were carried piecemeal down to the Ganges to be ferried in a little canoe to the blue-eyed barge moored in the middle of the swollen river. Because the men emptying the godown could only carry a few guns at a time, in case anyone saw them, the first stream of workers going to the mills were on the streets before they completed the task, and several loads were left behind for moving the next night. Secretly, however, after the last load of the night was delivered, the bulk of the guns were transferred again by Lal Singh and another Sikh to a smaller boat, a battered old green one with a covered cabin on its deck. Though exhausted, the two Sikhs then sat alone in the little cabin waiting for first light so they could set sail.

They were casting off when Vikram Pande went into his mother's room and told her that most of the guns had been taken away. 'The rest will go tomorrow,' he promised.

She sighed. 'Good. I hope this doesn't cause trouble for you with the plotters, but it had to be done.'

He nodded. 'I know. You're right. Don't worry. How do you feel, Mother? You look very frail.'

'I am frail, very frail and very old. My time is almost over.'

He took her hand and said, 'Don't say that. I love you.'

She smiled. 'Don't grieve for me when it happens. I hate being ill like this, and I'm not frightened to go. You've always been a good son, and though I didn't give birth to you, I love you as my own child. Dowlah Ram felt the same. I'm glad you won't forget us.'

★ ★ ★

Every now and again through the working day, Jenny's mind went back to the telegram and she mentally checked in case she forgot exactly what it said. She felt as if the Begum was in some sort of mental communication with her, insistently reminding her about it. Fortunately the typhoid outbreak proved to be a scare, as Allen suspected, and the flood of patients eased off by late afternoon. At half-past five she had the choice between going home to rest, or hiring a tonga to visit the Begum. She chose the latter option.

For the first time in their acquaintance Vikram Pande did not seem pleased to see her. 'My mother is very tired today,' he said when she walked into the silk shop.

'But I've some news for her that I'm sure she'll want to hear. It might spark her up in fact,' said Jenny brightly.

He frowned. 'I'm worried about her. She's fading away.' His eyes looked mournful.

'I lost my father when I was young and I know what a sorrow it is to lose a parent,' she said sympathetically.

'I call her my mother, but she is not. She is my uncle's wife. My father was his brother, who was shot during the Mutiny. My mother died when I was two years old, and the Begum and Dowlah Ram adopted me as their child. I love her as I would love my real mother – even more perhaps,' he told her in a rush of confidence.

331

'That was a good thing for all of you,' said Jenny.

'Yes, indeed it was so I want to protect her now. If I could defeat death for her, I would.'

Jenny shook her head. 'Unfortunately that's not possible. I'm very sorry. If she's too ill to see me, I understand, but I might be able to cheer her up with my message. It's very short.'

'You won't stay long?' Not only was he worried about tiring the Begum, but he did not want Jenny to be in the vicinity when the transporting of the last guns began again.

She assured him that her visit would be short, and at last she was admitted to the Begum's presence. It only took one glance to tell her that the old lady was indeed fading away. She lay in the big bed, white-faced, her lips tinged with violet. When Jenny walked into the room, however, she looked up and smiled.

'My favourite doctor, the bunch of flowers,' she whispered.

Jenny sat down on the mattress beside her and took her hand. 'And you're my favourite patient. I've brought you some news. Do you remember wanting to find out about my father's parents? I have the information for you. My mother sent me a telegram yesterday.'

The Begum's eyes sparked into life again. She still retained her marvellous capacity for producing another surge of energy even when it seemed she was completely drained. 'Yes. Tell me,' she said eagerly.

'My father's father was Matthew Garland, and his mother's name was Lucy. Before she married her maiden name was Crawford. They both died in India in 1857, but I don't know where...'

'I do. Oh I do! It's what I hoped for. Matthew died in Meerut and Lucy here in the Bibighar. She was my dear sister.' Tears began running down the Begum's wrinkled cheeks and her voice quavered as she spoke.

They stared at each other for a few seconds and then Jenny leaned across to hug the thin old woman. 'Does that mean I'm your great-niece?' she asked.

The Begum hugged her back. She was sobbing loudly now. 'It does, it does. You are dear Lucy's granddaughter. Oh, my dear, this is the miracle I hoped for.'

'So Lucy was the sister you told me about? The one who was with you in the Bibighar?'

'And your father was her baby Bobby. The one I smuggled out. The ayah must have got through to Delhi with him. Thank God, thank God! This is so wonderful I can hardly believe it. Ever since I left Lucy, I've wondered about Bobby.' The Begum was highly excited and smiling as she wiped her eyes with a handkerchief that Jenny handed to her.

'If he'd stayed in the Bibighar, he'd have died anyway, but in his mother's arms. That used to make me feel so sad,' she went on. 'But now you can't believe what this means to me, Doctor Jenny. Just to know that he was given life, even a short life, was better than death in the Bibighar. The first time I saw you I called you Lucy, didn't I? I wasn't wrong, was I? It's your eyes. You have Lucy's eyes. It's a miracle. Tell me about your father again, tell me everything.'

Jenny felt stunned. 'This is amazing. Are we really related?' she said.

The Begum laughed. 'It's not entirely a surprise to me but I wanted it to be confirmed. Your name gave me the first clue – Garland is quite an unusual name. Tell me again. How did Bobby get back to England?'

'Mother put that in the telegram too, though I'd heard the story before. He was sent back to his Garland grandparents by someone called Uncle Richard – none of us ever met him and nor did my father after he came home, but they must have kept in touch because mother knows that he died in an insane asylum in Brighton in 1905. He was the one who left the money that was used for my education,' Jenny said.

The Begum laughed, a deep husky laugh that belied her age. 'Uncle Richard. That's Dickie! My husband, Richard Maynard. I'm not surprised he went mad. Serves him right. He was never entirely sane anyway. At least his money was put to good use. I'm surprised he didn't drink it all. Oh, my dear, you have no idea how much this means to me.' She was glowing with delight, and clinging to Jenny's hands as if she never wanted to release them.

'I can hardly believe it,' Jenny said again.

'Believe it, believe it. There's no doubt. I'm so glad I didn't die without knowing you. The gods must have sent you here. So many times I've thought about Bobby – wondering if he was caught by mutineers and murdered on the way to Delhi. Dickie didn't bother me at all but I wish I'd known when he died because I could have married Dowlah Ram. He wanted that so much.' The Begum's tiredness was forgotten and her eyes sparkled with a surge of febrile energy.

Jenny, pleased at such a reaction to her news, said, 'I'll ask mother to try to find more out about Uncle Richard if you like We might have some information in our family papers. But I mustn't tire you out any longer. I promised your son I wouldn't.'

The Begum waved a hand in the air and said, 'Don't bother about Dickie! My son is your cousin now. Call him in for me please. I want to tell him this news.'

Vikram Pande came quickly when Jenny waved to him, and as soon as he stepped into the room, the Begum said, 'Hold hands you two. You are cousins, and must always be friends.'

He looked astonished, but Jenny, who was getting used to this new situation, laughed and said, 'It's surprising, but true. I'll let your mother tell the story, because I've been here long enough and she will be tired out very soon.'

From the bed came an imperious voice. 'No, don't go yet, Jenny. There is something else I must do. Come back, please, and sit beside me.'

Jenny did as she was bid and the Begum raised both hands to the back of her neck to unhook the clasp of her necklace. 'This is for you. It was your grandmother's. Her husband, your grandfather, gave it to her on the morning of their wedding and she gave it to me in the Bibighar just before she was killed. I always thought I'd give it back to Bobby one day and now I want you to have it. Please don't argue. Take it and wear it always,' she said, handing the glittering chain to Jenny.

The gift sobered her and she looked at the Begum with swimming eyes as she whispered, 'Thank you.'

Carefully she put the necklace round her own neck, conscious of the old woman's eyes watching every move she made, devouring her greedily as if she could not watch enough, soaking up the memory as if it would have to last for a very long time.

'Never take it off. It will protect you as it has protected me. The only time I didn't wear it was when Dowlah Ram carried it and it protected us both then,' the Begum said when the necklace was in place.

'My new cousin must go. It's going to be dark soon,' Vikram Pande reminded his mother anxiously.

But still the Begum would not give in. 'I want her to stay with me a little longer. We have more to say to each other,' she said, waving her hand to dismiss him.

She was not used to her wishes being refused and, when he left with a warning glance at the guest, Jenny sat still, saying, 'All right, I'll stay, but only for a few minutes.'

The Begum reached out and touched the golden links round the girl's neck with the tip of her finger. 'Dowlah Ram hid that in his boot for six months before he gave it back to me. I loved him so much. He taught me that love is a gift, more valuable than anything else.'

Jenny nodded and said, 'I know.'

'Good,' said the Begum, 'I'm glad you know. When I was a girl we were not meant to know about things like loving a man in the physical way. It was all hearts and flowers romance. We were kept in ignorance in case we liked making love. That would have been unseemly.'

'There's still people like that,' agreed Jenny.

The Begum's face was enraptured as she remembered. 'When Dowlah Ram was mourning for his dead brother, I wanted so badly to comfort him. I put my arms round him and kissed him. It was wonderful. I hope you know what I'm talking about.'

Jenny only nodded. She knew too well for her peace of mind. 'I miss James,' she said.

'But you're young. Marry again. That's what I want to tell you, live your life to the full, savour every minute. I'm an interfering old woman, but I feel it's my duty to advise Lucy's granddaughter.'

'Someone has asked me to marry him,' Jenny heard herself saying. The Begum was the only person she could tell about Ross's proposal and she wanted to see how her great-aunt reacted.

The old woman clasped her hands in delight. 'Good. Is it that doctor with the long face who came here to see me? He's been through a lot and needs help but he's not as gruff as he pretends,' she said eagerly.

Good heavens, she means Allen! thought Jenny, shaking her head. 'No, not him. It's a policeman called Robert Ross, an inspector based here in Cawnpore,' she said.

The Begum made a disapproving face. 'I'm not keen on policemen. Is that doctor married then?'

'Not as far as I know, but—' said Jenny.

'But what?' interrupted the Begum.

'But he hasn't asked me, and the policeman has.'

'I don't know your policeman but I think that thin doctor would be the best man for you. Don't wait to be asked. You ask him. I was still a married woman when I seduced Dowlah Ram and never regretted it once.' She laughed wickedly.

Jenny laughed too and said, 'For a great aunt, you are a very bad influence on me. What do you want me to call you, by the way?'

'Call me Aunt Emily. Before I go to sleep, let me hear you say it...'

'Goodbye, Aunt Emily. Lie down and rest now. I'll come back tomorrow.'

While Jenny was sitting with the Begum, Balraj, in Ross's office, closed up his desk and hurried out into the gathering night. His destination was Mary Mullins' house.

Sadie was already there when he arrived and her face darkened at the sight of him.

'Can't you leave us alone? Do you have to be here every night?' she snapped.

'Tonight I am on very serious business. The Sikhs have sent me a message that the guns will be shipped out tomorrow. If anyone comes here asking what to do, tell them to lie low. No one is to go to Celestial

Silks, except the people who are shifting the guns.'

He was not his normal giggling self, but a different person altogether, so much so that there was a trace of respect in Sadie's eyes when she looked at him. 'Do you know why Vikram Pande backed out?' she asked.

'Because his mother refused to have the guns in her compound.'

'She should be punished for that,' said Sadie.

'There are more important things to deal with now,' he told her.

She went into the room where she and her mother slept in two narrow metal beds that she had borrowed from the hospital. Closing the door behind her she stripped and before she put her sweat-stained uniform into the washing basket, she pulled Jenny's telegram out of the pocket. Smoothing it flat with her hand, she read it, smiled and carefully folded it in half. From a hook behind the door, she took down another clean uniform and put it on, slipping the folded telegram into the breast pocket.

When she re-emerged into the sitting room, Balraj had left and her mother was alone. She looked at her daughter in surprise and said, 'Are you going back to work so late?'

'Yes, there's an emergency. They think typhoid has broken out in the chawls round the Elgin Mills. More people will be coming in.'

Mary clicked her tongue in irritation. 'There are too many risks in that job. You might get typhoid yourself.'

'Don't worry. Stay here and pass on Balraj's message to anyone that comes. It's important that people keep away from Celestial Silks. I'll be back as soon as I can.'

She mounted her bike and rode off into the busy streets, but stopped at a sweetmeat stand that was set up every night at one of the main crossroads. Propping the bicycle against a wall, she went over and pored over the goods on offer. Big squares of bright yellow marzipan, sickly looking blocks of coconut ice, bright green chunks of pistachio fudge, milky globes of *gulab jamuns* glistening with sugar syrup, and whirls of deep fried pastry garnished with red jam, made a mouthwatering display under the gleam of two paraffin lamps hung from the stall roof.

The proprietor of the stall was waving a sheet of newspaper over the sweets in an ineffectual effort to scare away thousands of tiny flies. 'That, that, and that,' said Sadie, pointing out three different delicacies to him and he put them into a paper bag, which he handed to her. The cost was six annas. Dropping the bag into her canvas reticule, she mounted the bike again and rode into the heart of the bazaar.

Vikram Pande was sitting in the middle of his treasure trove of silk when she climbed up from the street. He and his assistants in the store stared at the pretty girl in her nurse's uniform but she walked calmly up and said to him, 'Doctor Jenny sent me with a message for Vikram Pande's mother.'

In one hand she carried the telegram, open so that he could see what it was. In the other she carried her canvas bag, the sort that local women used for carrying home small items of shopping.

'I am Vikram Pande, but my mother might be asleep,' he said solemnly. He did not think it odd that this girl was bringing the telegram Jenny had talked about only a short time ago.

'Then I can leave this by her bed. Doctor Jenny is most anxious that she receives it, and she'd like me to tell her what the old lady thinks about it,' said Sadie brightly.

The last of the gun runners had not started work yet, and would not be there till the bazaar closed down for the night, so he felt it was safe to let her in if she did not linger. She looked innocuous enough and obviously knew Jenny.

With a warning not to tire his mother, he led her through the back of the shop to his hidden compound. A light shone from the Begum's window and he headed for it, meeting his wife halfway across the garden.

'Is my mother still awake?' he asked.

She nodded. 'Yes, I have taken her some tea but she is very agitated, so I'm going to make her up a sleeping draught.'

'This nurse has brought her a message from Doctor Jenny.'

Vikram Pande's wife looked at Sadie and said, 'But the doctor has just left.'

Sadie smiled. 'I know. She sent me back with this telegram from England which she forgot to give to the old lady.'

They both nodded and Vikram Pande's wife said, 'All right. It's good you're a nurse. Will you stay and watch over her while I make up the sleeping draught?'

'Of course I will,' said Sadie in a kind voice.

The Begum was fidgeting, gripping the edge of the counterpane and turning her head on the pillow when Sadie was shown in.

'Who are you?' she asked sharply when the stranger leaned over her.

'I am Doctor Jenny's nurse. She asked me to bring you this telegram,' was the reply.

'But she's just been here,' said the Begum.

'She forgot to bring the telegram with her and she wants you to see it,' said Sadie quickly. She brandished the bit of paper and it acted like a lure.

The Begum stuck out a hand and said, 'All right, give it to me.'

They were alone in the room and as the Begum looked at the strip of printed words, she said, 'It's hard for me to read. Fetch my spectacles from the table.' She spoke in Hindi imperatives, as she had always done with servants.

Reddening, Sadie passed the glasses over without a word and stood watching while the woman in the bed pored over the telegram. Then she asked in a sympathetic voice, 'You don't look well. Are you feeling sick, madam?'

'A little,' was the Begum's short reply.

'Perhaps you need sugar. You might faint again if you don't eat,' Sadie said, and rummaged in her holdall to produce the bag of sweetmeats, which she held out temptingly. The Begum looked at the sticky contents of the bag and sighed. She had always been very fond of sweets, *gulab jamuns* in particular.

'Try one,' coaxed Sadie, lifting that piece out.

It tasted delicious. As the Begum licked her fingers, Sadie said, 'Another won't do any harm.'

By the time the three sweets were consumed, the Begum was already fainting. Weakly she lay back against the pillows and closed her eyes, floating into unconsciousness.

The bland, kindly expression left Sadie's face as she watched. Her features seemed to change and once more she became her grandmother. Leaning over the bed, she whispered, 'You're a wicked woman. Do you remember Dolly Mullins? Do you remember telling the authorities where she was hiding? I'm her granddaughter and I'm here to take her revenge. I hope you can hear me...'

The Begum only sighed.

With one swift movement Sadie lifted a fat pillow and pressed it down over the old woman's face. She only took it away when she heard the sound of the pattering feet of Vikram Pande's wife running up to the bedroom door.

As it opened she turned round, distraught, and weeping, 'Oh, look what's happened! It's awful! Your mother has gone into a coma and I can't bring her round.'

Pillows were scattered on the floor, the bed and the bedcovers tumbled, to show how she had struggled to revive the patient.

'Aieee!' cried the other woman in distress and ran towards the bed but it was too late.

Emily Crawford Maynard was only vaguely conscious of what was going on but powerless to do anything. She felt happy and weightless as if she was floating into the sky, up among the stars she'd always loved so much.

A tremendous peace filled her as she died.

Cawnpore, August 23rd, 1919

A few minutes before midnight, a man in a loosely wound scarlet turban and an all-enveloping white shawl that made him look spectral in the moonlight, leaned over the parapet of the bridge that carried the road from Cawnpore to Lucknow across the Ganges.

A latent theatricality in Robert Ross's nature made him seize every opportunity to dress up in Indian clothes, even when it was not strictly necessary. It was as if he enjoyed displaying the hidden side of his blood inheritance. Tonight his excitement was running high and he was quivering with anticipation as he stared downstream towards a bed of reeds and a line of skeletal palm trees on the river bank beneath him. In the reeds a line of police marksmen were hidden, and, under his feet, sheltering in the shadows of the bridge piers, two police launches waited for his signal.

Behind his back, an occasional cart drawn by hump-backed Brahmin bulls rumbled over the bridge but the dozing drivers paid no attention to him. The night was clear, with only a few clouds drifting across the face of a waning moon, so he was able to watch some fishermen paddling up-river with tiny lights glittering on the prows of their little boats. On the bank, other boats were tied up and a few faintly flickering lights showed a short line of men like black ants loading bundles into a shallow dug-out canoe. Every now and again it carried its load over to a long barge moored in the middle of the river. Since Ross started watching, it had crossed five times.

Its work was almost finished but where was Ali Bey?

Somewhere in the distance a bell tinkled and Ross felt a strange surge of blood to his head when he realised that the sound came from the Fisherman's Temple farther down river at Satichaura Ghat, the site of the massacre of 1857. That incident was about to be replayed, but this time the boot was on the other foot. This time the natives would be the victims. The thought made him smile.

But where was Ali Bey?

He looked at his wristwatch and saw that its hands stood at one minute to midnight. The damned man should have turned up five minutes ago. He was normally very prompt, but he'd been strangely sullen recently. If he didn't watch out he'd be back on the beat as a constable. After this was over, he'd be sent packing.

A slight noise behind him made him whirl round with his hand on the pistol he carried tucked into his trouser band. Ali Bey, also cloaked, emerged from the shadows like a ghost and stood without speaking beside him.

'You're late. And I heard you coming. I could have shot you. You're slipping, too much country liquor perhaps,' Ross said.

Unapologetic, Ali Bey stared at him for a few moments, the whites of his eyes glittering, and then said without any sign of respect, 'You know I drink no liquor.'

'More fool you,' said Ross. 'What's happening down there? Is it finished?'

'All the guns are out of the silk shop and the loading is nearly completed. In a few more minutes the barge will be full. Our men are waiting along the bank for you to give the order. When you fire your pistol, the ambush will start.'

'How many plotters are down there?' Ross asked, nodding towards the rickety jetty. He'd relied on Ali Bey to find out all the details about the Sikhs' plot, and so far the results had been satisfactory. Tonight they were going to gather in the lot of them.

'Five or six. One Sikh is on the barge already, and in another five minutes it'll be fully loaded, ready for picking off. They can't get away from us now,' said Ali Bey.

It was true and he knew about it because of the double-double game he'd been playing for the last few weeks. When it began he was unsure which side he would betray but now his mind was made up.

The green boat, carrying the bulk of the armaments and chief conspirator Lal Singh, was well down the river already. The other conspirators, and the residue of the arms, would just have to be sacrificed. That was their misfortune.

There was something about his colleague's attitude that triggered off alarm bells in Ross's head. 'You seem to have infiltrated their cell very efficiently,' he said slowly.

'Thank you,' said Ali Bey sarcastically.

'How did you do it?'

Ali Bey shrugged in a way that expressed nonchalance.

'Are you in it with them? Have you crossed over?' Ross asked, staring at his companion. Ali Bey's dark eyes were fixed bleakly on his face as he went on in half disbelief, 'Yes, that's it. You've known about the plans all along, haven't you? You knew where the guns were being stored and what they planned to do with them. If there hadn't been a hitch, would you have let it happen? Would you have stood back and let them slaughter us?'

Ali Bey spread out both hands in an attitude of non-belligerence. 'I would have told you eventually,' he said.

Ross reached under his cloak to stroke the reassuring barrel of his pistol as he asked accusingly, 'Eventually? Before it happened or after?'

Ali Bey nodded his head native style and said, 'After, I'm afraid, but before I killed you. I'm an Indian patriot and proud of it and I want rid of you and your kind, Inspector Ross.'

Ross couldn't credit what he was hearing. Ali Bey had always been his man, a puppet who jumped to his orders. Why was he suddenly taking on a life of his own? 'But we've worked together for years. We've relied on each other, and you can't be much of a patriot if you are handing your own people over to be shot down.' He was furious that his minion had turned against him.

'Though this plot has been defused, there will be others,' said Ali Bey.

Ross pulled out his pistol. 'Even if there are, you won't be around to see them. You don't think I'll let you walk away from this, do you?' With the gun in his hand, he felt dominant.

'You can't fire yet. Remember a shot in the air is the signal, and if you give it too soon, you'll lose the last load, and the conspirators. They'll be off into the night, and there'll be no witnesses. The fishermen will have seen nothing – they never do. It's safer that way.'

Pointing the gun, Ross stepped sideways and stared over the parapet again. Ali Bey was right. The last canoe was still tied up at the river bank, half heaped with bales.

'Don't worry. When this is over, even if you're dead, you'll be a hero,' said Ali Bey calmly.

'*Dead?* You'll be the one that's dead,' said Ross in a scornful voice. He even managed to laugh and that was his undoing, because as he threw back his head, he exposed his throat to a man coming up behind him, walking soundlessly on bare feet.

He threw a long cloth round Ross's neck and knotted it swiftly in both hands, turning it tight, tighter, tighter.

Ross's eyes were wide open and staring as his head jerked back. He gagged, his tongue stuck out and he struggled to free himself, one hand ineffectually grappling behind his head. As the strangling cloth tightened even more, the gun in his right hand jerked up to the sky and inadvertently he pulled the trigger.

Apart from the sound of the shot, everything was silent.

The man at Ross's back, face impassive, still twisted the cloth as Ali Bey, eyes bleak, watched. Thugs knew how to strangle, and the clerk called Jadhav, a Kali-worshipping Thug, son, grandson and great-grandson of Thugs, swiftly extinguished the life from

Ross, who slumped to the ground and lay there with his turbaned head lying on the roadway.

When Jadhav checked that his gruesome task was finished, he nodded to Ali Bey who grabbed Ross's legs and between them they heaved him over the parapet of the bridge into the river. Then they walked calmly away.

Ross's random shot was taken as the pre-arranged signal to start firing and a fusillade rang out from a posse of armed policemen hidden on the river bank. The police launches shot out from beneath the bridge and caught the barge in a pincer movement. In a few moments the arms intended for another Cawnpore mutiny were captured and the would-be mutineers were either dead or rounded up.

Only one fisherman noticed Ross's body toppling over into the water, where the splash it made was lost in the wake of the second police launch. When the excitement was over, the fisherman's catch that night was one body. He stole its fine red turban, before laying it out on the river bank and running to fetch a policeman.

In the confusion and weeping that broke out when the Begum's death was discovered, Sadie slipped away and made her way to the hospital. She guessed there would be work to do there soon.

She was right. By half-past twelve, casualties from the police ambush began arriving at the Mission hospital, which was the nearest to Satichaura Ghat. Jenny and Allen were wakened and when the first signs of dawn could be seen in the sky, they had dealt with five corpses and seven men with gunshot wounds.

One of the dead was Balraj. When Sadie drew the sheet off his corpse and saw his chubby face, she felt an overwhelming surge of relief, because he was probably the only one among the important plotters who knew about her or her mother and their involvement in the plot. The small fry, who had been told to report to them for details of where to pick up their arms, would go to ground and stay there. She and Mary were safe.

Jenny was pulling off her bloodstained white coat in preparation for going back to the bungalow for a bath, when she saw four policemen coming up the steps carrying another body on a stretcher.

Allen saw them too and said to her, 'Don't stay. I'll deal with this. It has to be the last one.' He walked behind the stretcher bearers who laid their burden down on a trolley in the outpatient room, and, as she was heading again for the door, Jenny heard him exclaim in surprise. She turned to look and saw he was staring after her with such concern in his face that she asked, 'Whatever's wrong, Fred?'

'Nothing. Go and have your bath.'

But she was coming back. 'What is it?' she asked again.

He was looking down at the body on the stretcher. 'I'm sorry, but it's that friend of yours. It's Ross, the policeman,' he said. It was obvious that he was afraid she would be devastated by his revelation.

'Robert Ross?' she repeated.

'Yes.'

'Has he been shot, too?' she asked as she walked towards him.

'I don't think so. They say he was pulled out of the river by a fisherman this morning.'

She joined him at the trolley and stood looking down at Ross. His dark eyes were wide open and staring. He looked totally surprised.

'He was in the river,' said one of the stretcher bearers again.

Allen pulled the wet shirt away from the corpse's neck. 'There's not a mark on him. I guess he was drowned. I'm sorry, Jenny,' said Allen awkwardly.

To his relief and her surprise, she only felt the sort of pity that would have been appropriate for any acquaintance who died by misadventure.

'Poor Robert, poor thing,' she said calmly. 'He must have been involved in that shooting business last night.'

The stretcher bearers all began to talk at once and Allen listened, nodding gravely before he told her, 'They say he was in charge of the operation to break up a gang of arms smugglers who were loading guns and ammunition on to a barge in the river. He gave the prearranged signal for his men on the river bank to begin firing and the police launches to take off – a shot in the air from the bridge apparently – but he didn't show up when it was all over. They think he must have fallen – or been pushed – into the river from the bridge.'

While he spoke he was watching Jenny carefully, hoping she would not dissolve into tears because he would not know how to cope with that.

To his relief, she showed no signs of breaking down, though she looked shocked. Instead she asked, 'Pushed? Do they mean someone murdered him?'

One of the police stretcher bearers who spoke English nodded. 'One of the gang might have done it in revenge.'

'I suppose this is how he'd prefer to die if he had the choice,' said Jenny.

Allen wondered if she was shell-shocked and might break down later. He'd seen it happen like that before. 'I think you should go for a bath and have something to eat,' he said to her.

She pushed a hand through her hair. 'You're right. I can't do anything here now, can I? What a terrible thing to happen. He had a good life in front of him.'

As Jenny turned to go, Sadie, who was standing by the door, said, 'I'm sorry but I've another bit of bad news for you, Doctor Jenny. Your patient in the bazaar died last night. I meant to tell you earlier but in all the confusion, I didn't have time.'

This time Jenny's sorrow was obvious. 'Oh no! I'd no idea she was so bad when I saw her – and that's only a few hours ago. It's awful that she's died so soon, especially now...'

Her voice trailed off and Sadie went on, 'She went into another coma. I was there when it happened because I went to the silk shop to give her the telegram form you left here.'

Surprised and suddenly suspicious, Jenny stared at the nurse. There was something bland and pat about the way she spoke that was disturbing. Why should she take it upon herself to meddle in private business anyway?

'You took my telegram to her?' she asked and Sadie nodded, innocent-faced.

'I thought you'd forgotten it and I heard you saying it would interest her. I had to go past the Celestial Silks shop on my way home anyway.'

'And you were there when she died?' For some reason Jenny felt angry about that.

'Yes, I was. She collapsed while we were talking. I tried to revive her but it was useless. She was pleased to see your telegram though,' said Sadie sweetly.

Jenny turned away. 'I wish I could have spoken to her again, but now I'll have to go to see her family and say goodbye to her for the last time,' she said.

Sadie looked through the open door and said, 'Then you must hurry. The body will be cremated very soon. They always take them to the burning ghat in the early morning. They'll be there now I'm sure.'

Jenny stared through the window and saw that dawn had broken. 'I must go too,' she said in a breaking voice and Allen realised she was far more upset about the death of her patient than she was about Ross.

Pointing at Ross's body, he said to the nurses, 'Look after him. I'll go too. Jenny can't go to the burning ghat alone.'

She turned to look at him in surprise and said, 'But there's work to do here. I'll be all right. I'll take a tonga.' It was obvious she wanted to go alone. He went with her anyway.

The burning ghats were down by the riverside. Every night many Hindus died in Cawnpore and already several pyres were lit, sending trails of grey smoke up into the lightening sky. When their tonga trotted up to the gate, Jenny jumped down and ran inside, saying over her shoulder to Allen, 'I'll be all right. Go back to the hospital please.' She was looking for Vikram Pande and soon found him, dressed all in white, by an unlit pyre and a trio of shaven-headed priests with yellow trident marks on their foreheads.

On the top of the pile of wood, the Begum, resplendent in a glittering shroud of mauve silk, with the end of it drawn over her hair and her proud face staring up to the sky, lay on a bier heaped high with flowers and gold and silver tinsel garlands. She looked majestic.

At the sight of her, Jenny stopped and stood staring, awed by the realisation that the woman on the bier was her grand-mother's sister – her own great-aunt, the only link she'd ever had with her father's family. Apart from her mother, her closest relative.

She turned to Vikram Pande and asked, 'Can I touch her hand please?'

His face was set but he looked at the priests who nodded, then he said, 'Please do. She would be pleased to know you are here to watch her taking leave of the world. You can help me light her pyre because you are her only true blood relative.'

With a shaking hand she accepted the taper he passed to her. 'We will light it together,' he said.

While the priests chanted and tiny bells tinkled, she and Vikram Pande walked up to the heap of wood and solemnly set fire to a sticking-out piece of wood that had been soaked in oil to make it flare. Then they stood back and watched the flames leap through the huge pyre. In a short time the heat was blistering and Jenny could hardly see for the tears that filled her eyes. She turned her head away when the inferno engulfed the body.

They parted at the gate and Vikram Pande solemnly shook her hand as he said, 'Goodbye, Dr Jenny. My family and I are leaving Cawnpore today. Business is taking me to the north.'

'So soon?' she asked in surprise.

'Yes, today. My wife's father is a silk dealer on the border of Nepal and we are going there. We were only waiting for my mother to die before we left.' He was not going to tell her the true reason for their flight.

'So we won't meet again?' she said sadly.

'Perhaps not, but we will always remember you. I will send you a message when we settle in our new home and one day you might be able to come and stay with us.'

She looked sad. 'I wish we had more time to get to know each other but I will always remember you too...and of course I'll remember your mother.'

He smiled. 'Think of her when you make decisions. She believed in taking chances. There is a lot of her in you, I think,' he said. Behind him a plume of grey smoke rose into the sky like a triumphal crest of feathers.

Jenny went home and lay on her bed weeping. The servants told the nurses about her grief and everyone supposed she was mourning for Ross.

There was another funeral at seven o'clock that evening. Daphne and Philip Villiers claimed Ross's body from the hospital and held a service in his honour in Cawnpore's largest church, which was packed out with their friends. At five o'clock, a puffy-eyed Jenny got up, dressed in a dark dress and set out. Through his office window, Allen watched her getting into a tonga and knew where she was going.

In the church Daphne insisted on treating her like a family mourner and installed her in the front pew beside herself and Philip. After the service, the congregation repaired to the nearby Cawnpore Club where Ross's police superintendent gave a speech about the dead man's courage and extolling him as a hero who died breaking up a dangerous conspiracy.

'He gave his life so that we could live. Without his brave actions, we could be the people lying dead tonight because the plotters' plan was to launch another mutiny

360

here in Cawnpore.

'Raise your glasses, ladies and gentlemen, to Robert Ross – our saviour. He did not die in vain. Tonight we must also honour his trusted sergeant Ali Bey, who was with him on his last adventure and will shortly receive a medal and promotion for his gallantry.'

At the end of the speech, Daphne went across to Jenny and put a hand on her arm, saying, 'I'm so sorry for you, my dear. This is your second bereavement, isn't it? Did you love him very much?'

What do I say? Jenny wondered. Do I pretend, or do I tell the truth?

She put her wine glass down on a convenient table and straightened her shoulders. 'I think I have to put things straight. He asked me to marry him, but I didn't accept. In fact I was going to refuse him.'

Daphne was astonished, 'Refuse him! But you couldn't do better than Robert.'

'I didn't love him,' said Jenny firmly, though she thought that Ross's funeral was perhaps not the place to say something like that.

Daphne looked around as if Jenny had uttered an obscenity. 'He loved you,' she said.

'No, he didn't. I suited his purpose but he didn't suit mine,' Jenny replied. She was putting an end to the gossip and speculation once and for all for she had no intention of being given the role of the permanently disappointed woman – the bad luck symbol.

'What an odd person you are,' said Daphne, walking quickly away.

Jenny did not join the mourners at Ross's internment in the church burying ground. One of the uniformed policemen who bore his coffin on their shoulders was black-browed Ali Bey. There was no sign of Jadhav.

It was a pleasant walk along a straight road bordered by shady trees between the Cawnpore Club and the Mission hospital. Feeling suddenly light-hearted in spite of everything that had happened, Jenny walked briskly, fair hair flying and looking straight ahead.

When Fred Allen, who was waiting under one of the peepul trees by the roadside, saw her coming out of the club doorway he thought that in a previous incarnation she could have been a Nordic priestess. Or Boudica might have looked like that, tall and fearless, a woman to admire and cherish. His heart lifted with the realisation that he was out of his valley of death and capable of loving.

As she drew near, he stepped out from behind the tree to join her and said, 'Is it safe for you to be walking alone in the darkness?'

She looked across at him, smiled and said, 'I'm not alone, am I? You're with me.'

4